Persimmon

Doc Pruyne

Mountain Springs House
Indianapolis

Copyright 2013 by Doc Pruyne

Cover Art: Tamara Sands
Editing: Lee Porche
Print Formatting: Lynn Hubbard

ISBN-13: 978-1940022239

Chapter 1

Damp, dark, and small. This is my life.

Six weeks in America and that's how sorry for myself and selfish I was, that I had such self-pity. I inhaled the air of our storage room, the acid tang of wet concrete cutting sharply through the light sweet scent of lettuce. Maybe those smells truly were like New York City and me—I had good reason to be sad—but there I sat trimming heads of lettuce, my job ever since we came to America, and it was my life. Six weeks of trimming lettuce. I sighed, I had no choice, and it did not matter that my back ached—I had to keep the knife shimmering in the gloom.

Hanging by a wire, one bulb spilled milky light over the sink that leaked onto the concrete floor. Bits of carrot greens and a sliver of apple peel dimpled the watery sheen below the leaky pipe. Stacks of crated lettuce blocked my view of everything except the stairs to the kitchen, the glowing floor, and rusty pipe. Bottom step, leaky pipe, sink, light bulb, ceiling pipes.

Pipes ran to the top of an open door, and beyond the doorway, in the light of our store, the cash register printed a receipt. My father said, "Sixty cent change." Coins tinkled in a palm. "Right change? Good, *ne,* uh-huh."

Appa-nim's voice rose and fell with a pleasant cadence, but because of him my chest felt hollowed out. I wrapped a moist green head with cellophane and grabbed another. My hands danced with the lettuce, the blade shimmered, and a globe of perfect green leaves remained before my eyes. Appa-nim said, "That be all? Four dollar ten cent total."

Lost in sad thoughts, I vaguely heard a truck backfire outside on the street, cracking like a gunshot. Inside our store a baby began to cry, and I understood when its mother began to coo and hush it in the language of mothers; but then a man's voice startled me.

"Yo!" I raised my head. "Veggie brain, yo!"

I rose and stepped into the lights of our store. A black man stood before the counter with anger hooding his eyes. He was staring at Appa-nim, who was behind the cash register, chin to his chest, his face clenched, shoulders hunched. I looked up into my father's face, his eyes squeezed shut.

He was whining quietly. I said, "Appa? Appa-nim?"

My father whispered, "Umma? Appa?" He seemed to be pleading with people who were not there. "Uncle Cho?"

His eyelids fluttered and he let out a whine of pain. The baby crying, the black man simmering, I turned to face the cash register. I rang up the man's bottle of soda. There were spots of white across the backs of his brown hands. He motioned with his chin and asked, "Whaddup with him?"

I did not answer. I did not know that there among our bright fruits and vegetables, red and golden apples, bosk pears, long green plantains, the big curves of melons and yellow squash, my father was suffering his very old demons. I gave the man his coins. When he left I said to an old woman, "Please, a moment one?" Irritation pouched her red mouth, but I didn't know what else to do. I said in Hangugo, "Appa-nim? This way." I tugged his sleeve. "Appa? Please?"

I led him into the shadows of the storage room, lettuce crackling under his shoes. He let out half a sob as I settled him onto the crate I used as a seat. He whispered like a little boy. *"Appa? Umma?"* Daddy? Mama?

I left him and hurried to the register. Three people were waiting, and the dowager with the pouched mouth had left. The people of New York City are impatient. I played the keys of the cash register, tallied prices of tomatoes, bean curd in a plastic tub, raisin bran, pomegranates, pears, a cold bottle of soda. Appa-nim's spells started after we opened the store, which meant that running the store was even more stressful than coming from Nun-yo to America. I took bills, made change, bagged chicory, avoided the bold stare of a Hispanic boy as he looked at my chest. I weighed his papayas and watched customers enter out of the brightness of sunlight on the street.

Our door was on the busy intersection of St. Mark's Place and Avenue A. Ten minutes passed. I glanced at the dark doorway of the storage room and clicked the keys of the register. Beep. Kumquats, soda, quart of beer, bouquet of flowers, coffee steaming in a foam cup. Beep.

I sold chewing gum to children who shouted and ran out and then there was only one customer, rolling the heads of lettuce in their bin. I stepped to the threshold of the storage room and peeked between the stacks of crates. "Appa-nim?"

Appa-nim mumbled, swaying so the crate squeaked. What's the matter with him? He was unaware of me. The crate squeaked as he rocked back and forth, suffering his awful visions; but then he raised his forearm to the crate. Two brass tines of a staple stuck out from the wood. The brass tines glinted and disappeared into his flesh, he jerked his arm, gasped, and his blood spotted the floor.

My mouth fell open but I could not breathe. Appa-nim raised his head. He was free of his demons and his cheeks glowed with the sweat of his struggle. He stammered, "Kee?" I was shocked, I couldn't move, and his voice faltered as he called my name again. He looked over his shoulder and glimpsed me. He said, "I...I cut myself."

"Stand up." I pulled him to his feet, blood leaking out from beneath his hand as he squeezed his arm. "Upstairs, come on."

"So stupid. *Chegiral!*" Damn! We bumped the sink and started together up the stairs to our apartment. Oddly, I felt like I was leading a little boy rather than my father. Then he asked, "Is the lettuce all trimmed?"

"Almost. Umma!" I pushed open the kitchen door. She was there, a bird in bright lights and steam. "Appa-nim cut himself."

"Not on purpose. Don't make it sound like—"

"I told you, Ki-Teh, there are demons here." The steam of garlic and odong noodles weighted the air. She clucked her tongue as they fussed by the sink. "Just the kind of accident an angry spirit causes. I told you we should have a *kut*, get rid of these demons. If you eat the salt you better drink the water."

Appa-nim snapped at me, "Get down there, hurry up."

I was my mother's daughter, I knew when to ask for what I wanted. "But Appa-nim, when can I visit Auntie?"

"Never. Get down there!"

I hurried out, and as I skipped downstairs, my hands bloody, I heard Umma say, "Why can't she? And why do you think they had a bloody eyeball over the door? To attract demons!"

Our store had been a heavy metal music shop, Bloody Eyeball Records & Tapes, before Auntie Yen rented it for us. I washed my hands at the bottom of the stairs, the leaky pipe dribbling like a goat's udder under the sink. I hurried into the store as a young woman strolled out onto the sidewalk, a bottle of our soda in her hand. Too late, I let her go, dried my hands on my pants, and said to a beautiful New York-type woman, "I help you?"

Umma came down the stairs in the storage room half an hour later, wearing low black heels and a dress with a white lace collar. She worked as a hostess in a restaurant for deaf people. The secretary at the Korean Business Association was excited when she called Umma about it, a good job for a non-speaker: learn sign language, on-the-job training, three dollars an hour plus tips.

Umma said, "He's eating. You hungry? I'll watch the register until he comes down."

I shook my head and accepted dollars for a bag of potatoes. "Thank you, thank you, please come again. Umma?" She kept building a pyramid of green apples on the island in the middle of our store. I asked, "Do you think he's acting odd?"

"He deserves respect!" Her vehemence startled me, but it faded quickly. She sighed and left an apple unstacked. "He's tired, that's all. Why do you think he brought us here and started the store? For you. So that you and Ling don't have to chop fish all day. Where did the Rhee twins take her? They go everywhere and he never complains."

"Six dollar ninety-two cent total." I accepted money from a Jamaican woman whose hair stuck out from her head in thick roots, a sight that still awed me. All we ever saw in Nun-yo were Koreans, and now and then an American Army guy, no Jamaicans, no blacks in baggy pants, no Indians, no Pakistanis, no punk rockers with pink spiky hair. I nodded as Appa-nim had taught me. "Thank you, thank you, please come again."

The Jamaican woman looked at Umma, looked at me, and left us with our tension. I broke it. "She goes everywhere with the Rhee twins and he won't let me go to Auntie's place. How is that fair?"

I needed to talk to Auntie Yen. She would listen to me, hear what I had to say about him.

Umma absently straightened a chocolate bar in a box. She was so busy now that she was absent even when she was with me; but then she hurried around behind me, lifted the phone, and dialed from memory.

"Yen? It's me." My struggle with Appa-nim, for this visit to Auntie Yen, had been going on for two weeks. Umma said into the phone, "Is there something you could bribe him with?"

Appa-nim appeared in the doorway to the storage room. White gauze and tape clung to his forearm. He jerked open the cooler to count the sodas. "Who's she talking to?"

Umma brightened. "Ah, so it's settled. Thanks, Yen!" Umma hung up the phone and said, "Kee can go down and pick up the TV, right?"

Appa-nim's brows dropped suspiciously. "What TV?"

"Your sister's giving us a little TV. Kee can go down and pick it up."

A muscle rippled beside Appa-nim's ear as he clenched his teeth.

He looked at me and snapped, "Get more co-cola!" I hurried toward the back as he pointed to the front. "Scheming wife, go to work!"

"All right!" Umma called, "Bye bye, Kee."

"Umma, wait!" I was in the dark where the sodas were wedged under the stairs, and when I scuttled out struggling with a heavy case of soda my mother was gone. I hurried out to say goodbye to her, but she was already down the street. She turned and waved, smiling, a glimpse of the mother I knew in Korea disappearing into the crowd of New York.

The crowds of the city. I stood there in the sunlight on the corner of Avenue A and Eighth Street, beside our bin of cantaloupes, to let the gloom of the storage room clear from my eyes. I stood there and watched New York City work like a big machine.

Mechanical workings. New York City's rhythm is like gears, cogs, whirrumblehonkhonk as traffic lights changed to green and drivers rushed ahead. A blue-haired grandma clung to her steering wheel. The car of a poor family limped along with a muffler that sparked on the tar beneath it, and pedestrians hurried from corner to corner, hurried along the walks. Busses rumbled on the streets, trains roared beneath them, scheduled by a man sitting at a desk somewhere below a huge clock, tock tock tock. Tick tick tick, planes crossed the sky like steel birds thrown by a slingshot minute hand.

Where is the rhythm in it? In Nun-yo the days were regulated by sea tides and daylight, natural rhythms, while New York City was governed by hours and minutes, by commerce. My back was stiff, my neck had a crick, pains borne from living against natural rhythms, and I was tired.

The stress of living with Appa-nim also tired me out. "Kee!" he shouted. "Trim more lettuce!"

I was already in bed when Umma came home at 10:30. I heard their feet shuffle up the stairs, heard Appa-nim drop the blue bank pouch onto the kitchen table, heavy with coins, and heard their bedroom door close with a clap of wood.

Ling, my little sister, giggled in the dark. We were not used to having a separate room, so Ling often fooled around instead of sleeping. She crept back from the window sill, her long hair wispy with faint blue highlights. Ling's hair was long and beautiful while mine was cut short, and she was cute and independent while I was plain and shy. Everyone loved Ling, a little force of nature they couldn't ignore.

She whispered, "He'll let you go to Auntie's. He's a jellyfish."

"A jellyfish? What's Umma?"

"An eel." Ling was eleven years old, but she was *yom-chae.* Precocious. She said, "Umma might be an eel, but Auntie is a shark. She always gets what she wants. She always gets Appa to do what she wants, and Harold the red-haired tomato too."

The red-haired tomato was Auntie Yen's boyfriend. I gazed up at the water mark on our ceiling, a faint blotch. Ling was right, so I asked, "What am I?"

"Cha-ra."

"Sea turtle?" I snorted. "I suppose you're an angel fish."

"I'm not a fish." She slipped beneath the sheet and pinched me. "I'm a plum. Appa says so."

We pinched each other and giggled, Appa-nim thumped the wall with his fist, and we stifled ourselves in the dark.

I was tired but couldn't sleep. I listened as Ling's breathing slowed, and when she was asleep I crawled through the darkness to our window. My throat clenched with the sadness that filled me when I was alone. I leaned against the window sill with its peeling paint, looked out into the air shaft, felt my throat clench and my cheeks tighten around my eyes.

A petal of a rubber plant, potted in a plastic tub, brushed my cheek. Five feet below me lay the tarred roof of our storage room. A doll there, with blonde hair, winked one eye at me. I felt like that doll, fallen and lost in the shadows at the bottom of the air shaft. In Nun-yo

I had developed inner stillness, my meditations and practice of martial arts were restful. Since moving to America my sadness was like an undertow, invisible to others, that dragged me down into resignation.

I whispered to the rubber plant. "I miss you so much, Chen-puin." My head sank into my hands as I thought about Ti-Lee. Why couldn't I kiss him? Would I still be in Nun-yo if I had? I remembered when big jiggling Ti-Lee had run huffing along the road to give me a present before the bus took us away.

Ti-Lee, I miss you!

I loved the sea and missed the rhythm of my days. I missed the stench that blew from the fish plant, a smell that meant Appa-nim was working, men and women were working hard to make a simple living. Always there was the honest salt smell of the sea. New York stank of boiled hotdogs, rotting garbage, gasoline, stinks that moved quickly on the nervous air.

If we were still in Nun-yo, I thought, right now I'd be in Peng Su-nim's school, practicing *komdo*. A "su-nim" is an enlightened teacher, a master, and "komdo" means "way of the sword."

I was the first girl in eight hundred years to study Way of the Dawning Sword, a special discipline that brings enlightenment. It didn't work for me.They told stories about me in Korea because I drove a snake out of Peng Su-nim's garden, and such things generate legends, but I was just a child.

Some legend, I thought, eavesdropping on people doing it. High on the air shaft, behind a window, the lovers moaned. Sex? No. No words came into my head, only the sense of a mystery that made me nervous. The doll at the bottom of the air shaft winked at me. One of its eyes was broken. Ling slept on. Air conditioners hummed, the lovers moaned with mysterious passion, and the world turned around the intensity of my sadness, my feeling of losing my life, my home, and my friends.

Was I just bitter and angry? Was that why I decided to betray my father? I do not think so, but not even the rubber plant wanted my sadness, its petals dry and hard against my cheek. Maybe the rubber plant knew my loss was a gain. I wasn't that wise, so I listened to the moans of the lovers that rolled around the air shaft. I wanted to follow those noises as they rose to the odd-shaped opening in the roof. I wanted so much to escape into the sky over New York City, into clouds as pink as mother of pearl, to escape back across the oceans to my sweet Korea.

I ached because I knew it would never happen.

Chapter 2

Five days before Appa-nim cut himself with the staple I had my first conversation with an American, a beery Korean *ajima* auntie with white spittle at the corners of her mouth. She was brown in the mouth from chewing tobacco, but she put hope into my heart after seventeen days of failure.

I had started to look for a martial arts teacher to replace Peng Su-nim. When Appa-nim was done rustling and crumpling the *Joong Ang Ilbo* and had thrown it down in disgust, I smoothed it out and read it, but saw no ads for komdo teachers. I quietly asked Auntie Yen, the one time we visited her place, "Are there any *komdo* su-nim here?" She stared at me blankly and changed the subject. In my desperation I grew bold. One bright day when Appa-nim was upstairs for lunch, a Korean man dressed in pointed black shoes, creased pants, and tall flat lapels came into our store. I said in Hangugo, "Do you know? Is there a komdo teacher here in New York City?"

He said, "Sorry, I don't speak Korean." He pointed to our rack of cigarettes. "Two packs of those menthols."

The next noon, while Appa-nim was upstairs eating, a Korean woman led a small child in through the doorway. She wore an emerald green dress with a ruby broach near her throat. I said in English, "Can you tell me? Is there a komdo su-nim here in New York City?"

She looked mystified. "Kom what?"

Can't Koreans here understand me? Didn't matter. I kept trying. Any Koreans who stopped at our store, if Appa-nim was upstairs eating, I asked them, "Is there a komdo su-nim here in New York City? Sword teacher?" For seventeen days I asked my question, but each person shook their head or shrugged.

One noontime, while Appa-nim was up in the kitchen, a boy and an old fat woman came out of the light of St. Mark's Place. The old auntie's mouth looked like a dent in a withered apple. The boy slammed the door of our cooler and brought her a can of cold beer. I said, "Can you tell me? Is there a komdo su-nim here in New York City? Sword teacher? Su-nim?"

The boy had nervous stork's legs and his reply was rapid English. My confusion must have been obvious because his grandmother shuffled close. Half of her front teeth were gone and she slurred the words. "There is a komdo su-nim in Chinatown, teaching across from a park." Some American habits disgusted me, and she had found one. Chewing tobacco. When she chuckled I saw her brown gums, and her tongue looked like a rotten banana peel. She said, "But he doesn't teach girls. That's what I heard."

My heart stopped. My lineage of komdo was the only one I knew of that excluded females. I was the first ever. The boy cracked open the can of beer and held it up to the brown-mouthed ajima. She grabbed it, and her lower lip quivered as she gulped. I asked, "Do you know if he teaches Saebyoke style?"

She lowered the can, sweating in the heat, and fastened her scowl on me. "Saebyoke is a myth. What my children said, what everyone in Choson said about New York was a myth too, a lie. My husband, dead now and worthless, said that Saebyoke never existed, that it's a lie. Let's go!" She paused in the doorway to snigger at me. "So many Koreans dissolve into New York City. They learn to lie like New Yorkers too!"

That old hag scared me. I did not want to dissolve into New York and lose myself. I already lost some business. After the old woman left I realized she never paid for the beer she drank.

I so much needed to find a new teacher, but nevertheless, going alone to Auntie's place scared me. In Nun-yo the white houses with their chicken pens and tethered goats were all plaited together by a few streets of grey concrete and cobbles. It was easy to find your way in Nun-yo, and it was peaceful. Gulls screeched over the clay tile roofs, rickety TV antennaes shivering in the wind that swept up off the bay. Though Green Dragon Bay was no more than a pock in the tip of South Korea, it seemed immense to me. Nun-yo seemed large, but on a map it was only a dot with three thousand people.

New York City had nine million people! Honking cars, shouts, barking dogs, rumbling trucks, and I jumped away the first time I heard a subway train roaring beneath a grate in the sidewalk. The streets all looked the same. I could not read street signs, everyone spoke so fast that my crude English could not keep up. People everywhere, tongues I didn't know—Polish, Farsi, French, Russian—but I had no choice. I had to go to Auntie's house alone. I had to follow the rumor of a komdo teacher, and I had to talk with her about Appa-nim.

At five o'clock on the evening after Appa-nim cut himself on the staple, I descended the stairs from the kitchen and entered the store. The bribe worked, Appa-nim wanted Auntie's little TV. He looked up from changing the receipt paper in the register. "You have directions?"

"Yes, Appa-nim."

A curl of white paper lay on the floor. "The map?"

"Yes, Appa-nim. Thank you."

Two people waited with vegetables in their hands. "Here." He slipped two subway tokens from his shirt pocket. An edge of guilt sliced down my chest. The map and the tokens cost real money. He said, "Be home by seven. And don't think I'm stupid. I know what's going on, why we're getting that TV. You three are conspiring against me!"

"Yes, er...no, Appa-nim." We had no savings, all our money was invested in the store, and I was going to Auntie's place to betray him, and there he was giving me money to go. I couldn't look at him as I took the tokens. Instead I grabbed a lopsided, spotted mango from the discard box under the register, in case I got hungry, and called,

"Thank you, Appa-nim!" as I hurried out onto St. Mark's Place.

I jogged up the street crowded with people old and slow, girls in the black skirt of St. Stanislaw's, black people with stockings on their heads, Jamaicans with branches of hair swinging as they walked. Mothers pushed baby carriages, a drunk sang to himself, a man perched on a stoop strummed his guitar, and green-haired men in black leather lounged outside a tattoo parlor, exhaling clouds of cigarette smoke.

I reached the end of St. Mark's Place and looked for the subway. It was all the way across the intersections of five streets, a crosshatching of cars and trucks hurtling north and south. In the center stood a huge black metal cube poised on one point. The bizarre sculpture was like the city itself, cold and hard looking, but somehow fascinating, and yet I was glad to get beyond it to find the subway.

The map Appa-nim bought was in Chinese, I couldn't read much of it. When I found the entrance to the subway I took the wrong train and got off at the wrong stop. I got lost. Look at these buildings! Looking for a way, I turned around and around, the rooftops spun, and I stumbled into a side street. The buildings stood black with soot, and run-off lines left by dirty rain led down to doorways where drunks had fallen down to sleep it off. What kind of world is this? My feet hurt, I stopped to rest. I wondered if there was a Korean drunk and if I could ask him for directions to Chinatown.

None of the drunks rustled their newspaper bedsheets. I lifted my head, hearing a sputter of piano notes and a gruff voice, somehow familiar. Music? I was lifted off the stoop. The voice caromed along the buildings that closed me in, closed in the song, and the music drew me eastward.

I came upon a man standing in front of a broken window patched with a sheet of plywood, his microphone clipped to a pole, a small box amplifier near his feet. He fascinated me. He needed a shave, his hair dangled in greasy strings, his voice cracked when he hit high notes, but he sang with rapture on his upturned face, as if he was serenading the pigeons that chortled on the rooftops.

I could see that he loved to sing, but he was old and poor. His grimy fingers stumbled through a melody on the keyboard of an electric piano with mashed corners. I understood no words, but I realized why the song, and his voice, drew me. The melody reminded me of a *sijo* sung by *obu*, fishermen, too old to go on the sea. That's how the street singer sounded, like a fisherman too old to fish.

He stopped singing. It was sad that a man so old as to be mostly bald, who loved to sing, had to sing in the street for coins. Then he burped and opened his eyes. The microphone caught the burp and it echoed off the buildings. Oh...he's drunk. I spotted a bottle poking from his hip pocket.

He saw me and held out a paper cup"Spare some change?"

I had a subway token and the spotted mango. Appa-nim told me to stay away from poor people. I crept forward, placed the mango on top of the box amplifier, then backed away. When he looked up from the mango his eyes made me stumble.

"What the..." He grabbed the mango and threw it down the street as I ran. "Rotten fruit? That's all you got, rotten fruit? Screw you!" I ran, and as I ran I glanced over my shoulder. That drunken street singer was twisting off the cap of his pint bottle, snarling and spitting swear words until he drank. "Screw you! I had a record, a hit. A hit!"

I ran to the next corner, stumbled, turned on the sidewalk toward honking horns, cars jammed under a red light, and that was how I fumbled my way into an intersection I knew from our visit with Auntie Yen. Canal Street! Rejoicing in my good luck, I stepped into the flow of people milling into the crowded heart of Chinatown.

Housewives hunted ginger root, rice wine, *mu shu,* chestnuts, soy sauce, garlic, and for their *Sangson guk*, their fish soup, they rattled oysters and clams in bushel baskets. Boys shouted over our heads. "Bluejean, fi'e dollar! Walkman, six-fitty!" Shoulders, faces, quick eyes. Banknotes, perfume, jewelry, scrimshaw, sneakers, evasive eyes, thieves' eyes, tourists with ten thousand heads bobbed east and west.

I could not see ahead. I stopped by a woman with a crate covered by a towel, a display for a dozen gold-plated watches. I asked in Hangugo, "Do you know of a Komdo su-nim here? Sword teacher? In Chinatown?" She shrugged. She replied in Mandarin, I did not understand her, and she shrugged until I pantomimed a bit of swordplay. I said, "Komdo su-nim? *Sensei? Sifu?* Teacher?"

"Ah." She pointed toward Mott Street. "There."

The buildings were soot-black, silly metal pagodas hooded the lights at the tops of posts, the curbs had curved steel edges, and the walks were crowded with mothers herding children, lovers strolling hand in hand. Everywhere the scent of bean sauce and grease hung in the air. My stomach gurgled. Why did I give my mango to that man? I wandered lanes paved with worn bricks, the air noisy with radio voices, the clatter of dishes, the whine of sewing machines from a top floor sweatshop. I widened my search, gazed at doors for a symbol of swordsmanship, followed an alley until it ended at a kitchen door, stinking dumpster, dead cat.

I knew I was lost when I came under the buzz of tires on a huge bridge. Three Asians smashed the window of a car. I ran as glass tingled in the gutter and they ripped out the radio. I ran until my lungs hurt. My feet hurt. Depressed, tired, I turned back toward Canal Street. East on Canal, north on Elizabeth Street toward white banners that announced Little Italy, and I was so relieved to reach Auntie Yen's building that I sat on the stoop a minute to rub my face and rest.

Auntie came to America when she was eighteen to study at Columbia University. When she opened her door she hugged me and cried, "I was so worried, you're late, come in! Let me get you tea."

Her apartment was full of silk wall hangings, ink paintings, a red lacquer chest three feet high, tables made of black tubes and smoked glass, and a Greek *flokati* rug strayed its tassels over the varnished floor. She filled a teapot and lit the stove in her kitchen, small like an afterthought.

"I wasn't thinking or I would've bought scones. Harold buys them for me, they're English, triangle biscuit things." She maneuvered me down between the black tubes of a chair and set out saucers and cups with blue and green dragons inside. "How is it going at the store? Have you made friends? Met any boys yet?"

Auntie was thirty-four years old but looked ten years younger, and she made lots of money as a translator at the United Nations. I said, "I'm always working."

"All work and no play makes Kee a dull girl." The teapot whistled. She filled our cups until the dragons swam like shadows under the tea. "It took me a while to learn this, but in New York there are two things. First, you find a job and earn as much money as you can. Then you get a boyfriend who will spend lots of money on you." She laughed and clattered the kettle on the stove. "I was so happy you wanted to come visit. I don't know why your father put up such a fight, but a TV, you need it anyway. How's Ling? Is she still running around with the Rhee twins?"

Auntie babbled on about how cute Ling was, how she already wheedled the Rhee twins into doing what she wanted, and I held my silence. I sipped tea. My feet ached in my sneakers. Eventually she noticed my silence, waited, sipped her tea, and batted her eyelashes. Finally I broke the silence. I said, "I heard there's a komdo su-nim teaching in Chinatown."

"I'm sorry, I forgot you asked about that when you were here." She rolled her eyes excessively. "I would've asked around, but ask me everything twice, I'm forgetful. What did you think of Harold?"

The tea tasted mildly of licorice. I tried to be polite. "How old is he?"

"Only fourteen years older than me...about." I made her uncomfortable, so she needled me. "That's why you wanted to come down here, to find a komdo master? But why? Don't you want to try American stuff?"

I fingered the gold rim of my cup. Auntie's *nunchi,* her intuition, was sensitive when she let it be, and she knew then to be quiet. She watched me and waited. I glanced up at her, but I still couldn't tell her the whole truth, that Appa-nim would've been furious if he knew I was looking for a Komdo teacher. Instead I said, "The other reason I had to come was because...well...remember he complained about the fish plant, that they wouldn't promote him? They wouldn't because he acts funny."

Auntie leaned forward. "What do you mean?"

"I don't know what he did at the fish plant, I only heard rumors, but—" It tired me to think about it. I pushed aside my cup. Auntie pushed aside her cup, clearing the table between us. She waited. I whispered, "Since we opened the store he's had three...um...spells. The last was the worst. I had to take over the register, and then he cut himself."

"Cut himself?"

"On a staple. To bring himself out of it. It bled a lot."

Auntie put one of her long red lacquered fingernails between her teeth. That told me she was troubled because her fingernails cost a lot of money to paint. Cars honked outside on the street. Shouts, grinding gears. She said, "Maybe I shouldn't have lent him money...to open the store. Has he hurt himself before? What time does he want you back?"

"No, that was the first time. Seven o'clock, am I late?"

Worry pinched a crease between her eyebrows. "Let's get the TV."

Each of us with a hand on the handle of the little TV, we rode downward in the elevator, crossed the lobby, and stepped out to the curb. The sweet smell of Italian pastries hung in the air. "Taxi!" A yellow car pulled over. Auntie hugged me and said to the driver, "Avenue A and St. Mark's. Make it by seven and she'll give you this too." She fluttered a second five dollar bill at the driver and gave them both to me. "If anything happens, call me. See you on Sunday!"

"Sunday?"

"He didn't tell you? The deal for the TV? Your mother's making pigeons and you're making your special carp for us. Harold's mouth is already watering. Bye bye."

The cab stank of exhaust fumes. I shifted nervously on the split-open seat, looked out at street signs, tried to recall the route, to see if we were going north, or if the cabbie was taking me someplace to rob me of those five dollar bills. But wait. Wasn't I supposed to figure out what to do about him? With auntie? Aiee, not good...so maybe when she comes. I could not relax until I spotted Thompkins Square Park, dusk gathering early around the black tree trunks and wrought iron fences.

The square of pathetic trees put an end to St. Mark's Place and faced the onslaught of all the traffic bustling north and south on Avenue A. Men shouted before the black iron gate. Bums lived in the park, drug sellers waited for customers—those hollow drug addicts who would kill me for a dime or a cigarette—and half-naked men played basketball on uneven courts. The cabbie stopped the car at the light and took a toothpick out of his mouth. "Here by seven. Comprendo?"

I gave him both fives, slid off the seat, grabbed the TV, and staggered with it toward our door. A siren screamed down the block, red lights of police cars flashed on Tenth Street, and two men who lived in cardboard boxes in the park slapped each other and argued. Our bins lay full of apples, peaches, trimmed heads of lettuce, melons, green peppers, oranges, and a rack near the door bloomed with bouquets of flowers. Those were Umma's idea. I hurried in, my face hot, my shoulder aching, and the tink tink of coin against coin greeted me, a sharp metallic scrape.

"I'm back." I hoisted the TV. "Look!"

Hangugo and English mixed in Appa-nim's mouth as he finished with a customer. "Thank you, please come again. Does it even work? Any trouble finding her?"

"Uh-uh. You want tea?"

He nodded. "Put water on and I'll take a break."

I climbed the stairs out of the dank storage room and stepped into the kitchen filled with shadows. Ling was asleep, exhausted by her adventures with the Rhee twins. I filled our kettle with water and put it on the stove to boil. Beyond an archway our shabby front room stood dark but for a square of street light yellowing the frayed edge of the rug below the window.

Umma wasn't home yet, and as I waited for the water to make a homey noise in the silence, I felt a touch of sadness. I missed my mother. I saw thousands of people every day in New York City, but few I recognized, few who spoke to me. The kettle snuffled, the water only as warm as Appa-nim preferred it, so I went down and relieved him from the register.

How can you be lonely in a crowd? Somehow I managed it.

He must have fallen asleep after he drank his cup of tea because he did not return for an hour. It was almost time to pull down the thick plastic curtains in front of our bins, haul down the metal grate, throw the bolts on the thick heavy door, and as I closed down the shop he counted the change in the register, each coin with its own metal clink or tingle.

I glanced back from the doorway to the storage room. "Good night, Appa-nim." Scrawny, tired, consumed by his work, he counted coins and did not respond to me at all.

Chapter 3

Umma and I hovered about the table and stove. She was known for *pidulgi much-him,* spiced pigeons, and we also made my special dish, batter-fried carp, and eggplant sandwiches, sunny lettuce wrap-ups, pear salad. My hands blurred, the blade flashed as I diced a dry red pepper, cloves of garlic, ginger root, and my eyes watered as I shredded green onions. Stir fry hissed on the stove, rice steam filled the air, the carp lay long and grew brown in the oven.

The pigeons turned crispy, and Umma and I worked like one person to mix the ingredients of spicy fish soup. I bumped into Ling. She snapped, "Out of the way!" as she filled our nine-part dish with hot green and yellow mustards, pickled bean sprouts, and different kinds of *kimchi,* spiced cabbage mixed with cucumbers, hot radish, carrot slivers, raisins, even mixed with dates and red peppers.

Appa-nim saw Auntie Yen and Harold on the street. He called out the window, "Hurry up, the food's hot!"

Ling clattered in her church shoes down the stairs to let them in. I tightened inside as I set the carp on the table. What if Auntie lets it slip that I went looking for a su-nim? I tried to calm myself by inhaling the savory steam rising from the soup tureen.

Harold was a big aging man, his stomach large and shaky, and he planted his scabby elbows on the table as we bowed our heads to pray. Appa-nim prayed in a droning voice for a long time, until Ling kicked a table leg, "Amen." Umma rose to serve fried bean curd and bellflower root, while I set out seasoned bean sprouts, soy sauce, red bean paste. Appa-nim watched Harold closely. I knew he was embarrassed that we were a three-*cheop* family, had only three covered dishes, and he looked away quickly when Harold glanced at him.

Harold surprised us. When Umma offered him eggplant sandwiches he said, *"Tae-danhi kamsa-hamnida."*

"I've been teaching him Hangugo," Auntie said.

Harold was red-faced from hard drinking, his hair white, and he had eight tongues, eight languages. He said, "She's cheaper than Berlitz, even if I did buy her pearls." An uncomfortable silence settled over the table as he stroked her jaw and fingered the pearls against her throat.

"Berlitz," Auntie said. "Language courses."

"Ah!" Appa-nim laughed hard and spoke in Hangugo to Auntie. "Why don't you teach English to Ling and Kee? I would let Kee go from the store, and if the Rhee twins weren't babysitting Ling I wouldn't have to pay them."

"They're not babysitting me! *Kimchi,* Haro'd?"

"Don't interrupt your father." Always the back and forth between languages. *"Kimchi,* Harold? Many kind."

Harold's elbows claimed half a side of our little kitchen table. He shook his head and pronounced flawlessly. *"Agashi-nim, wonch'i anssumnida.* Ki-Teh, are they the Rhee twins of the first attaché? Couple of brats. But he's a good connection to cultivate."

"They're teaching her about the city," Appa-nim said. Auntie Yen interpreted between them. "But if Ling went to Yen's a few nights a week I wouldn't have to pay them. I could give that money to you, Yen. Keep it in the family. Yen?" He offered a bowl of rice to Harold, who shook his head. "Yen? Kee knows the way now, and they could go together."

I stared at the garlic kimchi and felt my lungs empty. If Auntie agreed to teach us I could pursue the su-nim rumored to be teaching in Chinatown. Harold burped into his fist. He said, "You could tape the sessions, Yen, and sell the tapes. Now there's a bloody good business for you."

I waited without breathing. Auntie's eyes glittered. "Won't they get English lessons in school? I'm sure they'll have classes."

"They're not in school for the summer," Appa-nim said. "I'd pay for any books they needed."

"Of course you would." Auntie looked at him intently. "How are you feeling, Ki-Teh? Getting enough sleep?"

"Of course not." Appa-nim spread his stick-like arms, his fingers thinner than a spider's legs. "Kee and I put in sixteen, eighteen hours a day. She's my reliable turnip; but I'll let her go to your place a few nights a week for lessons. Why not?"

Auntie gazed steadily at me. "Why not? I'd love to see my nieces more often."

Umma offered me rice. I said, "No thank you."

Ling shook her head and waved her fork. "You don't say that here. Not say, 'no thank you.' Here you say—" She formed the f-sound carefully, planting her teeth against her lower lip. "Fook that!"

Umma, Appa-nim, and I drew back when Harold spit tea onto his plate and turned red. Auntie rolled her eyes and chuckled. She said, "Ling, good girls don't talk like that."

Appa-nim blushed. "Those Rhee twins taught you that?"

Harold chuckled. "That's black talk, Ki-Teh. She must've heard it from the street trash."

"Ah, black people." He shook his head. "Black people, uh-huh. Stree' trash."

Harold was still amused. "What have you been doing since you came to New York, Ling?"

Ling wore her hair in braids with fine red tail ribbons that fluttered to her waist. She smiled at Harold and said, "We go to Time Square. Try out for Broadway play."

"She already has the f-sound," Auntie said, her long fingers interwoven, eight glossy pink fingernails resting on the table. "You are *yom chae,* Ling."

Appa-nim smiled proudly when Harold chuckled and asked, "Did you get a part in the play?"

Ling shook her head. "They want Madonna yellow hair big boob.

We go Soho. Shop, um, for...um...masterchunk."

Harold's grey teeth appeared and his belly shook. "Master chunk? Oh, the art galleries. Masterpiece. Did you buy one?"

Ling flipped her hand dismissively. "Cho-Soo say it no go with hi' sofa. We go Boom Line, *chum bang.* How say? Um...oh yeah. Slam dance, punka rocka, so'd out show."

Harold's red jowls shook. "Who was playing?"

"Double bill. Steamy Shit. Chainsaw Toothbrush."

Before Auntie Yen and Harold left, Appa-nim gave them a bottle of rice wine. He said to Auntie, "Three times a week should be good for the lessons. Harold, *yong orl Hangugo heyo."*

They had emptied fourteen bottles of beer down their throats. Harold slapped Appa-nim on the back. "Thanks, old man. You're catching onto the English too."

"Yen, tomorrow I'll send them down at 4:30."

She paused at the door to the stairs that led down to the storage room. She asked, "Ki-Teh, are you feeling well? You look tired."

"I worked in the fish plant, and that was harder. Kee?" I looked up from scrubbing the platter and serving dishes. "I'm opening the store. When you finish there, come down and scrub turnips."

Customers were already rapping on melons and sniffing tomatoes when I skipped down the stairs and glanced out of the gloom of the storage room. Appa-nim stood behind the register. Beep.

Tomorrow, I thought. Tomorrow I go and find that su-nim!

I sat on the squeaky crate and took up the knife. Its blade shimmered, leaves fell into a crate, I yanked on the roll of cellophane, and it went *ssssspip* as I slit off a square. I trimmed and wrapped heads of lettuce, their cool moisture and sweet green scent on my hands.

I ripped open a box of turnips. The turnips were crusted with dirt and smelled of minerals, earthy like the mountains around Nun-yo. What is Chen-puin doing right now? She was my childhood tutor— Peng Su-nim's wife—and I saved her life. Memory pinched my adam's apple, and for a moment sadness held me in a spell; then I pushed my hands into the cold water gushing from the faucet and it shocked me back to New York City.

When I finished scrubbing turnips my back ached from bending over the sink. I lifted a crate heavy with clean turnips and carried it out the front door, to a bin beside the walk. After the dim storage room I had to squint even in the mild evening sunlight. Couples strolled without purpose, policemen stood by the park, old men pointed at a racing form and discussed horses. Regretfully, I turned back to our doorway, to the cash register where Appa-nim mixed Hangugo and English. "Trim a dozen bunches of romaine. Nine eighty-two total. Did you scrub all the turnips?"

"Not yet, Appa-nim."

"Scrub them good and clean because they're so ugly to begin with. Seventy cent change. Everything must look excellent."

"Yes, Appa-nim."

The next afternoon I climbed the stairs to get ready for the first English lesson I would never take.

I wondered if the Chinatown su-nim taught Saebyoke style. Probably not. So few teachers survived the Japanese occupation. I rummaged through the boxes of our clothes that we could not hang in the closet because of the radiator. In a box I found my canvas book bag, yanked it open for the first time since we left Nun-yo. I pushed in a white bundle tied with a black cloth belt. My *dobuck,* my uniform.

I was distracted. My period was coming, I was holding water, my arms felt full of wet sand, and my brassiere squeezed my breasts. I wished the boys who came into the store would stop looking at them. Ling came into the bathroom as I pulled tampons out of a box. "What are those for?"

"Umma didn't tell you?"

"Oh, that." Ling felt left out of komdo, Umma was not teaching her how to cook, and she felt left out of being a woman. She said,

"You're so special. Hurry up!"

"Who made you boss?"

I followed Ling down to the store, where Appa-nim's fingers blurred over the cash register, clickity-click-click. "Here, for the subway." Again, feeling guilty, I could not look at him as he counted tokens into my palm, precious, as if they were minted from his sweat. He said, "Tell Yen I'll pay her for your books."

"Thank you, Appa-nim."

As we stepped out the door Ling shouted, "See you, Appa!"

"Ahn-nyong, plum!"

We hurried west, toward the subway station in Astor Place, the square with the ugly black cube poised on one point. Poor people displayed paperback books, wrinkled clothes, and record albums for sale on ratty blankets spread over the curbs. Too busy socializing to sell anything, they waved their arms, gabbled, shook their heads, passed a bottle in a brown bag. I understood nothing, but they reminded me of the chatter of women hanging seaweed on the beach.

As we crossed the Bowery I reached for Ling's hand. She yanked it away. I felt lonely and irritable. English small talk all around us, conversations, greetings, shouts. Incomprehensible. So lonely here. A ripple of loneliness, as horrible as an intimation of death, made me shiver, and I purposely bumped against Ling. She asked, "Why do you have your dobuck?"

"I heard there is a komdo su-nim teaching somewhere in Chinatown." We passed a crazy man jabbering to himself. I put myself between him and Ling. "Please don't tell Appa-nim."

"That's not good. You're asking me to lie." She smirked at me. "What are you going to give me? A super grape lollipop?"

We put our tokens into the turnstiles and descended to the platform. We sat on a bench, and when a train rushed out of the tunnel the platform shook, the train thundered, hot stinky wind flailed my hair, and I squeezed my eyes shut. Ling shouted, "This is it! Hurry!" We got through the doors before they clattered shut. As we sat on a bench she said, "Don't let anyone see you looking at them. They'll kill you. They're all crazy, the Rhee twins said so."

Seated across from us was a huge woman with glowing chocolate-brown cheeks. Huge rolls of fat gave her body the layers of a pagoda. Too fat to wash herself, she stank like over-ripe nectarines and motor oil. I whispered, "They'll kill us if we look at them? Even fat ladies?"

"Especially fat ladies. They hide knives in their fat!"

We got off the train at a platform with grimy letters on the wall. CANAL STREET. We climbed a stairwell. Black spots of chewing gum. Stink of urine, cars droned, trucks rumbled, shouts, the singsong of Chinese spiked by commercial English. Low price! Over here! Hey stupid! The air seemed to hang gray, hot, and still.

Ling stopped before a window, the glitter of jewelry behind the glassy reflection of gray clouds and buildings. "I want to wear a million bangle bracelets!"

"You wouldn't be able to move. This way."

Buildings narrowed the sky over Canal Street, and when we passed Mulberry Street I saw to the south a place where the buildings fell away and the gray sky opened. That must be the park the old ajima auntie mentioned. I went with Ling up Elizabeth Street, and when we reached Auntie's building I pushed the button for her apartment. The door unlocked with a clack, buzzed, and I held it open for Ling.

"Auntie's on the third floor. I'm going to look for the su-nim. Tell her I won't be long."

"If Appa finds out you'll be sorry."

She was right, but I had to find him, this Chinatown su-nim. Mulberry Street was a sloping strip of pavement crumbling away to reveal the faded red brick cobbles underneath. The corner of the park was only a block from Canal Street. A chain-link fence surrounded children shrieking on swing sets, a slide, a worn see-saw that reminded me of Nun-yo, where I had ridden see-saws. Most of the park was tarred over, and the tall buildings that rose along the far edge notched the sky with sharp geometric corners.

I stopped. Four concrete steps. A glass door. Hangul lettering combined with English.

CHOI WOH-KUNG

SU-NIM/MASTER INSTRUCTOR

SEVENTH DEGREE BLACK SASH

SAEBYOKE KOMDO

Suddenly I was afraid.

A second glass door inside the first closed behind me to keep out the city noise. Silence. I felt swallowed. Before me were a closed wooden door and a teak chest, polished and pale. To the right lay an open floor, the practice area. A cabinet stood in the angle where walls of rough brick came together. Two flags hung motionless. The stars and stripes of America and the flag of the Republic of South Korea, with its yin-yang sign and characters from the I-ching, hung still above the glowing floorboards.

The air was silent and still. Pure silence. Still air.

As I bowed to the flags the door opened and an old man with glasses and thinning hair stepped out of an office. Fear tightened me. When Peng Su-nim took me into his school he had broken a very old tradition, one that this Chinatown su-nim probably still honored. To show my deepest respect I got down on my hands and knees and touched my forehead to the floor. The carpet smelled of mildew and the cement beneath it. When I rose the corners of his mouth were lifted disconcertingly. Peng Su-nim had never smiled, never overtly showed any emotion other than curiosity.

I bowed and stammered my request. "Choi Su-nim, sir, I have come to beg admittance into your dojang."

I felt the resonance of Choi Su-nim's voice quiver in my chest. "I'm sorry, it's not possible. Saebyoke Komdo is a masculine lineage. It is studied only by men." Maybe it was his *nunchi* I felt in my chest because I saw him go still. He was aware that I had studied

27

swordsmanship. His smile vanished. He said, "Though teachers in other traditions of komdo have admitted females, this lineage has been all male for eight hundred years. From its beginning."

I bowed deeply and looked at the floor. "I too, sir, have studied Way of the Dawning Sword."

Choi Su-nim turned fierce, his mouth crimped, his cheeks quivered, the air grew charged, and he leaned toward me over his cane. He snapped, "Who broke this tradition? Who was your master!"

"I...I studied with Peng Su-nim, of Kyong-Sang Namdo Province."

Choi Su-nim straightened. "Peng Ton-Yee? Of the dojang of Nun-yo? On Green Dragon Bay?" I nodded. His mouth tightened, lines deep across his forehead. "How long?"

"I raked the sands of Peng Su-nim's garden for three years," I said, "and for eight years I studied in his dojang."

Choi Su-nim scowled. He decided to test me. "Did he teach you the lessons of mindfulness?"

I bowed. "Yes sir...some of them."

Choi Su-nim leaned aggressively toward me. "Did he teach you how to see the chinese maple tree?"

I nodded. "If one focuses on a single leaf, all the other leaves will disappear."

He pushed up his glasses, which were too big and slipped down his nose. "How are the leaves of the maple tree like Kwannon, the goddess with one thousand arms and one thousand swords?"

I rejoiced when he used the Chinese name for the goddess, as Peng Su-nim had. I said, "If the swordsman asks, 'How do I respond to this sword of Kwannon?' it is like looking at a single leaf. His attention will be consumed by the one before him and he will be killed by all the other swords. If the swordsman does not focus on one blade he will see and respond to all the thousand arms of the goddess. He will see all the blades of Kwannon, go from one to another and respond correctly to each."

Choi Su-nim's face slowly lost its fierceness, the charged energy receded from the air, the dojang was again neutral. I dared for an instant to glance up at him. Choi Su-nim was studying me the way Peng Su-nim had studied me as a five-year-old child, after I drove a snake out of his garden. I felt Choi Su-nim's nun-chi probing me, but I was no longer nervous. I had nothing to hide.

"The Young Falling Water," he said. "You know about that?"

I nodded. "I walked it. One week before my family and I left Nun-yo."

His mouth lifted like the wings of an old pelican. He bowed to me and I bowed to him. He said, "I am Choi Woh-Kung, sometimes called Mulberry Street Su-nim." He chuckled happily. In that moment I felt it flow like an embrace all around me, the calm that surrounds teachers fully in accord with the great Way, as if they gave off warmth and light like a sun. He said, "Peng Su-nim and I apprenticed to the same teacher."

I nodded. "Su-nim Lee Chul-Cho, who split rosebuds on the throats of his students with his ceremonial sword."

Choi Su-nim revealed his yellow teeth in a smile. I could not hide my own happiness; I smiled too; but then I recalled my circumstances. I lowered my gaze to the floor, where a hole worn in the grey rug revealed the wooden flooring and cement beneath.

"Choi Su-nim, sir," I said, "there is a problem." The worn rug told me the dojang was not a rich one. "I have no money. I, my family, we...we're new here."

I glanced up. His eyes were distorted by his thick glasses. He shuffled along the edge of the practice area, opened the door of a closet to reveal a broom, mop, bucket, and sink. He said, "Mop."

Another test. He went into his office while I mopped the practice floor. I swung the heavy mop, my shoulders ached, but when I stopped there was not a speck of dust or a hair left to mar the glow of the boards. Choi Su-nim came from his office. He knelt and inspected a split in the boards.It had filled with dust and hair but I had cleaned it with my fingertips.

He rose with arthritic slowness. "Practice begins every weekday at five o'clock. Come early to mop."

"Yes sir. Thank you, sir!"

I jumped down onto the sidewalk. Bird song tumbled out of the park, children laughed, the wind carried the whisper of mothers passing secrets, and a Pekinese yapped at the world from a high window. I passed a woman with her hair dyed green and teased into a peak. The egret look? I chuckled. In the fish markets on Canal Street I inhaled the mud smells of clams, oysters, conch, the light scent of squid slime and octopus. Already I was less lonely for Nun-yo.

I have a su-nim! I have komdo!

I hurried toward Auntie's place on Elizabeth Street. It was a pleasure to feel my breath sifting up out of my throat, feel the joy of laughter as I ran, leaped black gutters, dodged people, laughed, and just as I reached Auntie's building Ling jumped up from the stoop. Auntie called from her window, "Hurry up, get home!"

"I found him, Auntie! I found him!"

She brought down her window with a rasping of wood. I was too happy to notice it much. Then Ling said, "She's mad because I told her."

"Told her what?"

"That Appa hates komdo. That part of the reason we moved here was so you couldn't do it anymore."

I sighed, I stopped, but I couldn't be mad at Ling just for being Ling. We turned back toward Canal Street as I said, "It's his fault. If he hadn't taken me to see Chen-puin I never would've started doing komdo. And now, if I don't start doing it again you know what'll happen? I'll go crazy."

Ling's eyes went wide. "Crazy like him?"

Chapter 4

I was five years old, a skinny little girl, when I became a legend.

I was playing with the other children of Nun-yo village, digging in the beach with clam shells, splashing in tidal pools warm from the sun, or playing hide and seek among the boulders of the breakwater and between racks of leafy seaweed swaying in the breeze. Suddenly Appa-nim appeared. He took me by the hand, and not knowing where he was taking me—to be punished? What did I do?—I started to cry.

"Stop crying. There's no reason to cry!"

Stinking of the fish he chopped that day, Appa-nim pulled me by the hand up the steep lanes of Nun-yo. We hurried along the high road of the village until we came to a gate between a house and a building with a stone foundation. The voice of a man counting numbers and the lisp of many feet came from the stone building. The gate creaked on leather hinges when Appa-nim opened it, and we stepped into a lush and private garden.

A stooped old halmoni grandma came out of the house. I did not like Chen-puin the moment I saw her. Wrinkles competed for room on her face, her shoulders were hunched, and her jowls quivered under her chin. She said, "Kee-Yong, this way," and led me away from Appa-nim, into the beautiful garden.

Every day I had to leave my friends to go see this tutor woman. Every day I climbed the slope of Nun-yo, smelled the pigstys, goat dung, and the sourness of compost fermenting among the houses above the sea, opened the gate with creaky leather hinges, and met her in the garden her husband, Peng Su-nim, had created over the years.

Though my quick little legs were frustrated by Chen-puin's slow shuffling steps, the garden, with its white gravel path, turtle pond and palms that rustled overhead, made me feel I had stepped out of Nun-yo and into a world created for her and me alone. We sat in the shade of a persimmon tree, at a table of teak aged to the color of a setting sun. Wind swished among the feathers of bamboo plants above us as the melodies of Hangugo passed between us. Chen-puin showed me how to spell my name, then brought out a book of lessons, and I worked hard, for while I learned to read and write I also learned to love Chen-puin. She never scolded me, as Appa-nim did, but when I was unprepared she gave me no black bean cookie for my walk down the hill.

We were reading the rules in my grammar book one day when Chen-puin suddenly froze. She whispered, "Get in the house."

Her fear confused me, then I grew frightened. I slid off the bench and peeked under the table. Dragon? I had never seen a snake, didn't know what it was, a viper undulating in the cinnamon bush near her legs. She was terrified, so I darted from the table, to the stand of bamboo, wrenched a shoot from the ground and rushed at the viper as it rose to strike at Chen-puin.

With all my strength I swung the bamboo, made it snap against the snake's body, and the snake hissed and lunged at me with its fangs unsheathed. I made the stick swish and snap against the snake's head, swish-snap! swish-snap! It hissed horribly and feinted back and forth. I beat the snake as it writhed and swayed, striking at me, until it knew I would not stop. With a last angry hiss it retreated beneath the bush.

I did not stop. I thrashed at the bush high and low, screeching through my clenched teeth. The smell of cinnamon filled the air. "Kee-Yong!" Chen-puin had climbed onto the table, so I dropped the bamboo shoot and clambered up beside her. We peered over the bush. Beyond the bush was a sculpture, a slender maple sapling at the center of concentric rings raked in the sand. Two wavy lines marred the rings. One mark was of the snake coming and one mark was of the snake going. We climbed down off the table.

Chen-puin shook me by the shoulders and squeezed me tight, chortling, "My great little Kee-Yong, you're so brave. You saved my life!" She pantomimed my beating of the snake, threw her arms around me and laughed. I laughed, happy not to be studying.

When Chen-puin got herself under control she gazed at me intently. Some awareness, an intuition, alighted in her thoughts. She said, "For your bravery, Kee, you're going to receive a gift that has never been given before."

"What? What is it?"

"You'll find out," she said, "after your lesson tomorrow." She gave me a black bean cookie and sent me home. At home that night and all the next day I wondered, what is she going to give me? An elephant? A big fish? A thousand black bean cookies? Surely no one has ever been given a thousand cookies before.

The next day, all through my lesson I begged Chen-puin to tell me what was my gift. She would not say. When our work was almost finished I couldn't sit still. I heard a sound in the house, sat up straight and craned my neck. "Is this it? Is this my present?"

She did not reply. Out of the house stepped her husband. I had never seen him before. I did not connect him to the stern voice that called out the names of *poom-sey,* moving poems, in the school of swordsmanship that formed the western border of the garden. He wore thick spectacles, tested the path with the tip of his cane, then shuffled toward us.

I thought, she's giving me a little old man?

Peng Su-nim and Chen-puin shared the mutual silence of many years together. When I felt him looking deep into me I huddled against Chen-puin's leg. He was not like Appa-nim. I could tell by Appa-nim's face how he felt. Peng Su-nim's face was as still as the water in the turtle pond, at rest a dozen feet away. He tapped his bamboo cane on the white pebbles, weighed my fifteen kilos, gauged my spirit. He glanced at Chen-puin. He said, "It is against tradition."

In Confucian society tradition is the ultimate master. But what was he talking about? Where is my present?

Chen-puin's hand tightened on my shoulder as she looked back at him. Understanding of what I had done, that I had saved him from great sadness—maybe he glanced up and saw the fruit of the persimmon tree, ripening, and realized the world was ripe for change—but some knowledge passed between them. Peng Su-nim tapped his cane amongst the white pebbles. He stepped past the table, studied the marks of the snake in the sand, nodded his head once, and turned toward the house.

That was how I became a legend, the first girl ever to study Saebyoke Komdo, Way of the Dawning Sword. The name means the sword is not a weapon, but rather a way to enlightenment, to spiritual knowledge. But how did Chen-puin know her husband would accept me as an apprentice? It was as if he disrespectfully cut the topknot off the male-only tradition, making it as much a thing of the past as topknots themselves.

Korea was changing. The giant factories were taking root, sucking young men out of the villages and into the cities like water out of the land. When I asked her, years later, how she knew Peng Su-nim would accept me, she said, "I did not know. It knew."

"It knew? What knew? What knew what?"

"It knew the time for change had come. The Tao expressed itself through us, and through the snake too."

No one in Nun-yo had ever heard of a snake behaving that way, sneaking into a garden to attack people, so the legend spread that a dragon was sent by the gods to bring about my apprenticeship. I didn't know if it was a dragon, though it was strange behavior for a snake. I certainly knew I was no legend. It was just my childhood before I grew up to be a homely girl.

Then I came to New York, where I knew for certain I was no legend. I sat day after day on a squeaky crate and trimmed the rotten leaves off endless heads of lettuce. No, I was sure of it. That was something legends never did.

Chapter 5

Day seventy-three in America, I woke into darkness. Insanity is the darkness of the past erupting into the present. Our apartment was very dark, and Appa-nim's insanity was about to ambush me.

Ling sighed in her sleep, air conditioners hummed in the air shaft, and trapped with the one-eyed doll below our window was a cricket that called to me, *speet-speet, speet-speet*. I fit my spine to the wall, crossed my legs into the lotus position, and closed my eyes to meditate.

I focused on my breathing, the rhythm of my body. Echoes of my heartbeat sounded in my temples and throat and flowed outward down my thighs. After seventy-three days in America, resentment, sadness, and fear were disturbing me. I was desperate to renew my meditations; but I could not focus. The voice in my head whispered, He'll be up soon. Breakfast. Back hurts. Breathe. Pee first. No, just breathe. Breathe. Breathe.

"Kee-Yong." I opened my eyes. Appa-nim leaned in the doorway, his face large and pale in the dark. I hadn't heard the knob clack or the creak of hinges. He said, "Get up, we have to go to Hunts Point. Hurry up!"

Hunts Point is the wholesalers' depot for produce from all over America. I yawned, crawled past Ling, pulled on my pants, socks, shoes, slipped into a brassiere, and yanked down my shirt again. He saw me with only panties and a tee-shirt on? The thin cloth could not have left much for him to imagine about my breasts.

Then I wondered, as I had the day before, why our bins were empty, why Appa-nim had not ordered another delivery of produce. I stumbled downstairs after him. The bolts on the metal door clacked like pistol shots as he threw them open, his brows hard, eyes sparking.

The rattle of the grate roused me; he closed it again—*shruggle-uggle-BANG*—and as we tramped around the corner I was fully awake.

He motioned. "I can rent a truck from a black man around the corner."

I stumbled after Appa-nim. It was early-morning-dark, the sidewalks deserted, artificial light thin and grainy under lamp posts and on the cracked stone stoops.

He waved to a black man. "Chack! Yo!"

Jack was a man with wide flaring nostrils and red eyes, smoking a cigarette, a cup of coffee in his hand, one sleeve of his green army coat hanging empty. He stood by a truck with wide round fenders, graffiti sprayed over the flat sides of its box.

"It's the gook with the good coffee." Jack drank coffee with the cigarette still in his mouth, a neat trick. "What's up?"

"Kayo t-hurong, um, Hontspont."

Jack snorted smoke. "I told you, Mister Ahn gook, I no speakee Chinese."

Appa-nim snapped at me, "You talk to him."

In Nun-yo School I learned to speak to our teacher, but talking English to empty sleeve Jack was much more difficult. I bowed to him as he flicked his cigarette butt into the gutter, waited while he held his coffee cup in his teeth like a white snout, waited as he slipped another cigarette from a khaki pocket and lit it with one hand.

"Sir?" I said. *"Chibe-nim* Jack...uh...Manager Jack, truck today ka-yo go, um, go Hunts Point."

"Fifty bucks, back by lunch." Appa-nim understood the slang for money, banknotes and keys changed hands. We clambered like monkeys up into the cab, high over the parked cars and street, higher than stop signs. The dashboard was dusty, cluttered with papers, the windshield tinted orange by nicotine. The seat jiggled and shook as Appa-nim turned the ignition key. Jack asked, "You know how to use overdrive?"

"Ne, lunch time!" The engine roared as Appa-nim pushed the gas

pedal. He shouted at me, "We go, hey hey!"

We chugged, stopped, the gears ground together, we trundled to the light and turned uptown on Avenue A. The pavement and sidewalks were ghostly grey and white in the pre-dawn. "Here's the directions. We're going to a different company."

"Why didn't they deliver more produce?"

"They said I didn't pay for the last delivery, but I did. They cheated us!"

We traveled north on F.D.R. Drive. The sun was still buried under Brooklyn and Queens to the east, and the South Bronx was a field of crumbling brown teeth west of the highway. The tires whined, the engine roared, and Appa-nim sat angrily, tight in his mouth, his knuckles white on the wheel.

Bang! I was thrown against the door as the truck hit a bump on the off-ramp. "The directions, what do they say?"

"Um...left here."

We rumbled through a set of gates. Street after street of wet and glowing black tar. Row after row of doors like open mouths, arc lights, loading docks, conveyor belts coming tongue-like out of trucks that disgorged boxes, crates, bags of webbing bumpy with oranges, grapefruit, onions. Men shouted from inside the trucks. Groaning conveyors, dickering men, broken crates, crushed rinds, flourescent lights, headlights, and the smells of fruit sugar and decay, the oily gasping of tar as trucks crushing the ruts even deeper.

Appa-nim's forehead shone and his armpits were dark with sweat, his knuckles white on the steering wheel. *"Chegiral!"* Damn! "Where now? That stupid manager!"

I peered at Appa-nim's scribbled directions. "Left at the gate. Street four. Bay eleven on the left."

Appa-nim yanked the shift lever, gears knashed, the truck shuddered. *"Chegiral!"* I was unsettled by the curses jetting out of his mouth. He turned onto the fourth street, and half way down we spotted a sign. HAN KOREAN TRADING CORP. Appa-nim stopped the truck, his hands shaking. "Don't leave the truck!"

He leaped up the steps to the loading dock and disappeared behind a tractor trailer. I watched burly men on the long platform hoist boxes to their shoulders, carry them into warehouses, pause to flick cigarettes into puddles of water colorful with gasoline. Other men gulped coffee and jotted on bills of lading.

Appa-nim climbed in behind the wheel. "Stay close to me. Don't open your mouth. These men are not fit for you to speak to."

He backed the truck up to the loading dock, beside a long tractor trailer like a giant praying mantis laying eggs. Boxes whispered out of its dark belly on a bridge of casters, heavy with cantaloupe, and when they reached the end, were carried into the warehouse by two Koreans. One of the men had a flaming skull tattooed on the swollen muscle of his upper arm.

Appa-nim's clipboard held a list of all the fruits and vegetables we needed. The manager came out of his warehouse. One of the men stumbled and dropped a box. The box split, the manager shouted, and the man with the flaming skull pursued the melons that rolled across the floor.

The manager turned to Appa-nim. "You said you'd be here by four o'clock so that we can—" He peered at Appa-nim. "Is something wrong?"

Who knows what caused the change in Appa-nim? It may have been the hectic atmosphere, stress, a truck that backfired, the manager's reproach; but whatever caused it, Appa-nim's mental state collapsed inside him and his face crumpled. "Appa?" he whispered. His shoulders jerked, he hunched as if ducking bullets. He cried, "Appa! Umma, it hurts!"

Appa-nim dropped his clipboard. It clattered on the dock.

Han Chibe-nim and I gazed at him. Appa-nim was split. Inside was the tragedy of his past while outside he knew he was stricken; but he was aware enough to slowly descend the steps to the roadway. He ambled out to the front of our rented truck and disappeared around a curving fender.

Han Chibe-nim and I looked down the side of the truck. Appa-nim stayed out of sight. Han Chibe-nim picked up the clipboard. He said to me, "Is this what he needs?" I nodded. He glanced toward the cab of our truck and pursed his lips. He went into the warehouse and gave orders to the men. Crates of vegetables and fruits made their way, on the shoulders of the two men, into the hold of our truck.

The man with the flaming skull, sweat glistening on his face, paused to leer at me. He said, "How do you do, Miss Nice-Pair-of-Oranges. Welcome to Mi-guk," the United States.

He laughed. I turned and went downstairs to the road. I found Appa-nim sweating in the heat of the engine that rippled the air before the grill. He was hunched over and clutching his wrist.

"What did you do?"

"Take me to the bathroom." He'd burnt himself, red blisters near his knuckles, but the spell was over. "Don't just stand there!"

I took him by the elbow and we started for the stairs. I led him up to the platform, we maneuvered between men loading the truck and found a door marked with a male symbol. In the bathroom he thrust his hand into water gushing in a filthy sink. I flattened myself against the door behind him. In the mirror I saw the hate and fear that glittered in his eyes, the clench of his jaw, and it frightened me.

"Don't tell anyone about this. Not your mother, not anyone!"

"Yes, Appa-nim, I won't, no."

I pulled open the door and slipped out. Han Chibe-nim was in his office, the truck was full. The man with the flaming skull winked at me, I dodged him, leaped down the steps, wrenched open the door of the truck, and climbed into the cab. I sat shivering. In the side mirror I saw the flaming skull man return Appa-nim's clipboard to him, and Appa-nim went into the office to pay for the produce, some of which had not been loaded. We had not been watching and we were cheated.

After a few minutes Appa-nim climbed in behind the steering wheel. The burn on the back of his hand was bright red, the blisters small taut bubbles on his skin. He was drenched with sweat, the skin of his face stitched around his eyes, full of suffering. Instead of thirty-seven, he looked fifty years old. He said, "God damn Koreans."

He jammed the stick, we lurched away from the loading dock, roared down F.D.R. Drive to the end of it. I sat clutching the door handle, kept myself against it, as far from him as possible. We rumbled between buildings and he swore when children on the way to school darted in front of us. I didn't know him, this crazy man. Who is he? He turned the truck off Avenue A, onto St. Mark's Place, yanked the brake stick as we stopped in front of our store.

"The truck has to be back by noon" He snapped, "Get the dolly!"

He unlocked the grate and the metal door and I ran past the cash register, into the storage room. I called up the stairs, "Umma!" I was so relieved I felt the muscles of my neck, tense as steel cords, go slack as I sleeved the sweat from my face.

The door opened upstairs. Umma looked tired, her eyes pouched, wisps of hair floating around her forehead. "You made it all right?"

I grabbed the dolly. "Appa-nim got burnt."

Her mouth went crooked. She didn't want to know, turned away and closed the door.

Appa-nim dropped crates and boxes from the tailgate to the sidewalk, I stacked them on the dolly, and he wheeled them into the store. Sweat dripped off my nose. I stopped a man at our doorway. "No open."

"Yo bitch, how'm I supposed to know?"

Appa-nim rushed up. "You no swear! Go! I call police! No swear!"

The storage room filled with towers of boxed oranges, apples, spinach, lettuce, tomatoes, carrots, peppers, cucumbers. Appa-nim wheeled in the last stack of crated fruit.

"Ki-Teh, lunch!" Umma looked down from the top of the stairs. He leaned over his knees to rest. She said, "Come and eat."

"In a minute." He backhanded sweat from his cheeks and flipped his hand at the stairs. "I'll take the truck back. You eat, then fill the sidewalk bins."

I trudged up the stairs. We had no breakfast and I was dizzy with hunger. The kitchen was hot, the air heavy with the steam of boiled rice, starchy garlic smells. I sat at the table as Umma filled a bowl with rice and covered it with vegetables and creamy sauce.

"He scares me."

"What happened?" I shrugged in response and filled my mouth with food. I crunched water chestnut and stared into my bowl. Umma turned from the stove and came to lay her hand on my shoulder. "Don't worry, he's just working too much. He's tired, but so are you, so am I. It won't kill us."

I ate rice and vegetables and she went back to her refuge, the American stove that stood too high and made her look small. Appa-nim's shoes rasped on the stairs, haphazard, he was hardly able to lift them from tread to tread. His forearms bore scratches from the crates. His eyes glittered a warning when he caught me looking at the hand he burnt on the truck.

I rose from my seat. "I'll fill the bins."

I closed the door and hurried downstairs. Behind the cash register, I lifted the telephone off its hook. Glancing toward the storage room, I pressed the numbers Auntie Yen had written on a slip of paper posted by the phone.

A woman's voice. *Korean Embassy*. "Auntie?" *Kee? Hi, what's up? You're coming for an English lesson tonight, right*? "Yes, but I'm going to komdo class instead, at the dojang I found. I wanted to tell you ahead of time."

Silence. Her sigh sifted through the phone lines. *I don't feel comfortable helping you do what your father doesn't want you to.* "He hates everything Korean, that's why we came here. But Auntie, I—" *Why do you want to do that stuff? What good is it? What do you get out of it? I mean—* "Auntie, please, I...if I don't do komdo I'll go crazy too."

Footsteps on the stairs. *I just don't*— "I have to go, bye."

I hung up the phone as Appa-nim's footsteps clunked on the bottom stairs. He appeared from the storage room, his brow furrowed suspiciously.

"Who were you talking to? Tell me!"

Chapter 6

Monday. Nervous, I moved more and more quickly as noon passed and the hour hand on the clock crawled from one to three. Appa-nim would be alone at the register all the time Ling and I were gone to Auntie's, so he went upstairs for a break. I grew so nervous that while I tended the cash register, "Thank you, please come again," I moved quickly enough to make urns of coffee, regular, decaf, carton of cream, new ice—"That be all?"—stir sticks, cups, tops, sugar packets, napkins. I broke open rolls of coins, wondered who the men on the coins were—Who cares? I know where the su-nim is!—and I flitted and bobbed over the register. "Sixty cent change. Thank you, thank you, please come again."

His voice in my ear, Appa-nim startled me. "Go trim lettuce."

I spun around so that he looked at me funny. "Is Ling bringing down the books?"

He said, "They cost twelve dollars each. You'll practice with her, won't you?"

"Yes, Appa-nim. Thank you."

At ten minutes after four o'clock Ling came down with the new books, and I could tell by the rounded bottom of my bag that my rolled-up dobuck was inside it. I gave her a thankful glance. Appa-nim tinkled four subway tokens into my hand. "Tell your aunt I said hello."

Ling called, "Goodbye, Appa!"

"Ahnyong, plum. Kee!" I stumbled in the doorway. "Watch that she doesn't run in the street."

"Yes, Appa-nim."

I hurried after Ling, toward the subway at Astor Place, across the avenues and up the walks until she stopped short. "Wait, come here."

"Come on or we'll be late!"

"This is the best shoe store. Look!"

I went back and glanced through the glass. Boots of all kinds stood among dried tree branches and little cacti in multi-colored pots. English riding boots; cowboy boots; boots with metal toes; black, blue and red boots; boots made from snakes and alligators; boots lined with animal furs. How stupid. I pulled at Ling. "Come on!"

"Why hurry? So you can mop longer?" I walked away. She ran to catch up, shouting, "Hey! Slow down or I'll tell Appa."

I stopped. She bumped into me. "You better not." An ominous tone in my voice. "That wouldn't be good for you, either."

"I was just kidding. Slow down!"

At the subway I fit tokens into slots so we could slip through the turnstiles. A train with a glowing eye rumbled out of the darkness. On the train I perched on the edge of a bench.

Ling poked my bag. "He'll make you stop. Appa will make you stop, Kee."

"Only if you tell him."

Rumble ride ride, screech of brakes, and we leaped upstairs, out of the gloomy station beneath Canal Street. People shoulder to shoulder, bleating cars, tubes of neon, glazed ducks, gold chains, shouts, Chinese words drifting on truck exhaust. I pointed toward Elizabeth Street. "Don't talk to anyone. Go straight to Auntie's."

"You're not my boss!"

"Ling!"

She was a red bow and flying black hair among the hips and elbows; so I turned onto Mulberry, followed the fence of the park, and crossed to the four steps of Choi Su-nim's dojang. Like a sparrow making its perch, as I stepped into the stillness inside the second glass door, my heart alighted and settled in my chest. The door of Choi Su-nim's office stood closed and the school was silent. Actually, I thought I heard a chuckle come from behind the office door, but I was not certain, and I wouldn't believe it. Peng Su-nim never chuckled. I bowed to the flags and went to the cleaner's closet. I winced when I banged the metal pail against the door frame. The dojang should be silent!

I carefully mopped the practice floor. I did not wear my dobuck while mopping because it would have been disrespectful of the uniform. When I finished I looked around. Because I didn't know where else to go I closed the door of the cleaner's closet and undressed in the darkness.

Blindness.

What's that? Boys laughing out in the practice area? Why aren't they sitting in meditation? In Nun-yo talking and joking were considered disrespectful of the dojang, a place for a calm spirit. I tucked a new pad into my panties, cinched tight the strings of my bottoms, tied my black sash with a four-corner knot, and stepped out of the closet.

The other students went silent.

I sat with my back to the wall of the carpeted area by the practice floor. They didn't know what to make of me, the first girl ever to step out of the closet. More students entered from the dressing room, crowded the carpet, talked, joked. No one sat near me. Whisper whisper. Look, a girl. Whisper whisper. What is she doing here?

Choi Su-nim emerged from his office, clapped his hands, flushed his students like quail onto the glowing boards where they arranged themselves into lines decided by seniority. Six students wore black sashes, and so I didn't know where to put myself. Choi Su-nim parted the ranks to make my place, second only to a tall man with a wild ivy mustache growing over the corners of his mouth.

Sinclair Ames with the wild ivy was a patent attorney, I came next, then a very good-looking young man who was moved to make my place. Irritation grazed Craig Donafrio's tanned face, as if I had usurped him. His hair was perfectly styled, his small nose tipped upward, and except for his irritation, he was cute. Beyond Craig Donafrio was an American, a red-haired man with blonde eyelashes and blue eyes—what a striking combination!—who never spoke to anyone, and I never knew his name. I was the only Korean among the black belts, the only female, and I felt different.

We spent twenty minutes stretching and doing sit-ups. Tito, a little Cuban boy with a sharply pressed uniform, went to a bristle of practice swords in a cabinet and brought a bamboo weapon to each black belt as the others picked for themselves. I smiled as I gripped the sword. I thought, feels so good!

We began with steps, kicks, thrusts, attacks, stances. Brightness filled me. My body knew the postures but resisted me, I was a bit stiff, but it was pleasure to be moving again.

Choi Su-nim barked, *"Poom-sey hanna!"*

Choi Su-nim's easiest poom-sey, his simplest moving poem, was identical to Peng Su-nim's. I was immensely pleased that Komdo transcended time and place. Choi Su-nim called out the names of poom-sey, and as I listened to and felt my body perform I was vaguely aware of blurring brick walls, feet slapping, the sweep of bamboo, and that we students moved almost as one body, outside time, outside place.

Choi Su-nim called for more difficult poom-sey. The newer students sat down, blue and red belts retired to the carpet, and for the final exercise we seven with black around our waists spread over the glowing floor. My body felt as loose as a liquid. Still I was rusty and it disturbed me to be out of step with the others; but mostly we moved like the facets of a kaleidoscope. I tasted salt, shouted ke-hop, we gasped, our clothing snapped about our ankles, feet lisped on the floor, and seven bamboos swished like one.

Choi Su-nim said, *"Pah-doe!"*

We returned to our places, returned our bamboos to the cabinet, bowed to both flags and to Choi Su-nim, and class was over. I felt the glow of my cheeks, the tubes of light on the ceiling glowed, the world looked bright, and Choi Su-nim smiled with his full set of yellow teeth.

"Your Crane Stance is very good," he said. "How do you feel?"

I bowed. "Very good, Choi Su-nim, thank you."

"Where did you change? In the closet?"

I bowed. "Yes sir. I didn't want to disturb you, sir."

"No no no. Get your things." He beckoned. Laughter spiked the air and loud talk burst from the changing room. Students, boys, businessmen, Caucasian, Asian, dark-skinned, watched as I grabbed my backpack from the closet. He pointed to his office. "When you want to change, knock. I don't want you using the closet."

Peng Su-nim was dear to me, I loved him, but he was not open, so Choi Su-nim's friendliness unsettled me. Then I was shocked: as I stepped into the office and closed the door, Craig Donafrio was watching me and tugging on the Korean flag!

The office. A desk, newsprint cartoons on a chair, and on the wall a yellowing photograph of a young Choi Su-nim and a woman in traditional wraps. His wife?

While I dressed I heard him outside the door, laughing with Sinclair, the tall mustached man. The clang of lockers, chuckles and low male voices came through the wall. What kind of dojang is this? No sitting? No meditation? But I was flushed with pleasure, acutely aware of my body, the pulse playing in my throat, the liquid looseness of my limbs, and with my bag in hand I stepped out of the office. I bowed to Choi Su-nim, "Thank you, sir," and hurried to the door, yanked on my sneakers, bowed to the flags and hurried out.

The sky opened above the park. The summer trees beyond the fence shook their leaves like models in television commercials, proud of their silky hair. I jumped down the four steps to the sidewalk. I knew why the children in the park chortled and screeched. Alive! We're alive!

I trotted up Bayard Street, past an old man chirping like a bird. He shook a bag of fortune cookies. "Dollar? Dollar?" I trotted on. I darted through the crowds on Mott Street. The class had run long, and the joy that electrified my body in the dojang, by the time I reached

Canal Street had changed into anxiety. We're going to be late! Oops! My hip knocked an umbrella off a vendor's table, he shouted, and I veered onto Elizabeth Street.

Ling ran toward me, trouble on her face. "What's wrong?"

"Appa's really mad, we have to hurry. Here!" She stuffed a five dollar bill into my hand. "From Auntie."

"He's upset? Why?"

"He called to see if we were going to tape ourselves, for him and Umma to listen to. We lied, we said you were in the bathroom, but he called again." She grabbed my sleeve, her chin quivered, she started to cry. "I told him. He made me! He knows you found a teacher. I'm sorry, he made me. I'm afraid! He's going to spank us, Kee. Spank us!"

I stumbled, stopped breathing. I stopped seeing New York City swirling around me. He knows. A truck rumbled past. Oh no, what am I...?

I remembered Ling.

"Don't worry." I pulled her close, her shoulders shuddering against me. "I'll take the blame. Don't be afraid. Let's...let's go."

"Where?"

"Um...I'm sorry...sorry I got you into this. I'll do something. Stop crying, it'll be all right." She sniffed and wiped her cheeks as we shuffled toward the subway station. "Don't worry. I'll make sure he doesn't spank you."

"Promise?"

A man jostled us from behind. "Promise."

In the subway station I bought her a purple super grape lollipop. We rode the train uptown. She sniffed and looked at me with red eyes, then bit the lollipop and crunched it. I felt more and more nervous. What do I do?

It was plain what I had to do, so I told her.

I touched her hand. "Okay, this is it." I explained to Ling that Appa-nim would not do anything with customers around. He could not leave the register and Umma would be home before he could spank us; then she would stop him.

New tears glistened in her eyes. "You didn't hear him. He was screaming into the phone!"

"I won't let him spank you." We were shuffling through Astor Place. "I promise."

She clung to my arm, the broken lollipop shivered in her hand, and the more I thought the more fear poisoned me. I kept walking, I don't know why, because I had to swallow the nausea that surged into my throat.

Ling asked, "You promise he won't beat me?"

"Yes, I promise. I won't let him beat you."

But how could I stop him?

Chapter 7

Beyond the doorway of our store Appa-nim tingled coins into a palm. "Thirty-two cent change."

His voice frightened me. We stepped back as a man with a yellow hat came out. I clutched the edge of the onion bin, my nerves as brittle as the shells caught in a low corner. "That be all?" he said. A bag crackled in the store, my nerves crackled, my insides hurt.

Ling whispered, "We shouldn't go in until Umma comes."

I shook my head. "You do what I said." Her fear made her look like someone I didn't know. "Go!"

Ling plunged over the threshold, her steps clapping on the floor, then I heard her thumping safely up the stairs. I exhaled slowly before stepping into the doorway. An old lady and a teenager stood waiting to pay. Appa-nim's eyes narrowed. A fist clutched my stomach and stopped my breathing. The little muscles around his eyes hardened into pebbles, his mouth sank down, and his fingers struck the keys of the cash register like hail.

The teenager left with his cigarettes. I crept to the island, kept its potato dirt smell between Appa-nim and me. He slammed the cash drawer. The old woman straightened, startled. A pink plastic handbag dangled from her elbow. Her fingers fluttered to her hair, curly silver with blue roots. She asked, "Do you have escargot? Snails?"

Appa-nim turned his glare onto me. "You lied!" His fist hit the counter, *bang*! The old woman stumbled back. "You lied twice!"

"I'm sorry!" I tasted fear. "Appa-nim, I need it, komdo, I—"

"That justifies it? Lieing to me? I'm your father!"

He stepped from behind the register. "Please," I said, "don't punish Ling. Don't be mad at Auntie. It was my fault."

"That's what disgusts me. You were all against me. Scheming!"

He swooped past the island and grabbed a handful of my shirt. He shook me, his teeth clenched. I covered my face and moaned. "Did your mother know?"

"Appa, please!"

He shook me hard. "No? Only you three lied to me?"

"Please, I'm sorry!"

The old woman said, "Oh my...please don't."

Appa-nim's teeth, clenched, bit off the words. "Get out." He let go of my shirt and I stumbled back. "Get. Out. Get out!"

"But Appa-nim—"

"Get out! Go lie to your whore of an aunt!" I couldn't move. He leaned over me and pointed to the dark door. "Leave! Now! Get out!" I crumpled as if he'd hit me. "*GET OUT!*"

His face was a burnt color. He grabbed a persimmon, scowling, and threw it down, *sput!* He grabbed another. *Sput!* He grabbed another, broke it on the floor, *sput! sput! sput!* as grunts of rage came through his teeth. I backed away, burst into tears, turned and stumbled into the dark.

Among walking people, policemen, a man begging, I stumbled, blinded by tears, I was in shock. I couldn't think, couldn't remember. I reached out to a telephone pole. "Ah!" Fire in my fingertip, a sliver of wood. The green blur of a traffic light changed to red as I veered across the street, into the darkness of Thompkins Square Park.

I sank onto a bench, slats carved and scarred, a garbage can chained to the armrest, branches shaking their leaves over my head. What do I do? What? What? Blood seeped around the sliver in my finger. I sucked the sweet blood and cried and could not think. Grunts, voices came from cardboard boxes that leaned against the chain link fence of the basketball court. I rose and shambled out past the black gates and leaned toward Chinatown. I leaned over my sneakers, saw them blurry through my tears, fractured lights, sneakers poking ahead, taking me somewhere.

Dark tunnel streets, headlights flashed, I hugged myself, wept, bumped into people. Traffic lights turned from green to red, I crossed in front of gleaming bumpers, but I saw little else as I shambled onto Elizabeth Street and leaned south. Auntie's window was a bright yellow square half way up a brick face. I pushed a button. The door buzzed open. An eternity had passed. My face felt clogged, my head ached as I climbed the stairs. Her door creaked open, light fell over me. Her arm circled my shoulders and she drew me in.

Her skin smelled of flowers and aloe and the air in her apartment was still, calm, settled. She sat me down at the table and stroked my brow.

"I knew something was going to happen, but I didn't think he'd throw you out. Your father—" Perplexity troubled her eyes. "—he's smarter than I thought. Or he's..."

She rattled the kettle on the stove. My headache ebbed as I watched her lower tea from a cupboard and set out cups. Her loose hair, strand by black strand, rippled like fine lace off her shoulder, blue lights shimmering up to the white line in the middle of her scalp. Everyone's eyes hide mystery, Auntie's too, but the perfect shape of her nose, the fruit color of her unpainted lips, did less than most people's features to explain her.

"Or what?" I asked.

She tapped her head. "Or he's sicker than I thought. But he does have a serious control thing with you." A crimp in her lips as she set down my cup told me she wasn't saying everything she thought. I hid my glance beneath the dragon in my empty cup. She asked, "Did you think he'd be that angry?"

I stretched my arm across the glass top of the table as she poured gurgling steamy water. Light glowed softly off the glass, different from the broken glittering spikes of light outside on the street. Strawberry steam rose as I uncurled my finger to show her the black sliver under my skin.

"From a telephone pole."

She went and got needles in a cloth booklet. "Did you think...?"

The telephone rang. She crossed to a rattan table. "Hello?" I noticed that her toenails were lacquered a dark blue. "Yes," she said into the phone, "and she's been crying. Kee, it's your mother."

She listened for a few seconds before shaking her head.

"It's not the same here, and we have to make him understand that. Besides, Kee's mind is made up. She's as hard-headed as he is. Stubborn. So we have to work out a compromise." She nodded. She chuckled. She said, "Good idea. You work on him that way, and I'll read him the riot act. Lay down the law. Okay, bye."

Auntie kissed the telephone to kiss Umma and let the receiver clunk in its cradle.

"Your father is going to notice how bad the food tastes, how dirty the house is, and on Sunday morning she'll be too tired for you know what." She sat down, cloaking me with her aloe smell and warmth, and turned up my hand. With a silver needle she pried at the black sliver. "Know what I mean?"

I nodded. "All you had to say was Sunday morning. They always do it before we get up for church."

"Ah yes, the romantic Korean male."

I drank strawberry tea until a shape of heat formed behind my navel. "Who's going to help him in the store?"

"That's his problem. I'll stop by there after work and pick up some of your things." She carefully slipped the point of the needle between the red of my flesh and the bit of black wood. "So? You started telling me last visit. Why do you need this sword stuff?"

She probed, I winced. "Because."

"Because why?"

"Because it makes me feel...right." She arched a curious brow and pried with the needle. I searched for words. "It makes me feel like I'm doing what I'm supposed to."

I winced as she probed.

"Did you think he'd be this angry?"

"Well...his problems at the fish plant were only part of the reason he brought us here. He was also afraid of causing a storm in Nun-yo."

"What would've caused a storm?"

"Ending my study with Peng Su-nim. Ow!" She needled me sharply. "It would've split the village, Catholics against Buddhists."

"And you think *he's* stubborn?" One end of the sliver rose up past the whorls of my fingerprint. "I wondered, but I never understood what drove him to become a Catholic."

"He fell out of Kim's shrimp boat. He got fired, and then he converted." The clock over the sink read ten minutes after eleven. The black sliver popped out of my finger, and she hummed with satisfaction. "We haven't gone to Mass here because we don't have the time. That's fine with me. In Nun-yo I never ate the wafer, uh-uh, I always threw it into the ocean; but I wouldn't know what to do with it here." I shook my head and stuck out my tongue. "The thought of taking a man's body into my mouth, yuk."

One corner of her mouth curled ironically as she closed the book of needles. "No time for church? Interesting." She lifted the the top of the red lacquered chest. "If you want to keep studying this sword stuff you're going to need time, and money. How many blankets? One be enough?" I nodded. She carried linens into the living room. "The floor or the couch?"

"The floor." She unfolded the blanket beside the sofa and dropped the pillow by the speaker of her stereo system. "Thank you, Auntie."

She kissed me above the eyes. "I'll see you in the morning."

She turned and disappeared into her bedroom. Closing her door, she left me as I never was before in my life. Alone in the dark, far from home.

Chapter 8

No! Please no! I was deep in a dream forest, the mottled trunks of eucalyptus trees standing around us. Please Appa, no!

It was dark as only dreams can be dark, his eyes wide open, glowing white, crazy, and he was surrounded by a red haze. I kicked my feet, my head was bursting, leaves crackled as I kicked against him, but I was small, too small, I heard a roar, the roaring loud like a storm or a truck, and I knew I was dying.

"No!" I sat up, gasping. "No!"

My chest heaved and the pressure in my head rushed south, leaving me dizzy, stunned. I sat confused. I was in Auntie's living room, her Korean art looking out of place among her couch made of chrome tubes and leather and her lamps with large frilly shades. Outside the window a car door slammed, a straw broom whisked the sidewalk. The morning sun burned orange along the top of the building across the way, but on the east side of Elizabeth Street Auntie's window was still in shadow. I rubbed my crusty eyes. Her clock said 6:03.

I lifted myself into a sitting position. As I had in Nun-yo, and for two weeks in America, I relaxed into still thoughtlessness. The air relaxed me, or maybe it was knowing Appa-nim would not be rapping on the door. I breathed deeply, slowly. Time stopped.

Time started again when Auntie's shower began to sizzle in the bathroom. She clattered cosmetics, her heels clacked on the tiles in the kitchen, I opened my eyes.

I was at peace, my thoughts settled like dust onto the liquid stillness inside me. Auntie dropped bread into the toaster. The trouble of the night before was history, the shambling trek downtown in the dark, crying, seemed a long time ago. The red of Auntie's lips matched her skirt and vest, and a button cover at the hollow of her throat matched her black hair. I rose from the lotus position slowly and let my leg bones, in my hip sockets, rotate into their place for standing. I asked, "Do you always go to work looking so beautiful?"

She kissed my head. "I try. Here, sprinkle cinnamon on your toast, it's good that way. I'm late. Here." She gave me keys. "One for the street door, one for mine. Anything you want from home? I'm going to pick up your things." I checked to see that my bag with my dobuck sat by the door. I shrugged. She nodded, sipped coffee, then threw out a slice of toast with a half-moon bitten out of it. "Gotta go." She grabbed a pocketbook and opened the door. "I'll be home at four. Bye."

"Bye."

My mind was still, no voice in my head. I washed the dishes and the sink. I felt peaceful. I wiped the table, folded the blanket, then found myself in a unique situation, alone with no plan for the day. I wandered about Auntie's apartment. I leaned my nose close to her ink paintings, which were very old, and bent to peer into a clamming basket woven of bamboo shoots. I opened the red lacquered chest and lay in the blanket I slept on.

The smell of mothballs, I wrinkled my nose.

An oddness caught my eye. Down on the bottom of the chest, under blankets and old clothes, I glimpsed an odd edge. Splintered wood. I reached low, dug my fingers under the hard edge, pushed aside the clothing, and lifted out a big book, heavy and thick. Hm. The cover was wood, one corner damaged, mashed and splintered, and I don't know why but I sensed the cover was very old.

I opened it. The first page was blank, made of thick compressed paper. I was right. The paper was so old the edges were cracked and yellowed. I turned it gingerly. "Aigo." I hummed over a beautiful watercolor painting, a picture of a Korean village. Behind the village was a large bamboo grove, green with yellow tassels, hard against a mountainside. There was a painting of a cultivated valley, a checkerboard of crops along a blue river. There was a portrait of a man and wife in peasants' clothing. There was the picture of a man looking at his reflection in still water, amused, and I liked it very much.

I raised my head. Traffic noises from the window reminded me. I was not in Korea, I was in Little Italy, in New York.

Will there always be a back and forth? Auntie's apartment looked like an indecision between Korea and America. After sixteen years here? She collected Korean art and displayed it among her chrome tubular furniture and blue ceramic lamps with frilly shades. But there I was too, even within a single sentence, going back and forth between English and Hangugo. Back and forth, back and forth, as if I was living in two places at once, as if I was split between cultures. Even the food I put in my mouth, I thought. Half American, half Korean. Burgers and kimchi.

What about dinner?

I locked the door, skipped down the stairwell to Elizabeth Street, followed its curb to Canal and crossed to the markets. I wanted to thank Auntie by making *ing-o t'hwigim*. The markets were thick with people. Shouts, morning greetings, a man hosing the walk, the air moist with sea stinks and a whiff of green tea. I gazed over icy beds of butter fish, salmon hacked into red butterfly steaks, albacore, eels, needlefish, conches out of the shell like two-pound garden slugs, and I breathed the calcium smell of clams, oysters, the iodine pungency of crabs.

I inhaled those smells deeply. I was happy, alone, and still in the crowd. I watched a seagull drift above the rooftops. I was flooded that moment with pleasure, I felt joy in my body, my chest and throat and muscles light with love for my being there, my life. Along with that lightness came an understanding. I stood on tiptoe to glance over all the heads of the crowd bobbing around me, past me east and west, awed by a sense of the perfect clockwork movement on the street, as if I was immersed in a perfect and lovely mechanism. I sensed that powers greater than me, than my father, than my aunt, had brought me to that place. But why?

To shop, of course. I began to barter. I had only the four dollars left after buying Ling a super grape lollipop the night before. It was enough. I pointed to a carp, waved my hands, shook my head. "Oh well," I said, "too much money," turned away.

The fishmonger waved a hand with four-and-a-half fingers. "Hey girlie!" I turned back. "Okay!" he said, and so I left the markets with a blank-eyed carp wrapped in newsprint. I also wheedled for vegetables, filled my bag with wild leaf chinese lettuce, six water chestnuts, four sweet carrots with green hair, half a pound of snow peas, and twelve tender pearl onions.

I was the first girl ever to practice komdo, a masculine art, but Umma was careful to teach me to cook. We moved about the kitchen in clouds of aromas and steam. Umma's mother, Grandmother Bong, had taken great pains to teach her fish cookery because she said Umma was a plain girl, they were a poor family, she needed something extra to bring to a marriage. When Umma was demanding of me in the kitchen I knew the hidden meaning—I was plain too—but there was more than just the joy of doing it. I learned that cooking delicious food to feed the bodies of the people you love also feeds your own soul.

It was strange to me that as Ling got older Umma did not engage her in the cooking. She explained that Ling would not be one to boil rice. Neither was Auntie Yen. Her kitchen was a rectangle of tiles, row of cupboards, sink, a midget stove. I found eggs and old hard butter in the refrigerator, an unopened sack of flour in the cupboard. Not a vial on the rack of spices behind the stove had been opened. I could not read the labels. I broke open all fifty seals and smelled every spice—dill, marjoram, sage, ground pepper, even the orange of saffron.

I flopped the carp onto a cutting board, slit it open and happily dragged out its guts. I raised the liver into the light. Umma's best friend, Mansin With a Bump—Witch With a Big Tumor—told me you can predict the future of he who eats the fish by the color of its liver. Auntie's carp liver was the reddish brown of dried hen's blood. Ah yes, good omen.

As I made long strokes to scale the carp I recalled sitting with Grandmother Bong in her kitchen as everyone cooked for the Spring Festival. I sat on her knee and chewed roasted almonds as the old women told stories. There was the story of Chung, who sacrificed herself to the Dragon King in the river so that her blind father could see. She rose on a giant lotus blossom into the human king's garden, where she became a queen. There was the maiden who woke her lover from a curse by weaving a tapestry, or the girl that loved her hair, but who, when her mother died, cut it off.

I mixed the batter for the fish.

My favorite tale told how a plain village girl saw a prince, in the garden of the king's compound, and fell in love with him. The next day she went to meet him, but was stopped by the king. The king said, "You're too plain for my son. He can have any princess in Korea!" But the girl begged to meet the prince—I had a dream!—which gave the king an idea. He said, "I'll let him see you, but first you have to bring me the most beautiful gift in the world."

I doused the carp with white batter and put it aside.

"The most beautiful gift? What could that be?" the girl asked. The king said, "I'll know when I see it. Go see what you can find, and you better hurry." The girl knew what she had to get, the biggest pearl in the sea, so she went straight to the shore and started to dive.

I washed pearl onions and snow peas, and sliced water chestnuts. I was giving the finest pearl onions I could find on Canal Street to Auntie Yen. But will I ever meet a boy? Was Ti-Lee the only one who can love me, as homely as I am? Oh yes! Thinking of Ti-Lee made me recall the ivory figurine of Ganesh, a dancing elephant god that Ti-Lee gave me before I left Nun-yo. Yes, I must have Ganesh! I took the vial of garlic powder off the rack. I had run out of money before I could buy fresh cloves of garlic, so the old yellow powder had to do.

The girl in the fable dove in the sea. She found a giant clam, and somehow she knew it held a treasure, a gorgeous pearl. The giant clam asked her for the secret of her life, of all life. The girl's heart was full of love, but her chest was empty of air, so she couldn't speak; but the old clam heard the yearning of love in her heart and opened its stiff lips.

The people of the village knew she was crazy when she refused to sell the pearl for a fortune. Instead she took it to the king. He cried, "What? You bring me an ugly persimmon!" He saw a simple piece of fruit. But the prince heard him shouting and entered the room. He didn't see a persimmon. He saw the pearl, he saw the girl, and insisted that she become his wife.

The telephone startled me, jangling. Should I answer it? Slowly I lifted the pink receiver. "Hello?"

Kee?

"Umma?"

Are you all right? He didn't hit you, did he?

I started to peel a carrot at the sink, the telephone clamped between my shoulder and my ear. "He would have if I didn't run out. Did he spank Ling?"

No, but now he's got her working in the store. He called the Korean Association and they sent a boy over. I'm calling from the restaurant, I can't talk long.

Clattering pans, voices, a crackle in the wire, I knew something was wrong. "Umma? What is it?"

Why didn't you tell me you were looking for a su-nim?

"Because I knew you'd tell him. I'm sorry, Umma, I was afraid. I'm sorry."

Her sigh sifted through the telephone lines. *"I just want you home. Don't worry, you'll be back soon. A family is a family."*

I was tempted to say, Why rush?

You know what they say: He can see the infection on his finger but not the abscess in his heart.

"Yes, Umma." I kissed the phone the way Auntie did the night before. "I love you."

I love you too, Kee. Tell Yen I said thanks.

When I finished preparing dinner I sat in meditation for an hour, then knelt by the window to watch the foot traffic below—so many strange haircuts!—and at three minutes before four o'clock Auntie entered in a whirl of red, white, and black.

"You're cooking?"

I nodded. "Batter fried carp. And vegetables in garlic sauce."

"Oh." I dumped a bed of rice onto a platter and drew the fish out of the oven. Auntie said, "I'm supposed to have dinner with Harold." I stopped. I began to apologize, but she said, "No no no. This smells too good. Is it ready?"

We sat at the table. I waited as she divided out a square of fish, the batter crunching. The fish passed her lips, and she withdrew her gleaming metal fork. "Delicious!" She hummed and swallowed. I began to eat as she savored the vegetables. "The sauce is perfect. Enough garlic, not bland."

I asked, "Did you stop at the store?"

She chuckled and swallowed. "He's running around like a maniac. He yelled at Ling, so she stopped working, and he wanted to kill me when I said there are child labor laws, that he'd be arrested. He knew better. I brought your clothes."

"What's Ling doing?"

"Ruining cauliflower in the storage room. By the way, when was the last time you bought new panties?" I stopped chewing. "Those bras you have, they don't give you any support. We're going shopping. If you're jumping around in martial arts class, with what you're wearing now, you'll be drooping before you're twenty."

"Be what?"

"Your boobs will sag to your navel. Men cringe at a sight like that. What's your mother been teaching you?"

The blank-eyed carp told me what to say. "How to cook?"

"That's something. I didn't know how to boil rice until I came to New York."

I hurried to clean up and Auntie reapplied her lipstick in the bathroom before we left the apartment, she to meet Harold, me with my bag over my shoulder.

"Take your keys. I may not be home by the time you get back."

"Auntie, um..."

The clack of tumblers as she locked the door echoed in the hall. "What?"

"Do you have money for a subway token? I need to get something from home. I forgot about it. I need to get it."

"Oh." After I spoke she often said oh, as if she didn't understand my thinking. She gave me a five dollar bill. "I don't know if he'll let you in, but you can try."

"Thank you so much, Auntie. Tell Harold I say hello."

I stuffed the bill into my pocket and ran toward Canal Street. I reached Choi Su-nim's dojang, stepped out of the city bustle into silence as thick and still as liquid. In the closet I filled the rolling bucket with water that gushed steaming out of a faucet, but I could not be mindful as I slung the gray mop over the dull floorboards. Being in the present was hard because of my good mood. I caught myself humming a melody I heard on the street.

A moment after I settled into the lotus position, near the wall of the changing room, Choi Su-nim appeared from his office. I began to rise, but he shook his head to stop me. In respect I gazed down at the rubber foot of his cane. He leaned on the hook of it and asked, "Do you sit in meditation only before class, or at other times too?"

I bowed my head. "Yes sir, in the morning."

"Relax. This dojang is not as formal as Peng Su-nim's."

"Yes sir," I said, though I kept my gaze on his rubber foot. I did take the liberty to ask a question. "Sir, why don't you teach meditation to the other students?"

"Because America is different from Nun-yo, hectic and fast-paced. Parents expect their children to do many things in a day, so quiet practices are difficult to promote in them." His hand closed over the top of his cane. "Everyone in America wants to be a stand out."

"We sell beer to people on their way to work. Umma said it's because they work too hard."

Choi Su-nim shrugged. "I've taught here for thirty years. Only seven of my students have reached the point of Walking the Edge of the Street, the final exercise." A teenage boy, a black leather knapsack over his shoulder, rattled the door, kicked off his shoes, bowed to the flags and to Choi Su-nim, and ducked into the changing room. Choi Su-nim continued to speak in Hangugo. "Of the seven who Walked the Edge of the Street, only four awakened out of the American Dream. I guess Walking the Curb isn't as effective as Walking the Young Falling Water." He shrugged and smiled. "Or maybe the American Dream is more confusing than the Korean Dream."

Choi Su-nim shuffled into his office. I sank into the lotus position and focused on my breathing. His words echoed in my head. Walking the Young Falling Water. It terrified me. But why didn't I awaken? What's wrong with me? Disturbed, I couldn't relax and be still. As the other students crossed to the changing room they joked, chuckled, then slammed the door. The area around me filled with noisy boys. I kept my eyes closed and remained in the lotus position.

Choi Su-nim came from his office and we lined up to begin class. Too much noise, no meditation, thinking too much—or maybe talking about the Young Falling Water—made me distracted. Whatever the reason, I couldn't sharpen my focus on the stretching routines, stances and attacks. A feeling also began to color me, a sense that someone was staring at me. The thought condensed into a presence in my mind.

I glanced over my left shoulder. No, not there. We completed the warm-up exercises, and as we started the first poom-sey, the easiest moving poem, the identity of my observer slowly became known to me. I glanced over my right shoulder, and he looked away. It was a boy in the last line, a beginner's yellow sash around his waist. A finger of anxiety touched me: he was brown. Choi Su-nim called for more advanced exercises, Monkey and Boar, Lotus Petal Poom-sey, and I forgot the brown boy, forgot everything as I dissolved into the flow and rhythm of those more difficult moving poems.

We seven black belts finished and returned to *Choon-be,* Starting Stance, panting, arms straight, swords vertical. I felt like a waterfall, pitching spray, irrepressible energy rippling in my arms, humming in my throat, shivering up through my vertical bamboo. My face glowed hotly, sweat tickled my lips and I wanted more, my fingertips abuzz; but the energy was going to slip away, class was over.

Choi Su-nim said, "Tiger and Crane Poom-sey."

Tiger and Crane? He teaches Tiger and Crane!

The young man next to me, Craig Donafrio, remained standing beside me, while all the other black belts sat down. Tiger and Crane Poom-sey is very difficult, with spinning attacks, leaping roundhouse kicks, complex footwork. The Tiger Stance is an aggressive attack, low to the floor, while the Crane Stance is high, the swordsman poised on one foot, his sword rising from his forehead.

Craig Donafrio and I began our dance. My bamboo whistled, cloth snapped at my ankles, my feet surrounded by the white blur of cloth. I rose into Crane Stance and dropped into the Tiger, slashing, my bamboo splitting the air. "Ha!"

My ke-hop, Craig's ke-hop, echoed. Our feet slapped the floor like one foot, our bamboos whistled together. Then I noticed nothing more of him because the demands of that poom-sey condensed me into my body. Lights smeared. Lungs hurt. Tendons stretched in my groin, my arms ached, my hips rankled, my feet flexed. My dobuck snapped at my ankles and my sword hissed, air sifting with a grainy texture over the bamboo that became an extension of my senses.

Finally I turned slowly onto a standstill and raised my bamboo to poise it with readiness before my eyes. I planted my feet flat on the floor, in the Choon-be Stance where I began, and the energy pulsing down into my feet went like roots through the flooring, into the cement, into the bedrock beneath. Panting, I smelled the salts of sweat, heard the beating of the heart inside my ribs. It thumped, Home home home! Home home home!

Approval glistened in Choi Su-nim's eyes. He clapped his hands and we hurried to our places. We bowed to the flags, to him, and were released, tired but complete.

In Nun-yo, when Peng Su-nim released his students from class we left the practice floor silently. We knew we had taken part in an ancient tradition. Choi Su-nim's students instantly took up what they were doing before. As they gathered around the cabinet to stow their swords they jabbered, laughed, hummed tunelessly, and two men engaged in backslapping. I sensed the brown boy's eyes watching me. Craig Donafrio—he was watching me too, but slyly. Very good with the sword, I thought. He's very good.

Little brown Tito hurried to take our bamboo swords, a respect accorded to black belts. Craig Donafrio said, "Catch."

"Don't!" Tito's hands were full so Craig's sword rattled on the floor.

He laughed, stooped for the sword, and handed it to Tito. Craig had the flawless good looks of a young man on a beer commercial. He followed me off the practice floor and touched my shoulder as if he knew me.

"I'm Craig. Who are you?"

I looked down. The cuffs of his dobuck were stark white against his sun-tanned ankle. "I be…um...Ahn Kee-Yong."

"You're pretty good, Ahn. I've been slicin' and dicin' for nine years and I can tell, you're good." The smile he bestowed on me opened like a bright banner across his face. "Real good."

Choi Su-nim interrupted, gesturing to his office. "Your turn, Kee-Yong. Very good poom-sey."

I bowed. "Thank you, sir."

Acutely aware of my own senses, I felt the eyes of the skinny brown boy on me until I was changing in Choi Su-nim's office. He was a skinny boy with acne spots on his cheeks, his teeth too big for his mouth. I closed the door. The clang of lockers, laughter, male voices came through the wall.

Outside the office I bowed to Choi Su-nim and Sinclair Ames, the stockbroker chewing the ends of his wild ivy mustache. I skipped down the four steps and down the decline of Mulberry Street. A dog barked and children screeched joyfully on the blacktop behind the chain link fence. I looked up Bayard Street toward the market where I bought the carp, slipped between the shoulders and elbows that crowded Canal Street, hurried down the gum-spotted steps to the subway. The thought of seeing Appa-nim sent nervous energy skittering through me.

At the turnstiles I reached deep into my pocket. Where is it? That five dollar bill! I grasped, delved at the seams, felt my thigh through the cloth, slapped my chest pockets, back pockets, rifled my bag. Auntie gave it to me, but where is it? All I found was the change from my trip to the market. I looked into my hand, a nickel, a dime. Lost it? Five dollars? I grunted with disgust and turned toward the stairs.

Stupid! What do I tell Auntie? So stupid!

I stopped. The brown boy, the yellow belt, stood at the bottom of the stairs. He had changed into jeans, and his street clothes made him look even skinnier. He held out a token balanced on his fingertip. "Here," he said. "I have an extra."

The letters stamped on copper glinted, the aluminum center shimmered. I shook my head. "Um...I not can take those."

"I have extras." His nails were clean pink tablets at the end of chocolate brown fingers, his fingertips and palms a pale butterscotch color. "You headed home?" he asked.

A train rumbled in the tunnel. "I...um...cannot speak the English much."

"Here." He pressed the token into my hand and passed through the turnstiles with another. He beckoned. "Hurry up." The rumble of the train became thunder as its nose plunged past the line of steel pillars, its long silver body shaking and jerking until it settled along the platform. Still he waited for me. "Come on!"

Doors opened. People got off and on. I glanced toward the stairs—Long walk, I thought—then I jammed the token into the slot. I budged through the turnstile, we jumped downstairs; but the train doors rattled shut. Running beside me, the boy shouted, "*WAIT!*" Like magic, the doors parted. We leaped into the lighted car and he shouted, "Yeah!" Everyone looked at us. My cheeks warmed with embarrassment...and excitement? The doors closed, he laughed and looked at me, the good humor in his eyes glittering, and he said, "That was perfect. *We* were perfect."

No one ever called me perfect before. His spirits were so high that he seemed to glow. My heart beat hard as I leaned against the closed doors. "Where are you headed?"

I looked at the floor. "English I speak...not much." And when I do, I thought, I sound like an idiot.

"I can understand you." His teeth were white, but too big for his mouth, and the acne spotted his forehead too. "Where do you live?" he asked. "Are you going home now?"

"Yes, uh-huh. St. Mark Place and...and Avenue A."

"Is that where your family lives?" He spoke slowly so that I could follow. I nodded. The glints of goldfish swam in the brown liquids of his eyes. Nervously I looked out through the windows, but all I saw was myself, reflected in the glass. He smiled. I looked at a placard with a dead roach and a grinning housewife. "What's your name?"

The train slowed jerkily. I looked out for the station name. "Ahn Kee-Yong."

"Pleased to meet you, Ahn. You're incredible with the sword. You're even better than Craig." He put out his chocolate and butterscotch hand. Spring Street. I glanced down and did not know what he wanted. He reached for my hand and shook it, which I thought only men did with other men. "Good to meet you, Ahn. I'm

Ricky Tibbs."

I touched my chest. "Kee. Kee-Yong." I turned to the door. It wasn't my stop, but I needed to get off. People rose around us, doors opened, I ducked my head. "Thank you. Is good to meet you and...and token, thank you for it."

I stepped off the train, feeling like an idiot. Where's my English when I need it? The doors closed between us. As the train ruckled and rumbled away on its track he waved to me through the glass in the doors. His friendly smile made me nervous. I owed him a token, that made me nervous, or maybe it was what I realized as the train rumbled away into the dark tunnel. He likes me.

But why?

Chapter 9

I glanced over as long bony feet in black socks got plugged into oxford shoes, then tall skinny Sinclair Ames knelt beside me like a folding lawn chair. His nose, a toucan's beak above his wild ivy mustache, seemed to disappear into his face as he looked over at me. The same as Choi Su-nim, his eyes held calm amusement. He said, "Good night, Kee."

I finished tying my sneaker. "Good night, Sinclair."

I bowed to him, a senior student, bowed to the flags, and skipped out and down the four steps to Mulberry Street. After the class a warm egg of energy hummed below my navel, my thoughts pleasantly silent; but it was still a shock to step out into New York City. The street smelled of oil, trash filled the gutter, gulls pecked at a pizza crust, and the trees in the park stood like emblems of the natural world that was gone from there. Buildings notched the sky, telephone lines, poles, signs, and lamp-posts cluttered the air. Even the curb had a hard steel edge and the cobbles of the street showed where the tar had crumbled beneath the pounding of Chinatown life.

"Kee! Kee-Yong!"

I stopped at the corner where Bayard Street rose from Mulberry. It was the boy who gave me the subway token, whose name I had forgotten. He ran after me from the dojang. Caution tightened me, but I needed to be polite. We were deep into summer, his forehead wore a sheen of sweat, and his too large teeth reflected the sunshine.

"You always charge out of there so fast it's hard to catch you. How are you?"

I nodded, "Good," and turned up Bayard Street.

He hurried after me, into the crowds on the sidewalk. "You're not going uptown?" I slowed to a shuffle as shoppers bunched up before me. I didn't know what to say. How could I tell him I was thrown out of my father's house? I felt uneasy as he spoke over my shoulder. "How long have you been practicing komdo? Did you start in Korea?"

"Uh-huh. Nine year." Shoulders packed together ahead of me so I slipped past a parking meter, out between bumpers of cars and into the street. It struck me that I was acting rudely. I stopped. "How are you, um...your name? Your name is?"

"Ricky Tibbs. I'm fine. Where are you headed?"

"Auntie Yen. Hers place." I strode, he hurried to catch up, and we reached Mott Street. I pronounced carefully. "'lisbeth Street."

Ceramic dragons roared behind glass, a child spoke Mandarin, a toothless old man opened his gaps to laugh, and somewhere oil hissed in a wok.

Ricky struggled through the crowds to keep up. "Did I tell you? I live on the Upper East Side. Yeah, my father's a stock broker. He works on Wall Street. He crunches numbers all day."

"Crunch numbers? Like…um…cereal?"

Ricky chuckled. We reached Canal Street, the bank on the corner built like a pagoda, tiers of red rooftiles dull with soot. I waited for the light to change.

"He makes stupid money," Ricky said, "but I don't think he likes it. My mother samples cakes for a living. She loves it, but she's also getting kind of hefty." The light changed, a flock of people started across, but he plucked my sleeve. "Wait."

Ricky licked his lips nervously. "We should do something. You wanna? This weekend? We could see a movie or, yeah, go to the park. Why don't we check out Central Park?"

Central Park? The heart of New York City? I clutched the strap of my bag, looked toward the flock of people striding under the traffic light, tension damming in my chest. I couldn't think, my throat tightened, and suddenly my head was shaking. I blurted, "No," and hurried into the street.

Horns blared, I skipped out of the way of cars, and glanced back.

Heading toward the subway station, Ricky Tibbs was still gazing at me. His glance met mine, then he bumped into a table full of medicine roots. An old crone screeched, he grabbed for tumbling roots, and I couldn't help but chuckle.

He's nice. He really likes me. He stepped around the table and waved to me, grinning like a fool, but for the first time I thought he was cute. Not the way black belt Craig is cute, I thought. But he is nice.

I jogged east on Canal Street, north on Elizabeth to the doorway of Auntie Yen's building. Up the street a singer had his keyboard set up on the walk, crooning behind it. I squinted. He was the drunken man who threw my persimmon back at me. His cheeks were covered with dark stubble, his eyes hidden by sunglasses, his hair tied in a ponytail. I unlocked the door and hurried up the stairwell.

So many angry men. Angry women too. As I unlocked the door I heard Auntie's voice.

"She works seventy hours a week! Ki-Teh, you're not being—" She looked at the receiver in her hand. "Damn you!" Clack, she slapped the receiver into its cradle. "He hung up on me, your father, again. Tea?"

"Yes, please. What did he say?"

"Your mother's cooking is so spicy it makes him sweat." She swished water in the pot, then made a circle of blue flames appear beneath it. "He caused the problem. You're an asset, you deserve equal pay. I asked him if he shouted at the new man the way he shouts at you."

"What new man?"

She glanced over her shoulder at me and nodded. "He hired a helper, but he can't tell if he's half retarded or just quiet, so no, he doesn't shout at him." She kicked off her heels and sat down. "I talked to your mother. She said he doesn't want any more Korean food."

"But he loves Korean food."

"Let's go to Macy's. The water's hot." She pushed buttons on the telephone as I poured steamy gurgling water into our cups. The dragons disappeared as the tea darkened. She said into the telephone, "Ki-Teh, listen to me. Working at a pizza joint seventy hours a week—"

I said, "Eighty hours."

"—she'd earn five hundred dollars." Her hair writhed down her back as she shook her head. "I'm not lying. And the new man has already cut himself, trimming lettuce. Kee never cuts herself. Your insurance rates, what if Mu slices his finger off?" Her eyebrows pinched together as she verbally pinched Appa-nim. "Be reasonable. She deserves—"

She glared at the buzzing handset, then hung it up. "Tough case, but I'll get him." She slung a clam shell pocketbook over her shoulder. "Forget the tea, let's go shopping. Hurry up."

"Should you be putting so much pressure on him?" I carried the cups to the sink. "I don't have any money, and Appa-nim won't pay you back."

"He's not fragile, and that's precisely why I'm bargaining so hard, so you have some money. Business is business. It's good for business if everyone involved is justly rewarded." She locked her door. Echoes of our footsteps bounced up and down the stairwell and along the wooden hand rails. "I've got twenty-five thousand dollars tied up in that store. Whatever is good for that business is good for me, and it's only good business to keep a valued employee satisfied. Valued employee, that's you."

Late daylight warmed my face as I followed Auntie across Elizabeth Street. Three pigeons squabbled over a squashed cannoli. An open door revealed a man hammering on the sole of a shoe. We reached Broadway, where Auntie raised her arm.

"Taxi!"

From the moment we walked into Macy's I had to keep closing my mouth. Glittering chandeliers, neon, mirrors, mannequins, chrome, two restaurants, travel agency, hair salon, a flower shop that perfumed the air, people perfuming the air and crowding the aisles. Staring, I bumped into Auntie. "Be careful."

"That dummy moved."

Auntie walked over to a mannequin dressed in a slinky blue cocktail dress. She asked, "How much?"

The mannequin, a woman model, struck a pose with a hand on her hip. "Two Sixty-Nine Fifty. Ladies apparel, second floor."

We rode the moving treads of an escalator, my head turning as lights flashed, spotlights lit up famous names, and then Auntie stepped off and away so fast that I had to hurry. We came upon rack after rack of brassieres dangling from golden hangars. I looked at the price tags as she riffled them with a practiced eye.

"Thirty-seven dollars? For one?"

A saleswoman approached, dressed in a man's black suit, her earrings jingling faintly. Auntie waved her away. She chose four sports brassieres, five simple white ones for everyday, and one of sheer black lace.

"A black one? What for?"

"For the same reason you want one of these." She stepped across the carpet to a carousel of lingerie. Her fingers showed through the black lace of a boostey-something. "Want one? Men love them."

"Um..."

"Let's try them on." She chuckled over my expression. "Loosen up, have a little fun. Here." She handed me a hangar with red smoke draped over frilly straps and lacy cups, and at the bottom, lace panties inside a red mist. She led me into a changing room. Even as she closed the door she started unbuttoning her blouse.

I looked at the red smoky cups and panties. "Go ahead." Her skirt rustled down around her hips. "As your aunt, Kee-Yong, I'm ordering you to put on that bustier."

I had never taken off my clothes like that before, except in front of a doctor. Auntie giggled in her nakedness, and while I undid my pants she stepped into her black teddy bear and gracefully assumed it.

"I don't know if we're supposed to do this. Hurry up!"

She undid the hooks of my brassiere, between my shoulder blades, and when I straightened from pushing down my panties the mirror reflected my naked breasts, the dark hair in the funnel of my hips. Quickly she drew the bustier up my thighs, guided my arms through the straps, which she adjusted as I tugged the panties into place. Not that they concealed me.

"There," she said. "What do you think?"

I looked in the mirror and my eyes opened. I did not know me. I didn't know what to say, I was uneasy, but I couldn't look away. For the first time I saw my body as a place of...*aigo*...blatant sexual beauty. I mumbled, "I look like a..."

"Like a woman." I looked down at my nipples, peeking from under lace flowers, my breasts misty within the red smoke lace that shimmered over the flat of my stomach, the lace flowers of the panties darkening over my womanhood. Auntie giggled and fanned the black crepe that hung on her as sheer as tinted water. "Makes you feel good about yourself, doesn't it."

I stood like a store dummy, unable to express that kind of body language. "Is it supposed to?"

She drew my hair back as we looked at me in the mirror. "You're beautiful. You don't think so, Kee, but you're a pretty girl; and that fencing you do, it's given you a beautiful figure. See? Mine are already falling." She turned sideways to show me how her breasts had settled on her chest. "We've got the same breasts, but I'm getting old."

"Auntie, you're gorgeous. Everyone on the street looks at you." She drew her teddy bear off her right shoulder and cocked her hip. I looked at my breasts, at Auntie's breasts. I said, "How come we have big ones? Your mother didn't, and Umma doesn't have any."

"I don't know. Sometimes it skips a generation."

"Then we both wouldn't have them, would we?"

She shrugged. "An old American expression: don't look a gift horse in the mouth."

When we left Macy's it was dark, the buildings were tall honeycombs of light, golden windows stacked over the glow of the streets, the sky turned into a mother of pearl patchwork of clouds. A red bag crackled on the seat in our taxi. Auntie said, "Let's make a deal. We'll call it even if you make me *ing-o t'hwigim* once more. Okay?"

I glanced at Auntie. Lights flashed, I saw her face, then she went dark again. She was serious. "I'll pay you back, and I'll make you the fish anyway."

"No no no. Make me the fish and we'll call it even. Will you need more money?"

I shook my head. "I thought I lost that five dollars you gave me. Then I found the bill right in my pocket, after Appa-nim shouted at me." The night before I had gone to our apartment, above the store, to get the figurine of Ganesh that Ti-Lee had given me. I said, "He only let me go upstairs for two minutes."

"How did you get on the subway?"

"A boy from the dojang gave me a token."

"Oh. Is that why you were late getting back tonight?"

For some reason her words needled me. "No. He's just a boy from the dojang."

The milk smoothness of her brow flawed itself. "Remember what I said about your figure? He'd know you have a nice body even if you wore a fur coat over a nun's habit."

No, I wanted to say, Ricky Tibbs is too nice for that. Auntie was sure of herself, and I was in her debt—but then I saw lights flicker across her eyes. It became plain to me. There was a hardness about my Auntie Yen, an unyielding will. I felt it, but in the time I lived with her that hardness worked for me and I owed her more than I knew.

When Auntie Yen called the store, Appa-nim's face flushed, he shouted at the phone, banged down the receiver. Ling told me what usually happened. Appa-nim would storm into the back room, mutter curses and break wooden crates. It unnerved the new man. The new man's name was Seung Mu. When Appa-nim stalked into the storage room Mu hurried out to check the sidewalk bins.

When we got back to Elizabeth Street Auntie paid the cabbie, and as we climbed in the stairwell of her building I recalled what she said about Appa-nim's insecurity. She unlocked her door. I later came to know her life was a series of trades, bargains, sacrifices, one thing for another. She bargained with Harold, with me, with Appa-nim for me, and she was good because she was hard. I came to know that Auntie bartered so hard because she saw life as a shell game, and she played as if, under all the shells, there was no pea of meaning to be found, not anywhere.

My poor Auntie Yen had no Tao or God to trust.

She thought she knew Ricky Tibbs better than I did, and maybe so. She lifted the black brassiere out of the red Macy's bag and said, "Is he cute?"

"In a way." I shook my head. "But his teeth are big and he's as skinny as Appa-nim." She cut away price tags, snicking them off the bras and panties with a pair of scissors. I felt I had a touch of Auntie's beauty when I said, "He asked me to go to Central Park."

"Congratulations. When?"

"Want tea? I told him no."

"Why? It would be fun."

I lifted the red kettle. "Tea?"

"Don't change the subject. What else are you going to do? I'm going to Atlantic City with Harold, so you won't have to cook the carp. You don't have anything planned for the weekend, do you?"

I made excuses. I had no money. She put twenty dollars on the table. I could not find my way around the city. She produced a map with all the street names written in Hangul. In the morning she spoke as if sleeping was only a pause in her argument.

"You could rent skates," she said, "and make him chase you around the reservoir."

Skates? Calm after meditation, I rose as she ate her bite of toast and tossed the crust in the garbage. "I turned him down. He won't ask me again."

"Men are gluttons for punishment. Put your sword down and loosen up." She swept a crumb off the front of her dress, which clung to the contours of her figure. "Learn to have a little fun. Life shouldn't be all work."

"Speaking of work," I said, "I'm going to buy a *Hankook Ilbo* and check for jobs. Appa-nim's not going to give in."

"If I play with him enough, he'll cave. Boys are fun to play with too, as long as you maintain control." She fluttered a blur of red fingernails. "Oh well, do what you want. Bye."

I washed the dishes and went out to buy the *Hankook Ilbo*. I spread its crackling newsprint on Auntie's glass table. The President of South Korea was quoted in banner headlines: THE NORTH SPREADS TERRORISM! I did not know if that was true. I only knew it was sad that a people could be divided against itself by little selfish men. Families had been splintered decades ago and were yet to heal. I flipped the pages quickly.

In the help wanted section there were ads for work as a seamstress, a cook, a maker of silk flowers, people to stuff mattresses, deliver pizza, serve ice cream, and to take care of old people. I could do that, I thought. I remembered the whine of sewing machines that descended from the sweatshops of Chinatown. I could do that. If Appa-nim won't take me back, I can find work. I peered at ads for Buddhist shrines, statues, incense, and cushions for sitting in meditation. I got out the map written in Hangul and looked to see where the Buddhist stores were located.

Forget it. No money.

Those ads reminded me, so I went to the wall below the window, by the red lacquer chest, and sat in meditation for a long time. My shoulders settled away from my ears, then the kinks of tension dissolved from my throat. The honking of horns came in from the street.

In my inner silence I sensed, as I had before, questions that pointed toward my bond with the world. Could I hear if there was no sound to hear? A tire studdered against the curb. Is there sound if there is no ear to hear it? I sat silent and listened carefully, and the answer came.

Honk honk, a driver goosed his horn on Canal Street.

Chapter 10

Kim hweseg. Grey seaweed. The mop looked like grey seaweed. Other than those two words my mind was silent as I pushed and pulled the mop over the floor—slosh and gurgle in the bucket, tendrils of hot steam around my hands as I rang out the grey seaweed—and the dojang was silent except for a chuckle that came from Choi Su-nim's office as he read the funny papers.

In the five days of taking classes and meditating in Auntie Yen's living room I had regained what I lost in the seventy days in New York when I was not practicing komdo. I felt relaxed, flexible, at peace. Ricky Tibbs was at the back, Craig to my left, but I did not feel their glances. My body moved without being ordered, I did not need to count the steps and phrases of movement during poom-sey.

Performing a poom-sey, a moving poem, is meditation in motion. You know you are performing properly when you feel too much to think. The body hurts, cries out for rest, but continues to move with the liquid quality of water. I felt no rankle of bones in sockets, the movement of my limbs and the bamboo was unified and automatic—the cuffs of my pants snapped crisply, my practice sword parted the atoms of the air, I felt them sift over my whistling bamboo—my lungs strained against my ribs, my ribs parted like the blades of a fan, and the poom-sey went on and on. Physical pain.

Spiritual purity. The body floats over a center rather than rushing unbalanced from one stance to the next, one direction or another. The mind observes. Pure awareness. It is purified by the million sensations of proper execution. Bones and flesh move through pain though the mind gives no commands and is not active. The body has wisdom of itself. Tendons stretch painfully, there is sweat, pain, the spine arches, colors blur, pain, lights, blurs, air, and cloth harsh against the skin, the body made of a million parts working through pain with beautiful precision.

When I finished Tiger and Crane Poom-sey Craig was still sweeping the air with his bamboo. He reached Choon-be, Ready Stance, and the dojang became silent except for his heavy breathing. Everyone ran to take places around us, we bowed to the flags, to Choi Su-nim, and class was over.

The lines broke. Voices echoed off the ceiling. Craig held out his sword to Tito. "God, Ahn—or is it Kee?—you were moving. Tito, hurry up." Tito had to juggle the sword Craig pushed at him. Craig said, "Maybe you are almost as good as me. I was fourth in the nation, two years ago." I walked, shyly looking at the floor, and noticed that one student, a bearded man, wore a gold chain around his ankle. Craig said, "I'm good. I'm really good."

I nodded, "Yes, uh-huh," and stepped into the office.

I did not see Ricky Tibbs. Will he try to meet me? That thought made me nervous, but differently than before. Auntie has fun, why shouldn't I? With my bag I stepped out of the office. I bowed to Choi Su-nim, "Good evening, sir," and bent to pull on my sneakers.

"Kee-Yong."

I stopped. "Choi Su-nim?"

"Very good Tiger and Crane Poom-sey. Very good."

"Thank you!" I bowed and smiled, "thank you, sir!" and hurried out and down the steps to the walk, pleased by his praise. A helicopter chopped the sky, bleached pale white by the heat of the day, and when I turned down Mulberry Street I could hardly stop my heart from laughing because Ricky Tibbs stood at the corner, leaning against a blue mailbox. He smiled with his big teeth.

"Kee, you were incredible. That last poom-sey, wow!" We started up Bayard Street. "You're a lot better than Craig. What did he say to you? He thinks he's hot stuff because his father's the Assistant District Attorney."

"Assis' what?"

"Assistant big shot. But you were too frisky, he couldn't keep up!"

We walked slowly. He smiled when he glanced at me. I asked, "How is you?"

"Fantastic."

He was glad to be with me, but there was also a quick piercing observance in his eyes, as if he was trying to decipher me, a new letter in his alphabet. On the corner of Mott Street two Chinese men threw toy airplanes that looped and buzzed like honey bees. Ricky Tibbs caught one, laughed, and gave it back to the man.

"You know," he said, "I'm going to keep asking you to go out with me until you say yes."

What would Auntie do? I had thought about what Auntie said all during the day. I said, "Yes?"

"Yes what?" He stopped.

I stopped. "Yes yes?"

"Excellent! That's so excellent! What do you wanna do?"

A man on a bicycle, okra in his basket, swerved to avoid us and rang his handlebar bells, ring-ling-ling. We started walking again. I said, "Centra' Park?"

"Sure. I could bring a friz. We could catch some rays in the Sheep Meadow." He skipped beside me as I watched shoes, work boots, sneakers, clickity-click spike heels. "What day?"

"Iryo-il? Um...Sunday?"

"It's a date, fat and fresh." We reached the corner below the pagoda bank. He skipped away through the crowd, danced along the curb, dodged between tables, waved and shouted, "One o'clock. Excellent! See you then, Kee!"

I ran up Elizabeth Street, leaped upstairs two by two, burst through the door and stumbled over the bag Auntie had packed for her trip to Atlantic City. She sat composed at the kitchen table, sipping pink wine from a bell glass.

"Guess what, Auntie!"

She smirked like a tipsy cat. "No, you guess what."

"No, tell me."

She flashed her white teeth. "Your father came around. He wants you back!"

I lowered my bag. "Already?"

"Already? It's only been fifty phone calls in five days. He came around, though. He agreed to let you go to Chinatown three nights a week. And get this: Sunday afternoons off."

"Then I can go out with Ricky Tibbs. Auntie, I have a date!" I grabbed Auntie, hugged her, we laughed and jumped around like school girls. "We're going to Central Park on Sunday. Thank you, Auntie, thank you!"

I stopped. I sat across from her and leaned on my arms. Uneasiness crept into me. Auntie and Umma did not convince Appa-nim to accept me back. It was something else. Something hard, inside Appa-nim himself, must have broken his resistance.

"Did he hurt himself?"

Auntie Yen shook her head. "I made him see that if you were fairly rewarded for your efforts, like anyone else, the business would be stronger. You're part of the business as much as you're part of the family. Don't worry, he's fine. Everything will work itself out. But I don't want you to go back home until he agrees to pay you cash too, at least a little." She touched my wrist with a fingertip. "And you have a date!"

"Oops," she said, "I have a date. Blackjack on the boardwalk. I'll be back Sunday night." She kissed me and grabbed her bag. She said, "Bye," and left me to dump her wine into the sink.

I'm going home. Pensive in the silence Auntie left behind, I held the bell glass up to the light. Like my life, I thought. Clear, flavored, but with what?

Flavored with a date! But what are we going to do? As I cooked my simple dinner, doubts squirmed into my head. What did he mean, throw friz? My English is so bad we can't even sit and talk. Starch mist rose from a pot of rice. He'll think I'm dumb. Ignorant. Unschooled.

Those thoughts went through me all day Saturday, and by Sunday noon I was so nervous I almost did not go out to the subway. Finally I did, and I bit my nails and had to go to the bathroom. What would Auntie do? It was hot on the train and the air smelled of sweat. Everyone looked angry. An old woman's flowery hat had wilted, so I stared at the grimy floor and thought grey thoughts. It doesn't matter what Auntie would do. She's beautiful. Not even Ricky Tibbs could think I'm beautiful. What if he's not there?

We had agreed to meet at the southeast corner of the park. I climbed up the subway stairwell to the intersection of Fifth Avenue and Fifty-seventh Street. _Aigo!_ Chrome buildings, marble walks, windows full of diamonds, furs, gold cigarette lighters and...and I was so relieved and happy to see Ricky Tibbs, across the avenue, waving to me. His white smile opened his dark face. He's cute. He wore big black and white sneakers with purple laces, and a bright green shirt with YO! stretched across his chest.

I chuckled. He is cute.

Somehow I stumbled off the curb. How embarrassing. The sky spread blue over the park, and Japanese couples bunched like bananas around a tour bus.

We met at the curb. I said, "Bathroom?"

"You have to...okay, come on." We crossed the street to where men in red tuxedoes waited by horse carriages reserved for people staying at the Ritz-Carlton Hotel. I hung back. Ricky leaped up the stairs toward the brass doors. "Come on!"

"No, we should no go there."

I followed him in, bumped into him as I looked up...up...up the grooved marble pillars to where chandeliers with four hundred lights scintillated. A man with gold buttons put out his white glove to stop us. Ricky said, "She's on the Korean team."

The white glove said, "Yeah, right," and let us go in.

A bathroom, wow. Gold faucets gleamed, gold circled the stone basins, and a saleswoman stood beside shapely bottles on a shelf. When I came out of a stall she said, "Have you experienced Prince Machiavelli?"

"Oh no," I said. "I am with Ricky. Date number one."

"Wonderful. Here, let me." Before I could say not to, she spritzed me. My eyes opened. She said, "Only eighty-nine dollars. He'll like it."

I saw myself in a mirror, looking foolish in that wealthy bathroom. I said, "I have not much to speak about. With him."

"Oh, it doesn't matter." She smiled, flipping her hand. "He's just as nervous as you are."

"Um...no way!"

We laughed, then I ducked out.

I almost bumped into Ricky Tibbs. "You smell delicious. I got the friz, let's go." We skipped out between the tall white pillars, out and across the soft tar avenue. He whinnied at a horse. "This is excellent!"

We crossed into the park. Excellent! Kids rolled on skateboards and in skateboots, bums begged, vendors sold ice cream, hotdogs, soda, pretzels with cheese, mustard, ketchup and sauerkraut. A man's short pants flapped open to reveal the white of his butt. We followed a road into the park, blocked to traffic. Joggers passed, people kicked tiny sacks from foot to foot, kicked soccer balls, batted baseballs, pitched, fielded, threw balls, or floated disks back and forth in the Sheep Meadow. I couldn't believe it. Women lay on blankets in the sun with almost no clothes on and the straps of their bras untied.

Ricky Tibbs took off his shirt and shoes, yanked a plastic disc out of his bag and ran away from me. He tossed the disc back at me. Friz? I dropped it. He made the frisbee float over my head and sink into my hands. I was clumsy. He ran to catch the frisbee when I threw it, or it stuck in the grass between us. "Sorry!" He laughed and flapped his hand to show he didn't mind.

After a while he pulled a big towel out of his bag and we sat down on the grass. His face glowed with sweat and his ribs and shoulder bones were moist. "Thirsty?" I nodded. He uncorked a bottle with foreign writing on the label. I gazed around at buildings like broken teeth around the park, as if we were sitting in the green throat of the world.

He filled a glass with wine. "Dad's good stuff. Stock brokers don't drink anything cheap."

Bitter! But I was thirsty, so I tilted the cup and emptied it. Ricky Tibbs lifted his eyebrows, refilled the cup and drank a little. I asked, "Stock? Stock broke...what?"

"Wall Street, the stock exchange. He's almost a partner in his firm. Wanna see the monkeys?"

"Monkey?"

"In the zoo. Let's go." We rose and followed the path where everyone walked, rolled, or jogged, pushed baby carriages, or stumbled after big dogs on leashes. We came up behind an old black man and woman holding hands, and suddenly Ricky grew quiet.

"What is wrong, Ricky?"

Ricky rolled his eyes. "My dad says he'll quit drinking when he makes partner, but my mother doesn't believe it. I think she's going to divorce him."

His cheeks tightened around his eyes, so I knew divorce was bad. I felt relaxed and dreamy. We reached a track of black cinders. Lovers kissed under trees, mothers chased toddlers, Poodle dogs sniffed each other and wagged their stubby tails.

"Kee," Ricky Tibbs said, "you are one helluva swordsman. Swordswoman." He looked at me the way he did on Friday, as if I was a mystery. "Nobody ever made me...you know...feel this way before."

I said, "Me too. No, one time, yes. Old man in Nun-yo." The wine loosened me. "Pu-Jong, he...um...wine. *Ne! Makkola hodoju chan*. Um...big glassa makkola. I fall out the door, got dirted."

"Somebody got you drunk?"

"Uh-huh, drunk!"

Startled, I laughed as two people with black caps rode by on glowing red horses, shod hooves kicking up cinders. "Appa-nim be mad, Umma mad. Me, I sing and go chirpy chirp chirp, caw caw as a crow." I waved my arms and ran in a circle. "I flies around the street and chirp chirp. I am, I was...um..."

"Wasted?"

"Uh-huh. Wasted!"

Ricky Tibbs laughed at my story. "I don't mean getting drunk." We bumped shoulders beneath a stone archway covered with vines. Birds screeched. A tank of black water appeared ahead. *Pfffffffff.* "Kee," he said, "I can't get you out of my head."

Pfffffff. "What that sound?" I ran ahead. Birds in a cage squawked, twittered, whistled as I ran toward the pool of dark water. Children pointed, a splash, I spotted them. Seals! Black glowing whiskers and noses, intelligent eyes. "Look!"

We stood by the tank as the sea children played in the filthy water. Little boys threw popcorn to the seals, but they only nosed the soggy kernels. My mood changed, and I said nothing when Ricky stood at my back and lay his hands on my shoulders. I watched as the seals swam in their black water trap. I'm trapped too, I thought. I thought of the glittering waves on Green Dragon Bay, of Nun-yo stepping down the mountainside to the beach, to the yellow sand where everyone in the village gathered around fires, sang *sijo* and ate pine nut candies. Couples flirted in the light, and though there were elders watching to stop them, slipped out into the dark.

The seals could never slip away. I said, "Trapped. They are trapped."

Ricky Tibbs rubbed my shoulders. Whiskers broke the surface, *pfffff.* Glowing black bodies vanished under the ripples. Ti-Lee and I had slipped into the dark, it was our turn, and thinking of him, I squeezed the figurine of Ganesh in my pocket, the tiny dancing elephant god he had given me. But with Ti-Lee I could not do in the dark what everyone else did. It made me sad.

I whispered it. "I miss Nun-yo."

Ricky Tibbs turned me away from the tank. He looked into my eyes. His eyes were very dark, goldfish scales glinting in their depths.

"Now you're in New York," he said. He kissed my forehead. "Think about being here, because that's where you are." He kissed my nose. "With me." He kissed my lips, which startled me. "I can't think of anyone but you. Really, Kee, I can't get you out of my head."

He's right, I thought, I am not in Korea. Ricky Tibbs was so serious he was almost scowling. I realized he was desperate with desire for me. I thought, I may never see Nun-yo again. He stroked the hair of my temple and looked into my eyes, searched them, as if reaching for a deep connection place in the middle of me. I could not look away, but I was maudlin drunk and about to cry. No, I won't ever again see Ti-Lee. Or Korea.

Ricky Tibbs, with his too-big teeth and bottomless black eyes, did not know I was thinking of everything but him. When he kissed my mouth passionately, his lips clasping, tugging gently, he got my attention. His warm wet lips consumed my resistance as he inhaled the warm breath of my reluctance, my anxiety.

I gripped his waist with one hand, then the other. He did not know the significance of the second hand. I had to release a dancing elephant god and pull my left hand out of my pocket. I responded with my mouth and kissed him. I was letting go of Nun-yo and Ti-Lee, I suppose, as I embraced Ricky Tibbs and New York. Or maybe I was trying to forget, with our kisses, the ache of loss that hurt so much inside me.

Chapter 11

Monday morning.

"He's relieved that you're coming back." From the bathroom, Auntie's words were distorted as she applied lipstick to her mouth. Appa-nim had finally agreed to her last demand for me, that I be paid cash for working in the store, so I was going home. The toaster coughed up Auntie's toast. "He did, he sounded relieved."

I was not listening. The ivory figurine of Ganesh, the dancing elephant god that Ti-Lee gave me before I left Nun-yo, lay in my palm. It was the symbol of Ti-Lee's love for me. I placed it on the shirttails of the dobuck with Peng Su-nim's insignia, to take them back with me to St. Mark's Place.

In Central Park, by the seal tank, when I kissed Ricky Tibbs I let go of the figurine in my pocket, as if trying to let go of my love for Ti-Lee. Unfulfilled love is the hardest to leave behind because you think it would have been wonderful. I touched the figurine, smooth against the rough cotton dobuck, and it reminded me of how my fingertips were first to feel something more than friendship for Ti-Lee.

We were sixteen, it was the winter rains, and Ti-Lee and I often hid under my umbrella. First I noticed that he bumped into me more often than before. Then one day, walking near the breakwater, our fingertips touched on the handle of the umbrella and we looked at each other. He bumped against me, his hand found mine, and I was thrilled by the touch of his thick soft fingers.

Happiness confused me when we were together. He laughed at my jokes and I found his puns endearing. Old women chuckled as we passed. Our friend, Sanggyo, teased me. "Kee loves Elephant Step! Kee loves Elephant Step!" Appa-nim scowled whenever Ti-Lee passed him in the lanes. In the dojang Peng Su-nim snapped, "Ti-Lee, mindfulness!" or "Kee-Yong, go sit!" Spring came. The rains stopped, I put away my umbrella, and fires began to roar on the beach at night.

It was Net Mending Festival, where the fishermen of Nun-yo drank *makkola* and mended their nets, the mending not so tedious because everyone gathered around bonfires, sang songs, told stories, roasted nuts, and gossiped. Waves fell in rumbling tumults, climbed the sand beach, then sank back with sighs of disappointment. Night after warm night we watched the married men drink, mend nets with hands that moved more slowly as the mountain valleys filled with darkness and the bottles emptied, watched the married women gossip, watched the old women as they sternly watched the young people, as year after year Ti-Lee and I had watched older boys and girls flirt in the firelight with their eyes. Flames snapped and leaped as if to burn the stars, and the children giggled.

Ti-Lee went to make water and a minute later I went to find driftwood. It was our turn. Childish giggles faded away, the warning words of folk tales faded, the dark surrounded us, and the breakwater raised its boulders against the stars in the blue-black sky. The flawed crescent moon shed its odd light and the waves of Green Dragon Bay were tipped with silver. We found a gap between boulders where the moonlight could not reach. Ti-Lee's fleshy arms encircled me. I rested my cheek against the vast warmth of his body. Ti-Lee was very fat. He was not inviting to look at but was surprisingly pleasant—large, soft, and protective—to hold in my arms. His arms felt like warm wings draped over my shoulders.

I couldn't do it, could not lift my eyes to look at him, see his eyes, because I knew that Ti-Lee wanted to kiss me. I felt safe but afraid, and I knew I could not kiss him. But finally I did look up at Ti-Lee and there was the glisten of love in his eyes. He lowered his smooth round cheeks toward me. His mouth hung as soft as a bud above the bump of his chin, but I hid my face against his chest. I pressed my cheek against the warmth of his fat, soft over his breastbone, until I could hear the sighing of his breath in his chest.

I held my body tightly to his. I knew what other couples did in the dark, but I could not look up to offer my lips to him.

"It's all right," he said. "We don't have to."

The moon's light turned the sand to cold copper. He thought we had the rest of our lives to kiss and get married, so he held me gently and rubbed his cheek against the top of my head.

The singing stopped, the fishermen stumbled home with their wives, grandmothers and giggling children departed, and the fire sank into an orange mound of embers on the sand. We turned toward our homes. Ti-Lee was not upset, he was happy, but I had changed in how I felt. I knew I would not be able to kiss Ti-Lee for a long time, if ever, and a weight of sad failure clotted around my heart. We unwove our fingers at the edge of the cold copper beach and parted.

When I reached home Appa-nim shouted, "Where have you been?! Are you trying to disgrace us?" I cringed as he shouted and slunk to my futon in the dark.

Why can't I kiss him? I said nothing at breakfast, and when Umma and I stepped out behind our house to the large urns that held our kim-chee, she noticed my difference. She said, "Don't mind your father's shouting. He worries. Once frightened by a tiger, always frightened by a cat." Gulls screeched in the sky, and Pu-Jong's radio, turned loud for his old ears, sent the twang of *sijo* across the street. "Kee?"

Should I ask her? I was so confused. No, not about this, she'd tell Appa-nim. I nodded. "Yes, Umma? More radish?"

A few days later I heard steps treading the packed dirt of the lane behind me as I left Peng Su-nim's dojang. I knew it was Ti-Lee. I took long strides downhill, but he overtook me. He touched my shoulder. "Are you going to the fire tonight?"

I glanced down at the rubble where packed dirt met paving stones. "I have to help make kim-chee."

Ti-Lee blinked. "I'll be there, if you change your mind."

The next time he mentioned the fires on the beach it squeezed me inside. It was outside our school building. He said, "There's a fire tonight. Do you want to meet me on the beach?"

I felt witheringly cruel. "I have to help Umma."

He knew then. He said, "Oh."

The last time he spoke to me it was Sanggyo who brought up the fires. Sanggyo talked in a fool's sing song, though he was intelligent, and he was handsome but for his mangled upper lip.

"Are you two going to the fire tonight?" he asked.

Ti-Lee shot a look at me. "Kim-chee again?" I nodded. Like mica in a tidal pool, anger glittered in Ti-Lee's eyes. He said, "I'm never going to those fires again. Ever."

He lumbered away with his heavy pained steps and did not look back.

"What's the matter? I thought you two were in love." Sanggyo liked to act the clown. He shrugged his shoulders to his ears and said, "Don't ask me, I'm Sanggyo the Hairlip." He started off with bouncy, clownish steps. "Everyone can't be wrong. But don't ask me, I'm just Sanggyo the Hairlip!"

Sanggyo wasn't stupid. Everyone knew Ti-Lee and I were in love, and they noticed when we were not. In a small fishing village such things are remarkable. Boys and girls grow up together, fall in love, get married, bear children, and live out their lives on the shore of Green Dragon Bay. It is life in the village. When a couple comes apart at the beginning of that process, it is remarkable. The gossips remark.

One afternoon I hurried from school because thoughts of Ti-Lee weighed on me, I felt as sad as he was angry. I wanted to cry. I missed talking to him. I ran up the lanes to where the cobbles turned to dirt, chickens clucked, and the air smelled of pig dung, until I felt the polished wooden handle of the gate to Peng Su-nim's garden.

The gate was eleven years older than when I first opened it. One large and three smaller turtles lived in the pond, the trees of the garden stood thicker in the trunk, higher in the branch; but otherwise I could have been bursting in on my first lesson with Chen-puin. Seated at the teak table, she and a little girl looked up from a lesson book.

It struck me how she had aged. Her teeth were worse, grey, two missing on one side, and her scalp showed through her hair. She said, "Kee, this is Soo Mei, my new student." The little girl looked at me fearlessly, and I thought of Ling. "Soo Mei, this is Kee-Yong, the first girl ever to study Way of the Dawning Sword."

"I know." Like Ling, she was yom chae. "She drove the dragon out of the garden and saved your life. Everybody knows that."

Chen-puin chuckled. "That's correct." Silence settled down from the branches of the persimmon tree, and when I did not sit down Chen-puin closed the lesson book. She slipped a black bean cookie from her pocket, gave it to Soo-Mei, and sent her out through the creaky gate.

Doves cooed near the shrine hidden by trees. She said, "What bothers you?"

I sat. "I love Ti-Lee, but I can't kiss him. Something stops me."

Sunlight flashing through the persimmon tree speckled the white gravel path, a shifting pattern of light and shadow. She brushed a twig off the weathered top of the teak table. She asked, "Does the dawn come because it's time for morning?"

Breezes whispered among the tree leaves. I said, "Yes."

Chen-puin shook her head. "Did you start to menstruate because you were thirteen years old?"

"Because I was thirteen? Not *because* I was thirteen. Chen-puin, what's wrong with me?"

She raised her hand to calm me. The joints of her fingers were swollen and knobby with arthritis.

"Hours and years are how we mark time," she said. "But they are not time itself. No matter whether you feel it is time for you to kiss him, it doesn't appear to be so."

"But I love Ti-Lee, I want to kiss him, yet I can't. Something stops me!"

"Then it's not time for you to kiss him." She spoke with a maddening certainty. "Relax and let the Tao express itself through you."

As bitter as tea left in the kettle, I snapped, "What's wrong with me? Is it because I practice komdo?"

She touched my hand. "Maybe so. Komdo attunes you to the Tao. In that way, when it's time for you to kiss a boy, you will. Nothing in the world will be able to stop you because the Tao will be expressing itself through you. But until then, don't fight against it."

"When I began to menstruate you said my destiny was to get married and have children. How can I, if I can't kiss anyone?!"

"I said you would menstruate so that someday you can have children. That's your ability as a woman, but it's not your destiny. Your destiny may be different." *Kee-Yong?*

"How can I know what my destiny is?"

"You can't," Chen-puin said. "It's revealed to you as you live your life. Maybe you have other things to do before you fall in love, other places to see." *Kee?* "None of us can know the path until it has passed beneath our feet."

"Kee-Yong?" I lifted my head out of my reverie. The dancing elephant lay on the shirttails of my old dobuck, on Auntie's sofa. Mascara and nail polish clattered in the bathroom. Horns honked outside the window. It took me a moment to adjust and return to New York City. Auntie asked, "Are you ready?"

"Almost." I rolled up the dobuck with the ivory figurine in the center. I used the faded sash to secure the dobuck in a tight cylinder with two black tails. Other places to see. How did Chen-puin know? I stuffed the dobuck into my bag. I zipped the zipper. "I'm ready." Other things to do? I don't think Chen-puin meant trimming lettuce on St. Mark's Place. "Do you really think he's happy I'm coming back?"

Auntie plucked toast from the toaster and dusted it with cinnamon. "He won't admit it, he's too angry. Here's your toast. Eat and let's go."

We shared a taxi for thirty blocks. Auntie filled the back seat with the smell of flowers. Sunshine lay warm across my lap. I asked, "What exactly did Appa-nim agree to?"

"You can go to Chinatown Mondays, Wednesdays, and Fridays, you get Sunday afternoons off, and fifteen dollars a week; but you buy your own subway tokens."

"Fifteen dollars? Every week?"

"I started at forty, but he wouldn't budge. I called him from Atlantic City, long distance, three times. Cabbie, pull over!"

I stepped out of the cab where it sat by the black iron gates of Thompkins Square Park. Across the street our rack for bouquets of flowers stood empty like basketball hoops, and the bin for onions showed its bottom.

"Thank you, Auntie." Everything was much the same as seven days ago, but everything looked...different. "Thank you for everything."

She reached out the window and touched my hand. "Don't let him slide on a thing. Stick up for yourself."

"Yes, Auntie, thank you. Thank you!"

I hurried into the store. Appa-nim stood stiff-backed behind the register, weighing a customer's peaches. "Hello, Appa-nim."

"Seventy-six cent change. Thank you." The coffee counter was a wreckage of napkins, stir sticks, sugar packets, and a toppled carton of cream. He said, "That be all?" *Beep!* "One dollar forty-two cent."

I paused in the doorway of the storage room. He's not going to look at me?

The storage room held the buzz of flies and the sickly sweet air of a citrus tree dropping rotted fruit. I ran up the stairs to our kitchen, burst through the door, dumped my bags.

"Umma, I'm home! Ling?"

Silence. Too early, they're not awake yet.

Downstairs, I wet a cloth at the sink, hurried to the coffee counter. In two minutes it was clean, there was a new carton of cream. When I grabbed the cream I saw the cooler was empty. I hefted a box of sodas from under the stairs, carried them out, stood them on the cold wire shelves. "Should I bother with stickers? Appa-nim?"

"Anio! Fill the bins, get it out there to sell. *Palli!"* Hurry up!

Cartons and boxes filled the storage room. I dragged crates of apples, oranges, peaches, and grapefruit out the door, dumped them into bins, then carefully arranged what he called advertising fruit, the finest, at the front. I wanted no reason for him to be angry. White onions thumped on bare wood and I tossed the empty netting to the curb. I hurried into the store, hot and sweating. He said, "Clean the island."

"Yes, Appa-nim."

I culled spoiled pears and spotted bananas. The green shoots of half the shallots had crinkled up brown and brittle. The starfruit had gone soft, and I said stupidly, "The starfruit didn't sell?"

They were his experiment. "Trim lettuce!"

I dragged a crate for the trimmings near to my creaky seat. The knife felt good to my hand, a trusty friend. I raised the blade, raised a head of lettuce, twisted it, and leaves fell into the crate. Slash cellophane. Wrap, toss, grab another head. Twist, slash, wrap and toss. I carried armfuls of shiny wrapped heads out to the proper bin, mounded them, hurried back and trimmed two more crates of lettuce. My stomach churled with hunger, but I was happy to see a patch of dark wet floor restored to the light.

Appa-nim's shadow fell over me. "You left this place disgusting. Clean it up!"

"Yes, Appa-nim." My back ached from hunching over the crates. I reached for a broom. "The flower rack is empty. Did you order more flowers?"

"In the back. You should've done those first. You know how fast they wilt. Did you forget everything in a week?" I started to sweep. "When you finish that, go eat. Your aunt and I agreed, half an hour for lunch. Hurry up!"

"Yes, Appa-nim, thank you." I swept furiously. Finished, I threw the broom into the corner, ran upstairs and burst into the kitchen. Things were different there too. Ling stood on a footstool, presiding over a pot on the stove. Seeing me, Umma's smile pushed up her cheeks. I said, "You're teaching her to cook?"

Ling asked, "He didn't kill you?"

"Ling wants to learn." Umma waved a wooden spoon like a magic wand, but I had a troubling thought. She looks so tired. There were dark circles under her eyes, her hand like a spider wrapped around the spoon. She said, "Aren't you proud of her?"

"Yes. So happy to see her too."

"I think it's done," Ling said, the cover of the rice pot in her hand. "Umma's going to teach me to make batter-fried carp. Auntie loves yours."

Umma said, "The water has to be all gone, then it'll be fluffy. Is he speaking to you?"

"Only to yell at me. What's that?"

Umma lifted a deep platter out of the oven, steam roiling white and sweet into the air. "Eggplant parmessan. Italian. Your father's been working himself to death." She was angrier with him than her voice revealed. "The one who eats the salt has to drink the water. *Aigo,* I'm late again."

"He hired someone?" I asked. She pulled on her shoes. "When does he come?"

"When we leave for Auntie's." Ling shook my arm. "I learned how to run the register. Mu can't get it right."

"You learned the register?"

Umma swung her cheap pocketbook. "Yom chae to the rescue. I'm so happy you're back." She touched my arm, which made me realize how western Auntie was to kiss me. Umma fluttered her hand from the doorway. "Bye bye."

When my stomach was full and quiet—Ling insisted on serving

me—I skipped downstairs. I boxed bean sprouts, washed Chinese lettuce, stacked apples, clipped vines into small bunches of grapes. At two o'clock Appa-nim barked, "Truck's here!"

I thought, if Ling knows how, why not? I climbed the stairs and opened the kitchen door. "Truck's here. Can you come down and run the register? *Putak-hamnida?*"

She was reading the English book Appa-nim bought us. She said, "In English it's 'please.'" She slid off her chair and threw down the book. "Auntie told us about your date. Tomorrow it's my turn to go to Central Park, with the Rhee twins. Did you kiss him?"

"Hurry up. You don't want to make him mad, do you?"

We scrambled downstairs, Ling to the register, and I went out into the hot light and helped Appa-nim unload and stack boxes and crates of vegetables for the truck driver's dolly. The trucker wheeled them into the storage room. The storage room refilled with towers of crates, leaves squeezing out between the wooden slats. I dragged the crates of old vegetables close to the door, to be used first, and the new towers swayed as the driver pulled the foot of the dolly from beneath them. Appa-nim did not speak, his face flushed the color of heated brass, and he grunted and huffed.

We finished at four o'clock. My arms ached and my face was hot. The work also consumed some of Appa-nim's anger, so he spoke to me evenly. "I'm giving Ling money for tokens. I suppose you want yours too."

I stooped for a bit of celery on the floor. I didn't know what to say. He took a ten and a five dollar bill out of the register. I couldn't look at him as he paid me, feeling selfish; but I also sensed that my few dollars was costing him more than money. His pride? His sense of security? Of control? Nonetheless, I took the money and hurried up the kitchen stairs.

"You can't leave until Mu gets here!"

Back to his old self.

Ling was by the sink, gulping water from a glass. "Get your

book." I pulled everything except my newest dobuck out of my bag. "When does Mu get here? That's his name? Mu?"

"He's supposed to be here at 4:15." She clunked her glass in the sink. "He's a bit slow, and he looks like Baby Huey."

"Baby who?"

"On the cartoons. Baby Huey."

Just then his voice came up the stairs. "Ling? I'm here." No accent? American born? I stepped to the stairway. At the bottom, beneath the dim bulb, stood a large Korean man, huge in the stomach, with a high forehead. He smiled and waved a wide hand.

"I'm Mu," he said. "You must be Kee."

Ling and I descended the steps, and she said, "What did Appanim tell you to do?"

"He told me to tell you I was here." Ling rolled her eyes. His face was smooth, ageless, fleshy, but his wrinkled dirty clothes made him look many years old, at least thirty. He said slowly, "He also told me to trim lettuce. I don't like trimming lettuce." He held up his fingers, badged with three bandages. "Cut myself. Easy to do with that knife. It's sharp."

I nodded. *"Cho'um poepkessumnida shillyehamnida."*

His face opened into a smile. "What did she say, Ling?"

"Goodbye. Goodbye, Appa-nim."

"Bye, plum. Kee, be back by seven. He works until *seven!"*

Appa-nim had to shout because we were out the door and running down the walk. I said, "Is he retarded?"

Ling shrugged and spoke all English. "Got me, Joe. He jus' a happy guy."

I was happy as we ran toward St. Mark's Place. We skipped downstairs. Before the token booth I was happy to pay the ten dollar bill to the token woman. She tossed a packet of tokens into the wooden gutter under the glass that separated us. That was the first time I ever spent my own money. How quickly it went. Those ten brass tokens quickly became nine, hoarded in my pocket as we hurried onto a subway car.

On Canal Street I went with Ling to the intersection at Elizabeth and watched her until she reached the stoop of Auntie's building. I turned toward Mott Street. I followed not only the streets but my new routine: mopping, meditation, class.

Class was different. I already knew the small differences in Choi Su-nim's poom-sey, moved in harmony with the others, which meant the difference was in me. I felt different about being watched by Ricky Tibbs. His glance touched me from behind. Part of me responded to his energy, I was pulled off-balance. My weight subtly shifted off the balls of my feet, onto my heels, as if Ricky Tibbs was pulling me, and I was letting him. The beginning of each poom-sey caught me flat-footed.

When class ended and the students broke out with their loud voices I ducked into Choi Su-nim's office, shucked my dobuck, dressed, and hurried out. I ran on Elizabeth Street until I saw Ling squatting on the stoop of Auntie's building. We were late. I shouted, "Come on!"

We ran like threads through cloth among the tightly knit crowd on Canal Street. We skipped down gritty shattered steps, stopped, I slipped a token out of my packet, with my stomach made the stile turn and stepped through. Flustered and rushing, I had to slow down and consciously squelch my smile. Ricky Tibbs leaned against a pillar on the platform below.

All of Ricky's protruding teeth appeared as he laughed. "Who's that? Yo mama?"

Ling caught up with me. "Ling is...um...sister?"

She looked at him, at me, and grinned. She said, *"Kuege komun."* He's black.

"Krok-he?" So? "He's nice. I think he's cute."

"His teeth are too big. Look at those lips!"

"Be nice." Ricky watched Ling, glanced at me, and licked his lips nervously. I said, "His name is Ricky Tibb."

"Ricky Tibb? Disney Mister Tibb?" She laughed and I cringed. "Monkey! In Disney movie, Mister Tibb be a monkey! Circus monkey!"

Ricky Tibbs laughed. "No no no, wrong movie. *In the Heat of the Night.*" A train rumbled into the station as he put on a stern expression. Over the roar of the train I heard him say, "They call me Mister *Tibbs.*" He laughed. "And you better too!"

Riding uptown Ling imitated a monkey, twirled around a pole, scratched her armpit, and said, "Me Mister Tibb!"

Ricky slipped his arm around me. "She's gonna be dead meat." A fat woman watched us. It was the same fat woman I saw before, who smelled of motor oil and rotting peaches. Her seven thick rolls of fat reminded me of my nickname for her. Pagoda Woman. Ricky kissed my ear. "Wanna do something this weekend?"

Ling said, "Kee like Elephant Step. Now she like Monkey Tibb!"

"Ling, *kamani kyese-yo!*" Keep quiet! The train slowed for Astor Place, our stop near St. Mark's. I pulled myself gently out of his embrace. "Our stop."

"You wanna do something this weekend?" Ling scratched her armpit and howled. "Shut up, you little fried noodle." He looked at me softly. "So?"

I said, "Um...maybe," as the doors of the car ruckled open.

Ling hooted like a monkey and said, "Me Mister Tibb!"

"Bye Kee. Goodbye, little fried noodle brain."

We hurried up and out into the evening on Astor Place. Clouds hung over the school building, the curbside junk sellers, beggars and businessmen going intently about their commerce. The neon signs of pizza joints and barrooms glowed red, dusky walks were crowded with evening couples out for a stroll.

Ling skipped along beside me. "Appa better not find out about him. Stop, I want to buy a bangle."

"We're late." She jumped down two steps under a porch awning to where baskets, boxes, and racks were crammed with hair ornaments, jewelry, cheap earrings. "That money is for tokens."

"Appa has lots of money. Here, this one." She handed a gaudy bangle and two dollar bills to a girl wearing a pocket apron. "Let's go, Joe."

She jumped up the steps and ran ahead. I caught up as we passed through the leather smell of the boot shop, passed a line of garbage cans where a man picked for bottles worth a nickel, passed brownstones, passed scrawny trees whose few dry leaves whispered about the hard life of leaves in New York City. At the threshold of our store we halted, out of breath and laughing. I stepped into the light, and all my good humor shriveled inside me.

A man stood before the register with a bottle of soda. His eyebrows pinched together, Mu picked for change among a mess of green paper money and coins on the counter. I hurried in. "Where is Appa-nim?"

Mu was so relieved his shoulders slumped. Ling shouted, "Where is Appa!"

Tiny beads of sweat glistened on Mu's forehead. He said, "He hurt himself. The man next door took him to the hospital."

Chapter 12

"Eight stitches?"

The back seat of a cab. Appa-nim and I had pulled the doors shut, outside the hospital, Auntie Yen and Umma between us. Broken shocks rattled, tires hummed, and I could smell the food smells Umma's dress had collected while she was working.

Auntie kept at him. "You call eight stitches an accident? A slip?"

"What do you call it?" he asked. "Intentional?"

"Do you really think he'd cut himself on purpose?" Umma spoke irritably. "It was demons. They were attracted by that ugly bleeding eyeball over the door."

Auntie touched my hand as lightly as she touched on the subject. "We've been...well..."

"We've been what?" Appa-nim's voice had a dangerous tone. I gazed out the window, "We've been what, Yen?"

Umma jostled me. "That bloody eyeball is the problem. We need a cleansing."

"No cleansing. We've been what, Yen? 'We' who?"

"You've been under pressure, working so many hours," Auntie said. "It's wearing you so thin, Ki-Teh, your bones all stand out and...well...you've been distant. So maybe you should see a therapist."

"Yes," Umma said quietly. "You've been distant. But no therapist. We need a cleansing."

"No cleansing!"

Appa-nim caught me looking at the white square of gauze taped to his forearm. He covered the bandage with his hand, but I could still remember the black threads, eight taut lines drawing the red lips of his flesh together as the doctor sewed him up.

"Distant?" he snapped. "You and Kee conspire against me, and you wonder why I'm distant? And what's a therapist?" Appa-nim's fist had clenched as the doctor stitched him, and though they gave him anaesthetic, his foot twitched from the pain. He asked, "What's a therapist?"

The cab hit a pot hole. We jostled against each other on the seat inside the crashing of metal, the cab's parts clashing against each other, rattling together. Auntie said, "Thank god I talked you into a good insurance plan."

"What's a therapist? Answer me!"

"A counselor!" She fidgeted. "You talk to them about your problems."

"My problems?" Appa-nim was so angry his cheeks quivered. He threw open the door as the cab reached our store. "If I need 'therapy' it's because you and Kee are driving me crazy!"

"It's our fault?" Auntie stuffed a bill into the cabbie's pay slot. "Keep the change. Ki-Teh, damn you, wait!"

Auntie caught up to him as he unlocked our door. His keys jingled, he cursed, she threw up her hands, he threw open the door and they disappeared inside, arguing. Umma and I stood on the curb. We listened to their voices. A switch clicked, light filled the store, fell out of the doorway, and they went upstairs.

The taxi pulled away. The corners of Umma's mouth curled down as she gazed into the future, one that seemed to be leaving with the taxi.

I touched her arm. "Let's go into the park. Umma?"

She mumbled, "Okay."

"I have to shut the door first."

We appeared to be doing business, the door wide open, the store lighted. I crossed the street and closed the heavy metal door. I turned toward the park, the corner where Umma stood, but how she looked, standing across the street, made me stumble.

Sadness spasmed through me. Her shoes were cheap and ground down at the heel. Her dress did not fit her, she was as skinny as Appa-nim, her hip bones like pieces of coral under her dress, and her shoulders were slumped. She gazed absently at nothing and plucked at her hair. She's only thirty-six? The strain of coming to America, of being married to Appa-nim, made her look fifty.

I ran to the corner and crossed to meet her in front of the gates to the park. It was a cool night, no sweat smell and stink of hot tar in the air, the park quiet. We strolled arm in arm. It was dark among the furrowed trunks of trees and over naked packed dirt. A man grunted inside a cardboard box beside the path.

"Did you go to class with your new su-nim?" she asked.

I nodded. "He's different from Peng Su-nim. He laughs while he reads the funny papers."

She made herself chuckle. Her gaze went down the tarred path. She breathed slowly, tiredly.

"Komdo is so important to you," she said. "We never would have come here if I knew how important. My feet hurt."

"But you did know. Umma?"

Umma touched my arm. We settled onto a bench with names carved all over it, and black graffiti signatures. The tang of urine stained the air until a breeze blew it away. She looked so wan and worn I couldn't push her further.

"Why don't you buy good shoes?" I asked. "Appa-nim can afford it. Remember the shoes the nurses had, with thick soles? Buy some of those."

"They squeaked." She glanced up at clouds as dark as squid ink. The door of a bar room opened on Seventh Street to let out a woman's drunken laughter.

"I never knew what to expect." She plucked nervously at her hair. "Sometimes he wandered off from the fish plant. Then there was the time he went up into the mountains, and you...you were too young to realize. Everyone in the village watched out for him. Grandmother Ahn loved him, and my grandmother said he was a special child." She sighed. "Then I saw it happen with you and Ti-Lee, you were falling in love. But you never asked me, so I thought you were talking about it with Chen-puin. That hurt me, Kee, but what could I do? Shout at you for not trusting me?"

A bad muffler popped on Avenue B. A homeless man mumbled in his cardboard box. "I'm sorry, Umma."

She squeezed my wrist. "He got drunk. When he worked on Kim's shrimp boat, sometimes Kim carried him home to me on his shoulder. After he got into the fish plant he drank with the rice farmers. The rice farmers brought him home in a wheelbarrow. But it was only once every few months; he wasn't as bad as Pu-Jong. Remember when Pu-Jong got you so drunk you fell off the porch?"

"Uh-huh. Last week I told someone about it."

She turned interested eyes on me. "A friend? Good. But whatever is inside your father, it's like a bad sore in his mouth, except that it's in his spirit." I looked at a crack in the tar between my sneakers. "I have a headache. That emergency room was horrible, especially that man with the gunshot wound. My head hurts from thinking about it."

Umma pushed herself up from the bench. She slipped her arm into mine as we walked on the path to the gates, onto the sidewalk, empty of people. We crossed the street, arm in arm, as we sometimes walked in Nun-yo. It was different. Umma was not leading me, there was a fine balance. She was balanced on my arm and I was balanced on hers. Brakes squeeked behind us as the light turned red and the traffic waited to flow.

"You found a friend at the dojang?"

"Uh-huh. A boy." On instinct, she drew me close. "Just a friend. He's nice."

"Good." I pulled open the metal door and we went in. I locked the door and turned off the light. We climbed the familiar darkness on the stairs to the lighted kitchen. Auntie was gone, Ling was asleep, Appa-nim had shut himself in the bathroom. "Good night, Kee."

"Umma?" She paused by the kitchen table. "Why didn't I know any of this before? About him drinking and running away?"

She shrugged. "Nun-yo protected you like a cocoon. People felt differently about your study with Peng Su-nim, but they all liked you, protected you." She pushed in the bedroom door. "No, you're not in a cocoon anymore."

New York was no cocoon. In the morning the harsh jingle of coins in a pocket woke me as the man who lived across the air shaft pulled on his pants. Air conditioners hummed, my throat was dry, and crabs of hunger pinched my stomach. I fit my spine to the wall and returned to the cocoon of meditation. I sat still until I heard Appa-nim moving in the kitchen. I dressed and slipped out the door. His eyes were red from lack of sleep.

"Good morning, Appa-nim."

He unlocked the door and went downstairs. I poured raisin bran into a bowl. The bang of the metal grate flew up the stairwell; I ate quickly and went down. Minutes passed. Tension tightened like wires between us. I glanced sidelong to see his mood. But still we worked like clock parts, filled baskets with grounds, urns with water, cleaned the counter, opened cream, stacked cups, stocked tubs with sugar packets, stir sticks, and sweetener, and the air filled with the rich aroma of coffee.

I started out to check the sidewalk bins. "Trim lettuce!"

"Yes, Appa-nim."

I drew crates together in the storage room. I did not mind trimming vegetables, if I didn't have to do it for too long without a change. But he allowed me no break. For four hours it was grab, twist, slash cellophane, wrap, and toss; twist, slash, wrap, and toss. Then I trimmed broccoli, asparagus spears, cauliflower, Chinese lettuce, chicory. My back ached. I rose and stretched, drank water from the sink, my shoe rippling the puddle below the drain pipe leaky like a goat's udder. I sat and knew he was punishing me. I looked wistfully toward the sunlit street.

What is Ricky Tibbs doing right now?

Appa-nim startled me. "Do the register," he said, and he went upstairs for his lunch. I hurried out to the drawer of money, the grid of numbered keys, the green numerals in the read-out. "I help you?" Customers lined up, my fingers flew. "Thank you, thank you, please come again. That be all?" People came in with the hot noon light, shoulders, bill caps, shiny tobacco brown cheeks. "Three eighty-six."

"That be all?" Click click click. "Four dollar and twelve." I thought: ask Mu about Appa-nim. I stopped the spattering of my fingers on the keys. I was thinking in English? That's a first. I finished tallying prices. "Two dollar even."

"—please come again." The rest of that day I stood on the mat behind the register. "That be all?" Click click *beep!* And the next morning it was the same because a truck came, blocked out the building across the street, dulled the sunshine, shadowed the threshold. A man wheeled in crates of green watermelons. They were too heavy for me to lift. In the storage room Appa-nim lifted and let them thump on a squeaky crate. "Exact change. Thank you, thank you, please come again."

His cleaver hacked the green rinds. I thought how, if he cut himself with the cleaver, it would take his hand off.

People flowed in and out. "Thank you, thank you, please come again." I waited for Mu to come. He was a little late, so I shouted up the stairs, "Ling!" and she hurried down with my bag and her book. When he lumbered in I whispered to him, "We talk? Outside?"

Mu looked down at us, one big jowl draped under his chin, his huge round belly curving between us. His eyebrows curdled with the effort of thinking. "I have to do something out there."

He grabbed the empty crates and cartons, and together we paraded with them out to the curb. He began to rip apart the crates. His hands and arms were thick, fleshy, but he snapped the wooden slats easily, his breasts of fat shaking on his chest.

"Mu," I said, "what happen when Appa-nim, um..." I passed a slashing hand across my forearm. "How?"

He shrugged. "A woman came in with a baby carriage. The baby started to cry, and he went into a dream. He was standing behind the register..." The memory made his cheeks rise around his eyes in a protective wince. "...and he started to mumble—Appa, Umma, Appa, Umma—over and over. I didn't know what to do."

"You see him do it?" Ling asked. "Cut?" Mu rubbed his forehead, his eyes troubled. Ling slapped his arm. "So? Tell!"

"He went into the storage room. He picked up the knife. He cut himself and it...brought him back. Then he put the knife down." He leaned close to speak quietly, glancing at the doorway of our store. Mu shook his head. "The old red-haired guy who lives next door, he was buying a soda, and he took your father in a taxi." He shook his head. "Your father's not okay. He makes me nervous, but I need this job. He told me not to tell you. My mother needs the money."

Ling said, "You is okay, Mu," and I nodded agreement.

Mu smiled down at tiny Ling and I saw that he'd learned to love her as everyone did, quickly. We waved goodbye and turned away up St. Mark's Place. But there was no smile on my face.

I knew it. Trouble ahead.

Trouble above? I glanced back to the doorway of our store. The ugly bleeding eyeball of the previous tenants still hung above the threshold.

What if there are demons here? I wondered. What if they followed us here from Nun-yo?

Chapter 13

Broken Heel Mansin gazed around at the ghosts floating below our ceiling, ghosts the rest of us could not see. She snapped, "The Grandfathers are upset!"

The beautiful witch limped across our living room and stopped before Harold, chuckling, and Ricky too, squeezed into a corner of the couch. Harold looked up at her and licked his lips like a dog. Broken Heel Mansin's hip was permanently cocked, her witch's mark, but her shoe heels were thin like spikes and her black fishnet stockings clung to her muscular legs. She was at least fifty years old but looked young, angry, and strong in her bright red dress.

She glared down at chuckling Harold. "You! You doubt that the Grandfathers are angry?"

"Not a bit." He looked sideways at Ricky. "Sure is a good-looking wench, I mean witch, isn't she, little Richard?"

Ricky said, "R-i-c-k-y. Ricky."

Every move the witch made charged the air with tension. Black fingernails, black lips, shaking a storm of black hair around her head, she limped to the left until she looked down at Appa-nim. "Before you left Korea—tell the truth!—you never consulted the Grandfathers. You did not!"

Appa-nim chuckled, "Of course not," but Umma hurried to the business at hand.

"Thank you for coming on short notice." She handed Broken Heel Mansin a can of beer, a dollar note tucked under the pull tab. "These demons are terrible. They cut his arm! Ki-Teh, show her the stitches."

Appa-nim sniggered, and he and Harold clinked green beer bottles. He said, "Dutch beer, Harold, mmm good."

Harold's belly shook as he laughed. "Yeah, let the spirits drink that American piss water."

Broken Heel Mansin pointed at Ling. "You take the dark one downstairs. Get the store ready. Light candles, get the record albums, check the champagne."

She opened the can of beer and tucked the dollar bill deep into her cleavage, framed by the V-front of her red dress.

"This is no joke, Ahn Chi-bi-nim," she said to Appa-nim. "These heavy metal rock and roll demons bring chaos. After concerts, whole towns have been destroyed. Riots, rapes, vandalism. Young people have killed themselves!" She slashed the air with her hand. Appa-nim's eyebrows rose. "These devil groups have been sued in the United States Supreme Court, highest court in America, for millions of dollars. And they always *won!*"

Auntie Yen said, "She's got that right."

Appa-nim blinked. "Demons, so bad. Right, Harold?"

Harold harrumphed. "Most definitely."

She turned away, glancing around the ceiling, her long black hair swirling around her shoulders. "Don't worry, Grandfathers, we will appease you. You—" She pointed at me. "—go down and check on the others. Now!"

I stopped in the doorway as she grabbed another beer from Umma, ripped the dollar note off a pull tab, stuffed it into her cleavage, lifted the beer to her lips, and threw back her head. Her throat jerked, beer spilled off her cheeks and blotched the front of her dress. A shiver skipped around the top of my head. She lowered the empty beer can. Her cheeks bunched around her eyes as she opened her mouth. *Buuuuuuaaaaah-agh-agh-agh...urp*, she burped, and Umma laughed and clapped her hands. Broken Heel Mansin ripped the dollar bill off a third beer, stuffed it into her cleavage, and pointed a shaking finger at me.

"Go light those candles!"

I closed the door behind me and hurried down into the store.

Ricky stood flipping through a box of record albums left behind by the music store owners, on the counter beside Broken Heel Mansin's boom box. Candles sputtered on shelves and around the walls of the store. I shut off the flourescent lights. Candle glow buttered the fruit that rose out of shadow, candle flames reflected in the glass door of the cooler. The square bins of the island stood in dimness, packs of garlic glistened, and shadow ghosts played on the walls.

Two men appeared at the screen door, dark silhouettes against the light. I said, "Not open."

They both had red eyes, like many people I saw that morning. I sold aspirin and stomach tablets to people bleery-eyed from Saturday night while Appa-nim, Umma, and Ling went to church. Auntie's deal made it possible for them to go to Mass while I ran the store; but that morning Appa-nim wouldn't speak to me as we made urns of coffee.

The man at the door scowled. "The Bloody Eyeball's gone? The record store?"

A wail from the kitchen. "They're coming!"

I grabbed two beers from the cooler and folded dollars beneath the pull tabs. Broken Heel Mansin's keening grew loud. She appeared on the threshold of the storage room, limping, her hair messy around her head, and she had her chest pushed out angrily. Appa-nim, Umma, Harold, and Auntie Yen crept behind her. Harold pinched Auntie's buttocks. She screeched and dodged past me. He chased her around to the cooler, and he and Auntie giggled and hugged, jostling the bin of red potatoes.

I asked, "Beer, Mansin-nim? Record album?"

Broken Heel Mansin hit a tab on the boom box. Drums beat, thumpa thump thump, thumpa thump thump. "They're—" She threw herself against the island. "—they're *here!*"

The tomatoes quaked in their paper cups as Appa-nim cried, "The oranges!" He and I rushed, but the pyramid of fruit unrolled through our hands and pummeled the floor. *"Chegiral!"* Damn it!

Broken Heel Mansin shouted, "Loathsome spirits, these are hard-working *people!"*

Harold laughed. "She's talking to a ghost?"

"Damn you!" She shrieked and stumbled against the counter, her hair flailing. "Ow!"

She knocked one of the prepared beers off the counter, grabbed it, and stuffed the dollar into her dress. When she yanked the pull tab the can hissed. A rooster tail of beer sprayed the ceiling and soured the air. Appa-nim swore. Umma stood wide-eyed as Broken Heel Mansin screeched and rolled across a corner of the island. Onions crackled, packages of garlic popped, and Harold stopped laughing when she dropped to the floor with a clocking of bone on concrete.

"Leave this place!" she cried. "Devils, your time has passed! You have no...no business...here!"

The witch rose like a phantom, seemed to float in the air above the onions, her robes thrashing red around her. Her hair brushed the ceiling pipes, she landed on her feet, grabbed something invisible, flailed her arm, and yowled like a cat in heat. One of the heavy metal music fans in the doorway cried, "Ozzy has her! Ozzy Osborne!"

"You clown," the other said, "he isn't dead yet."

Appa-nim opened a beer and guzzled. Broken Heel Mansin shouted, "Money? Beer? Cigarettes?" She shook her head, denying the extravagance of a child. "No drugs. Ah...*no!"* She whirled along the leafy greens, clung to the bins, shook like a wet animal. "All right! Money. He wants money!"

I shivered, I could feel the spirits.

"Here," Umma said. "Ossy, look!"

Appa-nim cried, "Not too much!"

"Shut up! You got us into this mess." Umma sprinkled dollar bills over the melons and green peppers. "Look, Ossy. Look at all that money!"

Thumpa thump thump, thumpa thump thump. Ling cried, "Let me feed Ossy!"

"Stay back! Ahn-puin, he wants money. Beer too."

Harold snickered. "Where's a ghost spend a quid?"

Auntie snapped, "Be quiet."

"Watch this." He tucked a bill beneath the tab of a can of beer and set it within reach of Broken Heel Mansin. He said, "Look, Ozzy, a fiver. A *five* dollar bill."

She ignored it, began to moan and toss her head, her black hair thrashing. With a gasp she clutched the edge of the island, gritted her teeth, fell back, and hit the floor with her legs falling open.

"You all want that too!" she cried. She shook, thrashed, wrapped her legs and arms around a blank space of air like a starfish clutching an invisible rock. My mouth hung open. Her black panties were edged with red lace that stood out against her inner thighs, paler than coffee with cream. She made the noises I heard in the air shaft at night, the screeches and grunts of lovers. The boys at the door clapped and whistled, Auntie and Harold laughed, but Umma looked stubborn, business-like as Broken Heel Mansin cried out, "I guess! If! If you...you have...have to! Oh! Ah! Oh God! Eeeeee-yah-yah-yah-*yaaaaaaah!*"

I pulled my mouth shut. I thought, that's what sex is like?

Howls, hoots, and laughter filled the store as Broken Heel Mansin slumped still, her face glistening with sweat and beer. One veteran helping another, Umma pulled her up and onto her spike heels. She shook her head, bedraggled, and as she lit a cigarette the flame of her match shook and she swayed dizzily, deep in a glassy-eyed trance. We watched, tense, waiting as she gazed dreamily at the ceiling and blew a smoke ring.

Her cigarette hissed as it burned orange, a nub of ash fell to the floor, smoke mushroomed against the ceiling, above the pipes, and Harold asked, "Was it good for Ozzy too?"

Broken Heel Mansin shook her head. "Albums."

"Everyone," she said. "Take an album." They took albums, but I hung back and watched Broken Heel Mansin step on her cigarette and slip a black record out of its sleeve. Thumpa thump thump, thumpa thump thump, the drums beat as shadows quavered across the walls. Broken Heel Mansin raised the record album over her head.

"This is not your place. You get no respect here. Out!" She swung the album down onto a corner of the island. Whunk! The record shattered onto the floor. "Out!"

"Don't!" Groans came from the music lovers in the doorway as the others swung their albums, whunk! "Aw man! Bummer!"

Appa-nim spilled beer as he hit his record, whunk! "Look, I can't break it!"

Harold took it and smashed it into a dozen pieces. "So much for Judas Priest."

Whunk! whunk! whunk! Shards of black plastic littered the floor as they enjoyed themselves. I stood aloof in the doorway and watched. Ricky, Appa-nim, and Harold especially enjoyed destroying those albums, made chips of plastic fly to the ceiling and walls. Then the box of albums stood empty and Broken Heel Mansin shut off the drum beat. Silence. Heavy breathing. Ling giggled.

Ricky asked, "Is he gone? Ozzy?"

"And his fans too." She pointed to the door, clear of music lovers. "But to make sure no demons return, everyone outside. Where's the champagne?"

"Here." Appa-nim drew two long-neck bottles out of the cooler. "What's outside? I don't want to be arrested."

I held open the screen door as Broken Heel Mansin, her red dress rumpled and stained, her hair stringy, hitched out onto the sidewalk. Everyone followed, squinting in the sunlight. People strolled by, oblivious to our ritual; then a woman saw Broken Heel Mansin scratch drunkenly inside her bodice, green dollar bills poking out of her cleavage, and skirted us with a disgusted face.

Umma ignored the ignorant. "Now what? The sign?"

Broken Heel Mansin pointed to the sign above our door, BLOODY EYEBALL RECORDS AND TAPES wrapped around an eye spurting blood. "We must deface it."

A man in old work clothes came out the front door of the next building as Broken Heel Mansin ripped foil off the neck of a champagne bottle. He was a black man wide in the body, his arms floppy with fat, and one of the straps of his bib overalls, unhooked, swung down his back.

"Redsy," Appa-nim cried, "hey you! Friend, good to see you!"

"Hey, Ki-Teh, how's the cut?" he asked. Redsy was the one who took Appa-nim to the hospital. He glanced around at us and said, "You should've seen it. I had to jump out and grab a taxi by the bumper to get one to stop. What's going on?"

"A Korean exorcism!" Ricky cried.

"We have to remove the sign and cleanse the store," Broken Heel Mansin said.

Redsy scratched in his red wool hair that was going ash grey at the edges. He said, "I'll help you get that sign down. Ugliest thing in the neighborhood. And the music, ouch."

Broken Heel Mansin said, "Yes, we could use your help, and thank you." I realized she must've been living here a long time to speak English so well.

Redsy stepped into a side entrance of his building. Two greasy bums watched with interest from the corner as Broken Heel Mansin popped a cork. She shook the bottle, champagne spurt from beneath her thumb, and as she sprayed the sign she cried, "I piss on you with goodness!"

She laughed like a crazy woman and turned the bottle on us. Auntie howled, "My dress!" We covered up as the champagne spray hit us, a sour smell in the air, and Ricky and I laughed together, behind the others, and bumped each other. Flat rubber feet poked out of the next building, rungs appeared, then Redsy the old wide-nosed man clumped toward us with his aluminum ladder. He stood it up on our threshold and kicked wide the legs.

"By the way," he said, "just call me Super Redsy, 'cause next door I'm the superintendent. Watch out." He started up the ladder, a cordless screw driver in one hand. He pressed the sign to the wall, fit the bit into notches, the drill whined, and screws tingled on the walk. He shouted, "Watch out below!"

The sheet of painted metal fell to the walk with a crash. Everyone cheered. Broken Heel Mansin dumped more champagne on the sign and cried, *"Kay-esso!* There they go!"

Super Redsy climbed down and nodded his head. "Well well, the Bloody Screwball is gone. Thrills and chills."

"Thank you, Super Redsy," Broken Heel Mansin said. "Now come upstairs and help us appease the Grandfathers. There's lots of Korean and American desserts."

"Super Redsy come?" Ling asked, pulling his hand.

"Not me." Super Redsy shook his head. "New toilet mechanism in 3G, I got to go." He folded his ladder and tilted it down toward his building as he walked. "Nice to meet you."

Appa-nim called, "Thanks, Super Redsy. Thank you!"

We trooped through the flickering candlelight in the store, through the dank storage room that stank of spinach greens and damp cardboard, up the stairs to our apartment. After the June sunlight on St. Mark's Place our apartment looked small and dingy, and I wondered what our beautiful witch saw.

I glanced at her. Auntie Yen exuded the soft beauty that entranced men, but Broken Heel Mansin had another kind of beauty, willful, powerful, and scary. Her lipstick was black, a stage performer's dramatic color, and when she turned her eyes to me I felt the intensity of her looking.

She lit a cigarette, its filter clamped between the smudged blacking on her lips. The cigarette was not for her. She lit a second cigarette and placed them smoking, lipstick on their filters, on the edges of two plates. The stink of tobacco smoke tainted the air as she and Umma filled the plates with fried date sweets, pine nut candies, squares of chocolate, flowers of honey cake, raspberry soufflés sprinkled with candies.

"Sweets for the Grandfathers," she said. She set the plates on the window sill; then she turned to Ricky. "And you? You are a native New Yorker?"

He chuckled. "That's right. Up and down, and out. What about you? You speak English better than I do. How's that?"

Broken Heel Mansin looked at the bleeding berry soufflés. "I came here when I was a girl. Who made the desserts?"

Harold hung his arm over Auntie's shoulders. "Wasn't Yen. She can't boil an egg."

"Shut up. Kee and Li, they're the cooks."

Broken Heel Mansin glanced at me, her eyes lingering until I felt the touch of her *nunchi*. Yes, I thought, now she knows my secrets. She lit a cigarette that she smoked as Appa-nim and Harold drank beer. Ling snuck around the table, reached, and quickly stuffed a whole glazed date sweet into her mouth. I followed the sharp rounding of Broken Heel Mansin's cocked hip and wondered what accident had caused it.

"Ow!" We all looked at her. "Oh!"

Umma leaned toward her. "Is something wrong?"

"Oh oh!" Broken Heel Mansin squatted down and grabbed herself between the thighs. "Oh oh!" I snatched her burning cigarette off the floor. "Hungry hungry!" She scuttled on all fours to the edge of the table, grabbed a handful of pears cooked in cream, and slathered her face as she ate them. When she turned toward us she looked like someone else, cream around her mouth and her lipstick smeared. "Hungry hungry."

Umma knew. "She's possessed! Who are you? What do you want?"

She pointed at Appa-nim. "Him!"

Appa-nim's eyebrows flew up. "Me?"

"Paego-buda!" Hungry! We all backed away as she scampered around, rolled her shoulders low to the floor and gamboled in a circle around Appa-nim. My mouth opened, I backed up to the sink. She

said, "Pick pick, pick pick pick."

Appa-nim giggled as she pinched his legs. Suddenly she clambered up his back like a monkey up a tree. Harold howled and bent over as Appa-nim reeled into the living room, hunched over, Broken Heel Mansin's red dress hanging around him, and he slapped at her half-heartedly, riding on his back. *"Aigo!* Get off!"

"Hungry hungry," the witch said. "Eat eat eat."

"Get off him!" Umma shouted. "You monkey bitch!" They all laughed as Broken Heel Mansin nipped at Appa-nim's neck and shoulders, and he staggered and spilled his beer. Ling rolled on the floor, but Umma was scowling. "Bitch monkey, get off him! He's a good husband, leave him alone!"

Around and around Appa-nim staggered, Broken Heel Mansin clinging to him, biting his neck, until he stumbled and dropped to his knees, onto his hands, his face flushed from laughing. Everyone but Umma and I were enjoying the show. Are they drunk? She's possessed! I stood behind the table, my fingertips white as I gripped the edge.

Broken Heel Mansin slumped on top of him and rolled off. She lay on the floor in a daze. The room went quiet except for Appa-nim, who was still laughing. She stared at the ceiling as he staggered to a chair. I plucked her cigarette, still smoking, from an ashtray and took it to her.

I knelt. "Broken Heel Mansin? Your cigarette?"

I put it to her lips. The end of it glowed bright as she sucked. Smoke spurt from her mouth and nose. The nicotine seemed to straighten her. She shook her head, slowly got onto her feet and stood up.

"Aigo. That one never got into me before. Don't know where it came from." She glanced around the ceiling, taking new measurements. "Over here."

Harold said, "Do you take tips?"

"Yeah, that was buggin'!"

I don't know what Ricky meant by buggin', but I saw Broken Heel Mansin's limp was more noticeable as she motioned for us to face the table. Auntie said, "Yes, amazing. You're quite an actor."

She snorted. "My husband is the actor, a soap opera star. Shut off the lights." We gathered around the table as she lit two candles, and we joined hands to encircle the desserts. Appa-nim grinned tipsily, flushed from laughing, his forehead burnished by the candlelight.

Broken Heel Mansin said, "Now I summon the powers of the five directions, North, South, East, West, and Center. Tangun, creator of the Korean peoples, urge out of the three nether worlds the spirits of the Grandfathers. Bring to us the grandfathers of this troubled family. Ahn Abuji, come to us!" Her voice put a shiver into my chest. "Bong Abuji, come to us!"

Thirty seconds passed. Voices came in off the street. A truck grumbled. Harold winked at Ricky and chuckled. Broken Heel Mansin said, "Grandfathers, come to us!"

My hand grew sweaty as I held Auntie Yen's hand. Tension tightened me. Ling shifted from foot to foot. Appa-nim chuckled until Broken Heel Mansin said, "Huh?" She made a disgusted noise. "What do you mean, you're the wrong grandfather? Aren't you Ahn Yong-Sool? Of Nun-yo village? In Kyong-Sang Namdo Province?" She glanced at Appa-nim, then into the air. "If you're not his father, who is?"

Appa-nim's lower lip trembled as if he'd been slapped, insulted, then he shut his mouth tight and spun away from the table.

Umma cried, "Ki-Teh!"

He yanked open the door, snarled an epithet, and slammed it. Wind from the door swept around the table, a candle went dark, and my father's steps drummed down the stairs.

Appa-nim's angry departure was so sudden we were all shocked back to hard realities.

"Let me go," Auntie said. She opened the door. "Ki-Teh!" No answer. Faintly from below came the clack of the screen door slapping its wooden frame, so Auntie Yen closed the door and went down.

Harold snorted. "You called up the wrong ghost, you booby."

Broken Heel Mansin glanced at Umma. Umma shook her head and whispered, "Not her fault. He gets like that. Pulls away, as if a tide pulls him down into himself." Ling shifted nervously from foot to foot. Umma was about to crack open and cry. "So...so we need the Grandfathers, we need their help. Try again, please. Can you still get them?"

Broken Heel Mansin nodded toward the window ledge. "One has already come and gone."

"What the bloody hell?" Harold walked over to the window sill. One plate sat full of desserts. The other plate lay empty except for a smear of berry juice, a dab of almond paste, a cigarette butt, and an unbroken line of ash. "The fag burnt down without being touched. Yen, come here, look. The desserts, they...they're cleaned out!"

Broken Heel Mansin asked, "Your father never smoked?"

"Cigarettes?" The cords of Umma's throat drew taut as she swallowed. "My father never smoked cigarettes."

Umma dropped her glance, her chin quivered, but Broken Heel Mansin touched her arm. She said, "Your father has left his blessing. As for the other grandfather...who knows?"

It felt like a storm hung over the table. Ricky broke the tension. "What's that?" He pointed at the raspberry soufflés, dark liquid around their edges. Umma slid one to a plate. He said, "Thanks, Mrs. Ahn. Um...my mother sees a good therapist. You want his number? For him?"

Umma busied herself by serving us. Ling loved sweets, but I never cared for them, so I took no plate.

"Korean culture is four thousand years old," Broken Heel Mansin said. "We know different things."

"Like what?"

"We know that the mind begins in the body. The body is

influenced by all the powers of the land, the spirits of trees and rivers, and the Earth itself...and by the long grasping hand of the past." She looked exhausted. "People think that everything should be understood. But the truth is that all our understanding, all that is known by man, now and in the future, doesn't even ripple the surface of the great mind."

"Yeah maybe." A moment of silence, then Ricky said, "Kee? I should be heading home, it's late."

Just like that, the kut was over and we all felt it. Umma said, "Good to meet you, Ricky. Thank you for coming."

"Bye, Monkey Tibb!" Ling cried, and Ricky rolled his eyes as we went to the door.

We stepped out of the store into sunlight glaring hot and harsh off the concrete walk. Appa-nim and Auntie Yen were across the intersection, near the entrance to Thompkins Square Park, waving their arms and arguing. Ricky and I hurried the other way, toward St. Mark's Place, through shadow puzzles made by sunlight shooting through the scraggly trees.

"That was wild. Thanks for asking me over," he said. We stepped into a doorway. "You wanna do something next weekend? How about a boat ride around Manhattan? See the Statue of Liberty, oil slicks, all that good stuff."

"Sounds wild," I said, imitating him. "Stainless, man. Totally buggin'!"

He laughed and took me by the shoulders, gently, and kissed me. It felt good, it felt right. He smiled at me with his big teeth, and I smiled to him as he waved and trotted toward First Avenue. Then I turned back toward the store and my smile faded. Auntie Yen and Appa-nim couldn't be seen. The good feeling faded out of me and was replaced by a feeling that slowed my steps. Dread.

He was in the store, and he was angry.

Chapter 14

First I heard his muttering. *"Chegiral!"* Damn!

I shuffled toward our doorway. The spilled champagne had dried up, but a ghost of the bleeding eyeball remained above the door, a rectangle of clean red bricks. The overhead lights glowed, the candles lay broken in a garbage can, the smell of burnt wax and beer lingering.

Appa-nim glowered at me from the cash register. "Sweep up the broken records. Now!" I grabbed a broom. "Heavy metal spirits, how stupid!" An old woman rolled cucumbers, frowned suspiciously, and a boy let the cooler door slam. "No let a door bang!" The boy hurried out. I dumped black plastic into the garbage can. "Trim lettuce!"

"Yes, Appa-nim."

I backed away into the damp air of the storage room. I washed my knife, twisted wires, flipped open the top of a crate, and the sweet scent of lettuce greeted me. The muffled sound of women's voices descended the stairs. I sat on my squeaky crate. I grabbed a head of lettuce, caught there, yes, caught there in the gloomy limbo between the women's voices and Appa-nim's furious muttering.

Greens fell as I sat hunched, worked, and sank into myself, took refuge in the simple act of trimming away the imperfect leaves. I grabbed heads, twisted them, let the damaged and rotted leaves fall, flipped the knife, slashed cellophane. Grab, twist, flip the glittering knife, slash, forget my problems, wrap and toss.

The problem came when my mind wandered, when I lost my mindful focus on trimming. I thought how Umma was too upset. She knew there was a bad problem with him. I grabbed a head, cool in my hand, twisted, leaves dropped—she wouldn't admit there's anything wrong!—slashed cellophane, wrap and toss. I thought of all those times in Nun-yo when he came home stinking of makkola, snapped at Umma, pounded the table, insulted our cooking. He was, and he still is a—

Something inside me hardened, a pain caught my breath. It felt like I swallowed a fish hook, barbs in my stomach; but then the pain broke open, swarmed up through me, seized me, and I was so angry my teeth clenched and my breath hissed in my nose. Why! Why is he so ugly!

Men's voices filled the store. "Stinks like a brewery in here. He's had a few." I leaned to look out. The two men wore jeans spattered with paint, dozens of colors. Struggling artists, they had scraggly beards, dirty tee-shirts, worn-out sneakers. "Pal, you been drinking on the job?"

Appa-nim said, "What you need? Hurry up."

Rasp-clunk, rasp-clunk, Broken Heel Mansin came down the stairs and stopped in the milky light of the bulb glowing over the sink. Her dress was splotched with beer, but her lips were repainted a soft red color, her hair was brushed, and she looked like a different woman.

"Watch out for the family," she said. I nodded. "If you need anything, call me. Your mother has the number."

"Yes, Broken Heel Mansin." She was settling a responsibility on me. "Thank you."

As she passed out into the store the painters stopped shopping to stare. She lifted her boom box from beneath the coffee counter.

"Be well, Ahn Chi-bi-nim," she said to Appa-nim.

Silence.

She let the screen door close with a soft cluck of its tongue, and I felt the leaving of her warmth and hope. All my energy and determination seemed to go out with her. No ruined leaves fell into the crate. I let my head hang heavy with thoughts, and because the anger did not come back to protect me, my chest ached. I felt bereft at the loss of something I could not name.

Appa-nim did not speak to me again that night and all the next morning, I felt the distance Umma felt, the sense of him drawing away and down into the dark inside himself. Noon came. Without a word he climbed the stairs, so I hurried out to the register, the drawer full of money, the grid of numbered keys, the green numerals on the read-out.

"I help you?" Customers lined up, my fingers flew over the keys. "Thank you, please come again. That be all?" People came in with the hot noon light, shoulders, bill caps, shiny dirt- brown cheeks. "Thirty-six cent change."

A woman poked in her purse. When she looked down I looked over her shoulder, and like a picture in an ad, I saw Craig Donafrio's handsome face. His perfect white smile flashed at me. "Howdy rowdy!"

I said to the woman, "Exact change, thank you," and held the bag for her to grab. "Please come again."

Craig stepped up to the counter, wearing a clingy shirt, his stomach flat and hard below his chest muscles. He said, "I see you have some fruits here. What do you recommend?"

"Um..." Something in me curled like a beached fish. "...pomegranate?"

He wrinkled his brow for a cartoon expression of deep thought. He tossed two pomegranates into the air.

"I used to juggle. Did I tell you I was in a 501 Jeans commercial? I banked sixty thousand dollars." He stuck the two fruits back in their cups and went to the cooler. He grabbed a wine cooler, came to the counter and leaned over it, which made me lean to the other side of the register. "Want to do something this weekend? There's a chillin' band playing at the Bottom Line."

Shoes clunked on the stairs. Umma? I made my fingers skip on the keys. "Sorry, I can no'...um...go. One dollar ninety-two cent total."

"Heavy bummage," he said. "Why not?"

Umma appeared from the storage room. I didn't show it, but relief washed through me.

"Eight cent change. Thank you, come again." I glanced at her. "No...um...thank you, I will be work, um, working. At that time." I closed the cash drawer as Umma watched from the watermelons. "How do you know to come here?"

"Ricky told me." Irritation kinked the corner of his mouth. "I didn't tell you when the show is, so how do you know you'll be working?" He stepped aside to let a woman with a purple head rag place her fruit on the counter. "Will you be working Saturday night, or going out with that bucktooth twit, Ricky Tibbs?"

The purple head rag woman was immensely fat, with folds of flesh flapping around her upper arms. "That be all?"

Craig wrenched the cap off his wine cooler and gulped. Umma watched. She said in Hangugo, "Your friend from the dojang?"

"Anio." No. I said to him in English, "Store will be open. Sorry. Four dollar sixty-nine cent total."

"Well hey, okay, I don't speak Korean, but I can take a hint." He gulped wine soda and backed to the door. "See you tonight at the dojang, Kee."

"Uh-huh. Thirty-one cent change." Ricky told him where to come here? They were talking about me? In the changing room? A pang of irritation, alarm, pride too that Craig had asked me on a date, made me look away when Umma's eyes caught mine. She walked to the door, smoothing down the front of her dress.

"Watch out for that one," she said. "No spot on the peel but rotten inside. See you."

When? I didn't think the words, how little I saw her, but in that moment I felt that loss acutely. There was little chance to talk with her, so I had a conversation with myself, in my head. I thought how Craig isn't that bad. And he asked me out on a date! He was angry that I wouldn't go...but who would've guessed?

So it was that I got on the train for Chinatown, hoping to see Ricky in the dojang but not wanting to show that pleasure. Rumble ride ride, clacks on the tracks, and I wondered as I strode up Mulberry Street if Craig would still be friendly. The dojang was cool, silent, and still. I removed my shoes and bowed to the American and Korean flags. I hurried to the closet. The mop was heavy, I was late arriving. I slung and flopped the heavy grey seaweed over the boards until the sweat broke out on my forehead. I left black water in the bucket and hurried to grab my bag.

I knocked lightly on the office door. "Sir?" A chuckle. "Choi Su-nim?"

He opened the door. The comics of the Daily Post rustled in his hand. He smiled and waved me into his office, and when I stepped out of his office, dressed in my dobuck and sash, he was still chuckling over a cartoon. "Thank you, sir."

"You're welcome." He surveyed the practice floor. "Now you sit in meditation?"

"Yes sir."

He gazed at some point beyond the ceiling. "You know," he said, "a mop can be just as useful as a sword, and a toilet plunger may be more useful than either."

I looked to see if he was serious. "Sir?"

He was serious, but that unnerving humor glinted in his eyes. "Mindfulness is about maintaining your focus whatever you do. Swords or mops or toilet plungers are only aids to the mental process, the focus on the present. What did Peng Su-nim say about the sword?"

I bowed sharply. "You do not wield the sword, the sword wields you."

Choi Su-nim nodded. "So it does. The sword is a handle onto the Way of the world that is offering itself to you. If you are willful it will weigh a ton and wear you out. If you lose focus it will cut open your hand. Mindfulness keeps your mind on the blade; and if you are mindful you will not think about the future or past, there will be no blocks to the flow of Tao, and the Way of the world will flow through the sword and through you. You will become the sword of the world."

A student barged through the doors, kicked off his shoes, bowed to the flags, to Choi Su-nim and to me, a senior student. I waited until he entered the changing room. I said, "I'm not sure what you mean about the mop and the plunger, sir."

"Use the mop, the toilet plunger, and the sword with full mindfulness and no thoughts will disturb your stillness. Hm. Better analogy than I thought." He nodded. "You get full of ugly stuff when you're plugged up with regrets about the past and fears of the future. So maybe mindfulness is a toilet plunger for the mind."

I bowed, amused but uncertain if I should be. "Yes sir."

Choi Su-nim turned with his rustling newsprint cartoons and retired into his office. I went and sat with my back to the wall by the practice floor. America has most definitely influenced him, I thought. Along with Way of the Sword, now he also wants me to practice Way of the Mop? Way of the Toilet Plunger? I laughed, and almost my whole meditation passed before I felt the good humor leak out and leave me as he described, still and quiet inside myself.

During class I felt Ricky watching me from the back line of yellow belts, his glance a fingerprint in my awareness, and Craig stood beside me without looking or speaking to me, and we began to flow on the floor, following the different currents of each moving poem. I fell out of rhythm. I don't know why, but for an instant I lagged a step behind.

Ow! A streak of fire lit down my back. I hurried to catch up, glancing over my shoulder. Craig? The tip of his sword? I edged away from him, out of step with the others, half a step quicker. He flicked me with his bamboo? We came to Choon-be Stance, stood with our practice swords at the ready, and I felt the ghost of fire on my back, as if someone had struck a match down my spine.

Choi Su-nim did not call for Tiger and Crane Poom-sey. I was embarrassed. I was so far behind that I had to be corrected like that? We bowed to Choi Su-nim, class ended, and as the dojang filled with talk and laughter Craig turned his calm glance upon me. He touched my shoulder as if he knew me.

"Jeez, Kee, sorry about zapping you," he said. "Did it hurt? I mean, if I didn't zap you, you wouldn't know you screwed up, and you did." He lowered his chin and his gaze became intense. "You did screw up today, big time. And I was nice about it."

Chapter 15

I was at the register, thinking about love. The lunch crowd had come and gone out like a tide, I was in no rush, so I was mentally composing a letter to my old friend and tutor. *Dear Chen-puin*, I thought, *I miss you*. Appa-nim and a driver were unloading a truck at the curb, waxed boxes smacked concrete, then came the crunch of cardboard and the mumble of loose fruit inside. Smack-crunch mumble mumble.

"Six dollar eighty-one cent," I said, but my thoughts were elsewhere. *I miss you. I miss Peng Su-nim, Ti-Lee, Sanggyo, and everyone else.* "Nineteen cent change." *I miss Nun-yo. New York City always stinks like burnt gas and tofu gone bad.* "Thank you, please come again." *I am writing to ask how you are, and how someone can tell if they are in love.*

When the truck was empty Appa-nim and the trucker started arguing. The trucker snapped, "There was eighteen crates of lettuce."

"Seventeen!" Appa-nim shouted. "Oh...the hell with it!"

He scribbled on the shipping bill, the trucker slammed his back gate, and Appa-nim stalked in past me. *"Shin chegiril!"* God damn! He stalked into the storage room and threw the clipboard. Papers rustled, it hit the wall, fell and clapped on the floor. In the loud silence he shouted, "God damn Koreans! I thought I wouldn't have to deal with them here!"

Here? In the United States? And why does he hate Koreans?

He rasped his shoes up the steps and slammed the door at the top. I let myself separate from the wall and became aware of a customer. My body relaxed a little as he looked toward the storage room with raised eyebrows. A small boy with big green eyes, he shrugged instead of saying it: Parents, they can be that way.

"A pack of menthols please," he said. "For my mother."

Tension settled out of the air as I tallied prices for collards, apricots, mineral water, potatoes, plums, wine sodas, granola, celery, beer. Heat rippling up from the sidewalk outside the door made me think of Appa-nim's anger, but I escaped by thinking about love. I know what Auntie thinks about love. Maybe I should ask Broken Heel Mansin what it feels like? I spilled coins like game counters into a pink palm, into many palms pale and creased. Did I really love Ti-Lee? I couldn't kiss him. If I loved him I could've kissed him.

"Three dollar forty cent." I certainly didn't love Ricky Tibbs; but how could I kiss him then? Well...I decided I better write Chen-puin. I said my singsong, "Thank you, please come again," thought about the letter to write, and looked forward to Sunday, when Ricky Tibbs was taking me on a tour boat ride around Manhattan. Maybe I should ask Umma? Her voice held such tired regret when we sat in the park. Does she regret marrying Appa-nim? That made me think another ignorant question. If she regrets marrying him, did she love him in the first place?

I composed my letter to Chen-puin, the days of the week passed, July ended, the nights of August fell a little cooler, and during the times of tedium I wondered about love. Every time someone bought persimmons, bright yellow or succulent orange, I thought of my favorite folk tale. The king sees a persimmon while the prince sees a pearl. Why couldn't the king see the pearl for what it was? Chen-puin told me to listen carefully to the old folk tales, they held great wisdom. What did it mean that the king saw the pearl as a persimmon?

Saturday morning. Ling stayed in the store because the Rhee twins were at summer camp. Appa-nim let her run the cash register, or she twirled and danced herself around the island, arranging fruits and vegetables. Her childish beauty surrounded her like a radiance. She nudged up to an old man wearing suspenders. "Mister, squash on sale," she said. She danced two squashes on top of the flat red stage of a halved watermelon. "Dee dee dee, dee dah dum. Appa squash, umma squash. Must buy two!"

The customer laughed, but he bought only one, breaking up the marriage.

I wondered what caused Appa-nim's problems. Mu mentioned a crying baby. What could a crying baby have to do with it? I watched Appa-nim across the distance he imposed, tried to plumb the silence between us with sidelong glances. Saturday afternoon he caught me looking at him. He snapped, "You didn't replace the matting under the onions, like I told you. It's infested with flies."

"I'm sorry, Appa-nim."

His brows were hard lids over his eyes, so I kept my gaze in the cash drawer. Ling saw and tugged his sleeve. "What did Umma make for lunch?"

"Noodles." Appa-nim lifted a whole watermelon and strode for the sunlit doorway. He stopped short. "I help you?"

In the August heat the man wore grey pants, a shirt with a patch. "Department of Health," he said. He turned a clipboard toward Appa-nim. "Inspector Berger. This is an initial inspection. This is your third month in business, Mr. Ki-Teh?" He pointed at the clipboard. "Ahn Ki-Teh, is this the correct spelling?"

Appa-nim jostled a customer to put the melon on the counter. "What you looking for? No bug. Clean store, no bug."

Inspector Berger said, "I'll see for myself." Appa-nim followed at his elbow. "Mr. Ki-Teh, just stay out of the way."

I said to a girl, "That be all? Seventy-nine cent." My fingertips tapped the keys, *beep!* and I nervously plucked coins out of the drawer. "Please come again."

"Clean store, no bug." Inspector Berger, a man with a red mustache and blonde eyebrows, glanced under the leafy greens, hovered his hand over the two-packs of garlic while Appa-nim spoke over his shoulder. "I tell you, clean store, no bug."

"Please stay out of the way."

Appa-nim followed him into the storage room.

"Hi Kee!" I looked around. Ricky Tibbs? He rapped his knuckles on the counter, a smile of his big white teeth splitting his face. My hand nervously jumped to my face, I rubbed my brow. Too many things at once. Ricky laughed. "There's the little fried noodle. How are you, Ling?"

I leaned over the counter. "What do you do here?"

"I was in the area. Something wrong?" I glanced at the storage room. Appa-nim's voice rose to an anxious pitch. "This is what you do all day? Run a cash register? Must be boring. Fried noodle, you can't hide from me, I see you."

Her eyes and forehead bobbed behind the avocadoes. I whispered, "Not a good time, Ricky. Buy something."

"How about a candy bar?" He ripped the wrapper off a chocolate bar as Appa-nim and Inspector Berger came out of the storage room. Appa-nim glanced over angrily. Ricky said, "I'm taking a test prep class over on Third Ave. Boring boring. My dad didn't ask me, he just decided I'm going pre-law."

Appa-nim planted his hands on his hips and stood in front of Inspector Berger. "I tell the truth. No bug!"

The wrapper of Ricky's chocolate bar crackled loudly. Appa-nim glanced over. I looked at the keys of the register. Ricky swung the chocolate bar like a sword. "You wait. They're gonna call me the black Bruce Lee."

"Well, Mr. Ahn..." Inwardly I groaned as the inspector lifted a bag of onions. Out of the matting rose a puff of fruit flies. "...you still insist there's no bug?"

I whispered, "Go."

"If you insist." Ricky bit the chocolate bar savagely, the wrapper crackled, Ling chuckled. "See you tomorrow. Oh yeah, I have to pay for this." He dropped a bill on the counter and spoke with a stagy accent. "Keep the change, kid."

Ricky skipped out into the sunlight, only to be replaced before the counter by Inspector Berger, running his fingers through his red wavy hair.

"This was only a preliminary inspection, Mr. Ki-the," he said. "You've got fruit flies and roaches, and you should keep the storage room cleaner; but otherwise you're in good shape. I'll be back in a few months to see if you've rectified the problems."

"Yeah, uh-huh." As the gray back of Inspector Berger disappeared outside the door Appa-nim turned on me. "See what happens when you don't change the matting!" He threw up his hands and stalked into the storage room. "Kee, I give up on you. The hell with it!" What does that mean? He appeared with a watermelon in his arms. "Now that I pay you, you don't care, so I don't care either. I do, I give up on you. I give up!"

When he reached the doorway he stepped aside for a customer: Craig Donafrio cried, "Howdy rowdy!" I wanted to hide with Ling. Who next? Choi Su-nim? Ling's chuckle came out of the avocadoes. Craig strode up until his stomach muscles, inside his skin-tight shirt, met the counter. "God! It is a to-oo-ubular day. Perfect friz weather. How's it going?"

Appa-nim snorted and spoke Hangugo. "At least this one isn't black."

He went out with the watermelon. Craig looked after him, his mouth hardening, he was irritated by the tone of Appa-nim's voice. Then he looked at me.

"I stopped in," he said, "to ask if you wanted to go to a Black Sabbath concert. How about it?"

Appa-nim became a dark shape on the threshold. "You go." He tapped Craig's shoulder and pointed to the door. "You, you get out."

Craig looked at me, looked at Appa-nim. "What's he saying?"

Appa-nim jerked his thumb toward the door. "You go. Get out. She work, no talk talk talk."

"Christ, dad, what's the zip code on your hemorroid?"

"No swear!" He herded Craig out the door. "You no come back.

No swear. I call police!"

Craig's muscled shoulders filled the doorway, his elbows went out like a rooster's wings, and he grabbed Appa-nim's shirt. He threw my father stumbling back and the island shivered when Appa-nim hit it.

"Bastard!" Craig shouted. "You put your hands on me again and I'll beat the *shit* out of you. You hear me?!" Appa-nim's mouth fell open. Craig's face was fiery red and ugly. "No comment, putz? Putz!"

"You putz!" Ling ran around the island. "Kee, 911. Call police! You putz! 911! 911!"

I was too startled. I glanced for the telephone behind the counter, and when I glanced back, Craig was gone. We stood in the silence of being shocked. A fly buzzed, caught in the uncoiled fly paper suspended in the corner, while little Ling stood in the doorway with her fists clenched. She shouted, "You putz!"

Appa-nim was the first to recover. He rubbed his hip and looked down as if to make sure he was not broken. He said, "Komdo hasn't done much for his temper. Ling, you were so brave. You drove him away when I couldn't."

She looked doubtful. "Well..."

"Well," he said, "I think we should go eat *odong*. Want to eat noodles with me, plum?"

She nodded and they went upstairs. I was still shocked. He pushed my father across the room! Alone at the register, I rang up what people brought to me, took bills, felt the milled edges of coins, let them tinkle into palms, and wondered what to do. Tell Choi Su-nim, I thought. Don't tell Ricky Tibbs. No, uh-uh.

On Sunday morning I did no meditation because Appa-nim, Umma, and Ling went down the block to St. Stanislaw's Church. As they marched out the door, past me at the register, Ling said, "Goodbye, fruit-head girl." I felt lonely as they went, but not only because they went without me. Umma seemed always tired and depressed, denied that anything was wrong, even though Appa-nim had a new scar. That pink line of scarring was thick like pursed lips on his arm. It made me nervous.

He treated me with pursed lips, so I was glad he could do the American thing on Sunday mornings. After church, at the Polish diner by the park, he sat with a *Hankook Ilbo*, read, ate potato blintzes, and drank coffee. That was good for him, the break. I think he liked how Auntie's bargaining worked out. When they returned he changed his clothes upstairs, and when he descended it was my turn to do the American thing.

"Thank you, Appa-nim! Bye Ling!"

I ran out to meet my date for a cruise. At the far end of St. Mark's Place, the square where the Cooper Union art school stood sharp, I shouted, "Ricky!" He looked up from a fat woman at a folding table, an orange scarf binding her head, a crystal ball before her. What's she doing?

He sprinted across the street, jumped to land on both feet in front of me. "He leaps the curb in a single bound and says, Nice to see you, Kee. Let's go."

"How...um...do you say that? Nice to see you?"

"Right. The fortune teller said we're gonna have a great time."

We reached the subway turnstiles. I said, "Nice to see you too."

"Put that token away, this is on me." Reluctantly I put away the tattered plastic packet, the four tokens remaining from my purchase on Monday. "I have Dad's credit card so we can charge the boat tickets." He kissed my cheek. "You smell delicious."

At the Hudson River, the pier like a flat finger of tar pointing into the water, Ricky Tibbs bought our tickets, we climbed a set of carpeted stairs, gulls screeching overhead, and I laughed aloud. The water stank of gas and oil and my laugh vanished into the pale blue sky. We climbed to the top deck and stood in the warm sunlight and let the sea wind cool us. Ricky Tibbs put his arm around me. I leaned against him. The engine thrumbled beneath our feet, the boat left the dock, and I smelled Green Dragon Bay.

Every ocean smells different. The Hudson River smelled enough like the bay before Nun-yo, though, that memories flooded me. I gazed out over the green humpback waves. Ricky Tibbs put his arms around me, from behind, but I hardly noticed. The tour boat was heavy with tourists, four languages mixed in the air, but I heard them only in the back of my head. In four months my memories of Nun-yo had become dream-like. They were not crispy real to me anymore.

Ricky Tibbs held out a copper coin balanced on his fingertip. "Penny for your thoughts."

I put the penny in my pocket. "I miss Nun-yo." It was a different homesickness from when we first came to America. I was looking back at a lovely place lost and gone forever. "I miss Peng Su-nim, his dojang, and Chen-puin, her, um, plant place."

"Her garden?"

I nodded. "Garden." I pointed to the Statue of Liberty, the giant green woman raising her torch. "Her color."

"So you miss your Garden of Liberty?" I looked up at him and smiled. He looked down at me. He lowered his face and kissed me softly on the mouth. He said, "I love you."

A firecracker of feeling burst in my chest, but I did not know what such a feeling was, so I said nothing. We went into the cafe inside the boat. He kissed me while we waited on the food line. We went back to the prow, he kissed me, and now and then he kissed me as we threw pretzel pieces to squawking sea birds. The boat passed through the Narrows and turned around a pier of the bridge to Staten Island. Cars droned over our heads. Ricky gazed deep into my eyes, searched for a part of me that would respond, and kissed me.

"Kee," he said, "I love you."

"Ricky," I said, "you are...oh...okay."

He stepped back. "I tell you I love you, and you tell me I'm okay?" He laughed. "When they say Asians are mysterious, they must mean the women."

I didn't want to disappoint him so I leaned up and kissed his mouth. That made him feel something acutely. For the rest of the boat ride he never released my hand or let me break out from the yoke of his arms. I inhaled the smell of the cologne on his shoulders, the smell of my first boyfriend, whom I will never forget. He kissed my throat, my cheeks, my mouth, his big front teeth like the edge of a shell inside soft flesh. I could not see past his collar, his mouth, his eyes, but I thought people must be looking at us. Then I felt the tip of his tongue touch my tongue with the sweet taste of persimmon fruit, and I didn't remember anything else until the boat courted the dock with a restful quieting of its engines.

As we were in a line of people clumping our shoes down the gang plank I heard Hangugo, a man's voice. *"Sonyo, taek."* You, girl. I glanced over my shoulder. It was a Korean man wearing a camera around his neck. He said, "Your own kind isn't good enough? You have to go out with a black one?"

Ricky asked, "What's he saying?"

I shook my head. We went out into the streets. I walked arm in arm with Ricky and felt that man looking at me from the parking lot.

We played mailbox, kissed when we came to a mailbox. We changed the rules to play parking meter, since they were closer together. Every six strides Ricky sang out, "Parking meter!" and we kissed. The tip of his tongue filled my mouth with the sweet taste of persimmon fruit, the same taste I enjoyed under the tree in Master Peng's garden when the fruit was ripe.

There weren't enough parking meters, so we forgot about rules altogether. I wanted to forget that man. I did forget him as Ricky Tibbs and I kissed. I tasted the hot fruit sugar taste of being a woman with a man. I breathed his breath until I was lightheaded and ate of his mouth—hot, sweet, liquid—like I was eating the most delicious fruit.

My body grew anxious. It felt good. I arched my back to keep myself tightly against him. His hands caressed my back, my shoulders, my waist, then rose to my ribs. I wore the black brassiere that Auntie bought me, and I knew Ricky could glimpse its lacy edges, which made me feel like a woman. His fingers traced a groove in my ribs, around from the back, beneath my arm, until the base of his thumb touched my breast. His hand opened and closed on me gently.

I wanted him to touch me there, but not where people could see us. "Ricky." He squeezed me tenderly, but I saw the street beyond him, people strolling on the sidewalk, a traffic light changing from green to red. I whispered, "No," but he pushed his fingers between my buttons.

I pulled away. "Ricky, no. No!"

"What, what's the matter?" He looked at me, bleery desperation in his eyes. "Don't you know what we're doing? What the hell? Are you getting me hot and bothered for the fun of it?" He held me away, the cloth of my sleeves bunched in his hands. "Is that it? All you're doing is teasing me? Well...damn!"

He turned his back on me. I reached out to him, my mouth still needy for his kisses. "Ricky, please..."

He snapped, "Damn, Kee, I'm frickin' horny. You can't get me like this and not do something about it. Dammit!"

Chapter 16

A chuckle came from Choi Su-nim's office. I thought that his English must be good if he could easily read the papers. Relax. Relax. I wiped sweat from the nape of my neck and in the silent cool of the dojang conformed the curves of my spine to the hard vertical of the wall, the bones of my buttocks like two knobs on the carpet. My shoulders settled away from my ears, my neck lengthened, and as I listened in the red darkness behind my eyelids, my heart beat slower, slower, a drummer slowing the beat.

Other students entered from the street with the rattle of the door, clucking shoes, laughter, the rustle of clothing. My meditation was as still and focused as when I sat in the lotus position in Nun-yo. Boys joked behind the wall of the changing room at my back. The door opened, the knob rattled as the door shut, but I was not disturbed.

Then something poked my thigh. I opened my eyes. Towering over me, Craig pulled his toe away. He said, "What's your father's problem? I know I shouldn't have pushed him, but what an asshole. You saw him. He threw me out for no reason."

Ricky Tibbs appeared, a second figure towering over me. "Hey," Ricky said, "can't you see she's meditating?"

"Can't you see I'm talking to her?" Craig gestured with his middle finger at Ricky; but then the crack of Choi Su-nim's clapping hands echoed between them. I rose slowly out of the lotus. Craig said to me, "I'll talk to you after class."

We hurried to our places, Craig and I to the front. We bowed to the flags, to Choi Su-nim, followed Sinclair's counting of numbers with his flat Hangugo accent—*"Hanna, duel, set, net, dos, yos"*— stretched our tendons, did sit-ups, poised in the basic stances, and whipped our kicks with the snap of cloth cuffs. Choi Su-nim strolled along the practice floor and before our front line, rested his knobby-knuckled hands on the head of his cane. He said, *"Kmbung-oh Poom-sey."* Poom-sey of the Goldfish, the simplest moving poem.

Craig's irritation forced itself on me. I was aware of Ricky Tibbs' attention, it did not bother me, but Craig's anger felt like a splash of blood on the waters. We completed another poom-sey. I was part of a triangle. Ricky loved me, Craig hated me—he does, I thought. He does hate me—and I...what was I?

I was stillness. I was there and I was not there. Ricky Tibbs and the other yellow belts sat down. More difficult poom-seys. Kee-hop cries burst from our chests, echoed, faded into a faint buzzing in my ears, our lungs went hissah! hissah! and I was with it, the flow. Students with blue and red belts sat to the side. Bamboo whistled and swished, cloth snapped about my ankles. I was with the Tao and my flowing stillness was complete.

I heard danger behind my ear, bamboo slicing the air, and pain like a flaring match burned in a line down my back. *Ah!* Craig's sword again! I thrust, kicked, shouted, and cut the air with my bamboo, I did not stumble, but nervous prickles danced on my skin. I kept expecting to feel the flaming tip of his sword, kept moving through the poom-sey. The flame did not come again. The poom-sey ended. I breathed deeply, Craig huffed, and I wondered, Didn't anyone see him do that? I snuck a glance at him. Red-faced, he was laboring to breath.

Choi Su-nim said, "Tiger and Crane Poom-sey."

To be safe I paced fifteen feet away from Craig. I raised my jointed bamboo straight before me, gripped loosely in my sweaty hands, the sweat cementing my connection with the sword, making it a part of me.

Choi Su-nim snapped, *"Say-sha!"* Begin!

As I think about doing Tiger and Crane Poom-sey, I recall what I was told in Nun-yo, which is on the opposite side of the world from New York City. Peng Su-nim told me that although the Earth turns the pond won't spill a drop. I didn't know why he told me that.

My body complained with a thousand pains—my back muscles clenched on my spine, ribs squeezed my lungs, the muscles of my legs powered me tiredly—yet I moved with the tranquility of the pond. No thoughts. The pond remained still as the world turned with ferocious speed, on and on—pain. Pain. The muscles of my thumbs ached as I gripped my sword, and when I slashed and heard it whistle it took more effort, as if I was slicing through cloth, not air. Then the poom-sey had passed through me and I was finished.

The reflection of the sky did not ripple on the waters of my awareness.

I brought my sword to the poise of Readiness Stance, but Craig's heels thudded for another few seconds. His gasps came loud off the walls when he stood in Choon-be and his sword wavered before him. Choi Su-nim let out his low ending command. "Pah-doooooo." Craig and I returned to the front, Sinclair stepped in beside me, the others behind us.

Choi Su-nim stood below the flags. He leaned on his cane and gazed at me. "Yes." He nodded. "Yes, you are ready."

Ready for what? We bowed to him, to the Korean and American flags, and he clapped his hands to end the class.

I stepped forward and bowed. "Choi Su-nim? Can we speak, sir?"

Sinclair and Craig watched as I held out my bamboo sword to Little Tito. Choi Su-nim turned, led me into his office and closed the door. My bag sat on the floor like a popped bladder. He settled into the chair behind his desk. Over his head and behind him on the wall, as if she was always in the back of his mind, hung the picture of his wife, long dead.

"Choi Su-nim," I said, "I don't want to cause problems." Choi Su-nim crossed his hands atop the red, blue, and green shapes of the newsprint cartoons. I looked at the floor. "Peng Su-nim told me the reason women were not allowed to study our Way…of the Dawning Sword… was to prevent problems like this."

Choi Su-nim pushed up his thick glasses. "What problems?"

"Craig 'disrespected' me with his bamboo, during poom-sey.*"

"Yes, I saw. And?"

"And he asked me out on a date, twice. I said no, and now he's angry. He came to our store. When Appa-nim made Craig leave, he got furious and pushed my father. Threatened him."

Choi Su-nim peered into his interlaced fingers. The trouble pulled the wrinkles in his forehead low onto his brows, sparse grey and white.

"Yes," he said, "Craig is troubled. When he began studying with me he was troubled by his father. Many American fathers care more about their jobs than about their sons. I've tried to show him the way of komdo; but he has other troubles too, troubles this city seems to breed. But Craig is not your concern."

Disappointment whispered inside me. He heard it and spoke curtly. "Have you chosen a Way?"

"Yes sir."

"And you know the commitment it takes, heart, mind, and soul?"

I nodded. "Yes, Choi Su-nim, I do."

"I also assume you know the path sometimes leads to enlightenment. In order to reach the freedom of enlightenment you cannot compromise your commitment. You cannot involve yourself with distractions. The path is not easy."

Uneasiness stirred in me. I bowed. "What should I do about Craig? How should I act toward him?"

Choi Su-nim shook his old grey head. "Don't act toward him at all. Continue on the Way you have chosen." He rose to leave his office, to give me privacy to change my clothes. "Don't forget that the way to enlightenment demands everything. There can be no compromises in your commitment."

"Sir?" He paused with his hand on the door knob. "What did you mean outside, when you said I was ready? Ready for what?"

"Ready to walk the edge of the street." He stepped out and silently pulled the door shut.

Walking the edge of the street? Sounds strange. I dressed and opened the door. Choi Su-nim stood waiting by the door to Mulberry Street. "Thank you, sir."

He bowed. His bowing stopped me. It is unusual for a teacher to bow to a student. He said, "Thank you for the confidence."

I went out, mystified. The treetops and tenements stood still beneath a sky torn and grey, a dirty blanket of smog draped around the tops of tall buildings. Children chanted as they jumped rope and basketballs beat on the courts in the park.

"Kee!" Craig stood below the sign for Bayard Street. His hair was combed and he smiled deceptively. He asked, "What did you talk to Choi Su-nim about?" I kept walking. He fell in step with me. "What's the matter with your father? You saw him. I walked in and he started screaming at me." He sniffed loudly, pressed one nostril and sniffed hard through the other. "He started screaming at me for no reason. You saw him, right?"

Fish scales glittered like sequins in the gutter. I turned up toward the crowded markets. He slapped my arm.

"What? Did Daddy tell you to stay away from me? Too good to talk to me now?" I put my head down and detoured between chrome bumpers, into the street. Craig stopped. He shouted loud enough to make people look. "Your friend, Ricky Tibbs, he said he *fucked* you in Central Park. Three times!"

Fucked? What is fucked? I heard a trucker use that word at Hunts Point, I knew it was not good. Where's Ricky Tibbs? Maybe he did say such a thing, so he isn't here. The serenity of the dojang was gone, a nervous hardening around my breath. I pursed my lips and followed Mott Street.

Among the crowds of housewives, baby carriages, tradesmen, couples, the rich smells of wax, garlic, and ginger, I thought of Ricky Tibbs. We kissed so much on the boat, and afterwards too, that I got excited. Pu-Jong's chickens. I had watched Pu-Jong's chickens often enough to know what my body wanted. That? With Ricky?

"Hey." Something flagged my arm, but I was not seeing. "Kee!" I blinked. The glittering brown of Ling's tiger eyes and the little peak of her nose came into focus. She said, "Thinking of Ricky, huh?"

I snorted. "Come on." We hurried down Canal Street, past windows with glazed ducks, radios, wrist TVs, buddhas, backpacks, scrimshaw. Ricky's kissing and Craig's explosions created a riptide of unease inside me. We barged through the turnstiles. I used the last of my tokens, but Appa-nim had paid me that day, I had fifteen dollars in my pocket. I remembered that Ling had used that word at the dinner when Auntie and Harold were visiting. I said, "What does 'fucked' mean?"

"Don' know, Joe. Stop!"

Ling stopped. She gave a dollar to an Arab caged in a kiosk, only his face visible behind a hundred different magazine covers, candy displays, racks of cigarettes. Savagely she ripped the cellophane from around a lollipop.

"Look. Mister Monkey Tibb is waiting for you."

I gazed down toward the oily steel pillars of the platform, the dark tracks beyond. He grinned and waved.

"Ling," I said. "Don't call him monkey."

Ling chuckled and skipped down toward him. Ricky hummed and said, "A super-grape lollipop. My favorite too."

"Not a lollipop, Mister Tibb. Kumquat, you canno tell?"

"Very funny, noodle." He leaned to kiss me. I leaned away. "I wanted to talk before class, but that Craig was bothering you. What was he saying about your father?"

A train filled the tunnel with rumbling, stopped beside us with screeching brakes, shivers running under our feet. The doors shook as they closed behind us. The faces of people desperate to get places appeared beyond the glass. The train rumbled and shook away from the station and the desperate faces turned angry. Ling licked her lollipop and Ricky Tibbs looked at me. I looked up at ads for a romance novel, night school, a Broadway show, roach powder.

On the bench across the car sat the huge fat woman I saw on the train before. Going home from work? No, too dirty. Who'd hire her, stinking that bad? Ricky watched me and looked upset. She stank of motor oil and overripe nectarines. Pagoda Woman, that's what we called her. Her head on top of her fat shoulders, her huge blubbery breasts, and four huge rolls of fat gave her seven layers, like the pagoda in Seoul. Seven layers to reality, seven layers to the fat woman. I felt Ricky getting agitated. I looked at him as the Pagoda Woman's eyes moved in her fleshy cheeks.

Ricky could not contain himself. "Kee," he whispered closely, "I'm sorry I got pushy Sunday. I know you were mad at me; but I...I got horny. I'm sorry. I am, I'm sorry."

"Mister Tibb, you not okay," said Ling. "I buy kumquat, you see lollipop."

I said, "Go away, Ling, please."

The way I looked made her chuckle. She licked her lollipop and crossed the car.

"I thought you liked it too," whispered Ricky. "You got horny too, didn't you?" Ling watched. The Pagoda Lady watched him whisper. "If it didn't feel good, why did you let it go on so long? Come on, Kee, gimme a break."

The lights of the car flashed on and off. "You grab me like a tomato." Ling's eyes spread open, my English so much better when I was angry. "I am no tomato, Ricky."

"Be real. I don't think you're a tomato. Well, maybe you are my little tomato." Ling chuckled. "No, if anything, you're a fruit. What's your favorite fruit?"

I thought of my favorite folk tale, the story of the prince and the girl with the pearl. I said, "Persimmon."

He nodded. "The yellow things with the stem like a little green hat? My mother calls them dessert fruit. Yeah, that's what you are. My sweet moonglow persimmon. Anyone tell you that? Your skin looks like moonlight is coming through it, like there's a moon glowing inside you."

As he talked he leaned closer and closer to me. He touched my shoulder and whispered into my ear. "I'm sorry. I'm sorry I grabbed you. I won't do it again. Okay?"

I did not like being angry with him, my only friend in New York City. The train jerked, lights flashed, we were slowing. I said, "Okay."

He pulled me gently into his arms and hugged me. "My sweet persimmon."

Ling pulled at my sleeve. "Our stop."

I looked up at Ricky. I said, "Okay."

He kissed my lips, a moist nibble. "I love you."

"Our stop!"

He looked deep into my eyes, kissed me, and then I noticed over his shoulder the watchful eyes of the Pagoda Lady. I smiled for him and stepped off the train. As the cars jerked and trundled into the dark tunnel he watched us through a window as we started climbing toward the light of the street.

We crossed to where art students sketched us as we passed. Ling sucked her lollipop, her tongue showing purple as she said, "I like Ricky too."

Too? We crossed to the sidewalks of St. Mark's Place. Thirty motorcycles stood in a row along the sidewalk. One motorcycle was covered with cowhide, the hair still bristling, and most had tassels and streamers of black leather dangling below the hand grips. The people standing on the sidewalk had black leather coats and fringe on their pants and boots.

"Jap, go home!"

Swaddled in my own thoughts, I hardly noticed. I thought it best to keep Ricky and Craig apart. Ricky's so much smaller, I thought, and Craig's a black belt.

We reached the store. "Where's Appa-nim?" Mu stood at the register, pushed a key, and squinted at numbers that appeared in the read-out. "Where is Appa-nim!"

"Upstairs, going to the bathroom." His brows relaxed, his forehead smoothed itself. "He's been in the bathroom for an hour. I'm better at the register. See? Only a few mistakes."

The anxiety only half seeped out of me. "Ling, please do the register. Mu, will you break crates?"

He followed me into the storage room. He crackled wooden slats, I watched and looked up the stairs to the kitchen door. I turned on the water in the sink, points of water needling my ankles as the drainpipe leaked. What's he doing up there? I waited, splashed water, washed a turnip, and glanced up to the kitchen.

After Mu had reduced a crate to a pile of slats and a wad of wire I lifted my sneakers up the steps to the kitchen door. I opened the door, dropped my bag in my bedroom, and crept across the cracked linoleum of our kitchen. The door to the bathroom stood shut. No sound came from beyond it.

"Appa-nim?" I knocked gingerly. "Are you all right?"

"I can't even do this in peace!"

Ducking my head, I slunk downstairs. "Thank you, Ling, I'll take over. You go watch TV."

"See," she said in Hangugo, "your English is getting better. Those tapes Auntie and I made are helping, right?"

I nodded. "A lot. That be all?" The customer wore five gold rings in his right nostril, a dozen in his right ear. "Thank you, please come again."

My fingers danced on the keys, faces appeared, vanished, and Mu came out of the storage room. He spoke the way he walked, slow and lumbering.

"Kee, I'm supposed to go now."

"Okay, go now." Clickity-click-click. "Please come again."

Appa-nim came downstairs. He studied the floor like a repentant boy as he carried broken slats past me, at the counter, to the curb, and he swept the floor without looking up. In the watery light I glimpsed the scar on his arm, rang up prices, and wiped the coffee counter. He would not look at me.

"I wanted to see," he finally said, "if Mu could do it, the register." He shrugged. "No good with numbers, huh?"

"If he can't do the work, why keep him?"

"Koreans take care of Koreans!" He changed from quiet to loud so suddenly that my fingers paused over the numbers. He snapped, "But you wouldn't know about loyalty. You only care about what you want to do." The broom clacked as he flung it into a corner. I stepped back from the keys as a last customer shuffled out. "Go on, I'll close the register."

I wanted to please him. "I could learn to close the register. There's no reason why you should always do it."

My offer softened him. His lips parted, he sighed, rubbed his brow, thread-like blood vessels turning the whites of his eyes to pink.

"It's easy," he said. He punched two buttons. Receipt paper curled out of the slot. "It tells you what happened during the day. Then you count the money and see if they match up. Go on, I'll do it." He waved me away. "Go on. You look tired. Go to bed."

I was tired. But I also had an important letter to write. I climbed the stairs and left the door open. Ling lay before the television, canned laughter coming through the doorway as I sat on our futon. I found a pencil and paper. Out of the shoe box I took Ti Lee's dancing elephant god. I rubbed its curving trunk. I wrote the date at the top of the page, and then my characters descended in columns.

Dear Chen-puin. I told her how I missed her and Peng Su-nim, how New York stank of rotten garbage, car exhaust, and the urine of bums who relieved themselves on the scraggly trees that grew beside the street. Then I got to the heart of my letter.

I have a question. How do you know if you love someone? I am dating a boy, but I don't love him. I like him a lot, but we're so different. He jokes and laughs, and he thinks I'm mysterious. I want to know for the future. I thought I loved Ti-Lee. Now I don't know if I did. I couldn't kiss him. You said it was not my time to kiss. Maybe I couldn't because I didn't love him? Now I kiss Ricky Tibbs, but I only like him. Maybe I'm not able to love him either. Maybe I'm not able to love anyone. What is love?

Please write soon.

I miss you very much.

Kee

I addressed an envelope and folded the letter into it. I found an international coupon in a drawer in the kitchen, put it on the letter, and hid it beneath the futon. I carefully bedded Ganesh, the dancing elephant god, in our shoebox of treasures, and because I could not sleep I crawled to the window, leaned on the sill, and gazed up the air shaft.

Dishes clattered. Water splashed. Sitcom audiences laughed on cue. A woman's voice. "Where's the seltzer?" A man's voice, low and seductive. *"Que linda, chica."* Girl, you're beautiful.

Below lay the doll with the broken eye. It had been in the weather so long its hair was changing color. Its blonde hair was changing to orange and I had too many problems to feel sorry.

Chapter 17

A clang and a rattle of chains outside on the walk. "Gimme a damn paper!" A businessman kicked a newspaper machine chained to a no parking sign. Heat rippled off the sidewalk. The sign wobbled at the top of a thin green post. The businessman kicked the machine with his black shoe, swore again, and walked away.

I wiped sweat from my forehead and watched bare ankles, sneakers, sandals, and high heels walk through the heat ripples. A pair of work boots appeared, raw leather at the toes, blue jeans worn to white at the knees, a purple kerchief wadded in a brown hand.

It was our neighbor, Redsy. Appa-nim laughed. "Super Redsy! Friend!"

Redsy wiped his face with the purple cloth. "Man, the sidewalk is steamin'!"

"You need a soda? Beer?"

"Tomato juice for the wife. How's the arm? Got quite a cut there." He drummed his fingers on the counter, his cheeks wrinkling around his eyes, and deep in his eyes I noticed glints the warm color of bronze. "You should've seen the blood. Sure is hot. Keep the change."

I said, "Thank you, Super Redsy. Come again."

He vanished through the bright white doorway. Appa-nim glanced at me as he arranged red halved watermelons. "Black people, they're not all bad."

"They are too!"

It was the brown-mouthed ajima auntie who told me about Choi Su-nim, a bulge of tobacco in her cheek. Her grandson snatched a beer from the cooler.

"Those blacks are black because they're rotten fruit. Don't trust them," she said. The boy cracked open the can of beer and gave it to her. "Fate was kind to the Han people, no blacks in our country. Disgusting is what they are."

"Ki-Teh?" Umma appeared from the storage room. "Your lunch is ready."

Appa-nim rolled his eyes and went upstairs. The old woman said, "Blacks are even dumber than those flat nose Cantonese rice farmers."

"Get out," Umma said. My eyes opened. Umma waved toward the door. "Pay for your beer, old hag, and get out."

"What did you say?" The old woman narrowed her eyes, fierce like a bulldog. "Don't you have any respect?" She said to the boy, "See? Right off the boat and already she stops respecting her elders."

"Nobody likes a biting dog." Umma beckoned. "Come on, pay for what you drink!"

"I'm disgusted. She loves blacks more than her own people!" The old hag bared her brown teeth and gave Umma a crumpled bill. She leaned to the boy. *"Hankook ke-yo."*

"Yeah." He looked back from the doorway. "Korean bitches."

"Don't come back!" The odd couple disappeared and Umma gave me the bill, shaking her head. "She always walks out without paying. Your father let her get away with it, but I won't."

"Once with me too. But Appa-nim wouldn't stop her?"

"Of course not." Umma feigned disbelief. "You haven't noticed? Women are stronger than men."

Appa-nim came down and I went up to eat. Eating hot Mexican rice and beans made sweat dust my brows, and stocking the cooler made my armpits clammy. I stood at the register, counted change, sodas were wet cold in my hand, my throat was dry, and I rolled my shoulders to unstick my shirt from my back.

"Refill the bins outside," Appa-nim said, "onions and oranges."

He took my place behind the register. I dragged a large bag of onions out the door, to the bin near the corner. I liked the faint sweet smell of onions much better than I liked their taste. I straightened and shaded my eyes against the sun. At Seventh Street and Avenue A a man stood strumming a guitar. His guitar case lay open for people to drop money into. Nobody stood watching, but he sang and it changed the mood of the street like a hint of a festival.

I struggled and lifted the bag of onions to the bin and emptied them in, then stood listening to the guitar player. The harmony of his strumming made the street less harsh. On impulse I grabbed an orange. I ran across the street and down the block to him. I dropped the orange into his guitar case and it rolled around among the glinting coins. I said, "Thank you!"

He laughed and kept singing.

"Kee-Yong!" I looked back. Appa-nim flapped his arm at the corner. "Truck's here!"

I ran around the corner bins, past the back of the truck where Appa-nim glared at me, into the store, to the register. The driver swore as he wheeled stacks of crates into the storage room. Sweat glistened on the throats of customers. Damp coins, limp bank notes, stained shirts. Three boys came in, chattering in Vietnamese. I couldn't understand except that they were four cents short. I nodded, shooed them away, and they were gone running out the door like black-haired bees.

The storage room stood full and Appa-nim signed the bill of lading. I trimmed lettuce until the door creaked at the top of the stairs and Ling followed the light that flooded down the steps. She carried her book and my knapsack, and we were free to fly because Mu had arrived, and we did. By the time we reached First Avenue I grew aware of a change, a difference in the city.

Silence.

Internal silence, it was a change in me. The quiet of the dojang was already filling me. We hurried past the black cube balanced on one point, down stairs, through turnstiles, waited in the hot and hazy tunnel. In Nun-yo the internal stillness filled me all day, but for so long it had been gone from me. Then I noticed the stillness settling into me in the midst of rushing through the busyness of New York. I was not upset by the heat, which made August in the city the big month for murders. I was not upset even by the fist fight.

Two men in front of us, at the edge of the platform, pushed each other. One man cocked his arm, his knuckles smacked on skin, and the other man stumbled back. Cursing, they grappled in a waltzing hate dance, their faces red, and they snarled, clawed each other, bared their teeth like beasts. I stood observing. So furious, and they looked like they knew each other.

Ling cried, "Look out!"

Locked together, the two men stumbled toward me. Their eyes were wild, large white, one man wearing half a mustache of red blood. I stepped aside, they waltzed past and slammed against the grimy wall. People closed over them, a policeman appeared, a train stopped with screeching brakes, and we got on.

Ling looked at me. I shrugged. She shrugged and made a silly face. I stood still and waited. The train swayed and *BANG!* hit a bump. Down in my shirt, sweat glowed between my breasts. Lights flashed on and off. Stillness. I was the calm eye of the subway storm.

My calm deepened in the dojang. I mopped the floor and sat in meditation. Tension seeped out of me like sand out of sea water. I felt it when Ricky Tibbs entered. Everyone lined up on the floorboards, and I was sensitive to Craig, to my left, Sinclair's tall bones to my right, everyone ranged behind us. Craig flicked me during the first poom-sey with his sword, fire down my back. I did not flinch. Craig and I performed the Tiger and Crane Poom-sey together, I experienced the paradox of stillness in motion, and the class ended.

I changed in the little office, Choi Su-nim's wife watching. Dressed, I stepped out of his office, "Thank you, sir," and hurried down the four steps to Mulberry Street.

Uh-oh. I squeezed the strap of my bag. Ricky Tibbs and Craig were at the bottom of Bayard Street, by the telephone pole and blue mailbox.

"You're a green belt," Craig said. "You don't know."

Ricky looked to me. "You should show respect for senior students. Right?" I strode along the walk, between cars, onto the warm soft tar of Bayard Street. They fell in step to either side of me. Ricky said, "It's not your business to correct her, so why don't you cut it out."

Craig stopped. "Did she tell you what I said?"

Ricky halted. Uh-oh. I stopped too, and he looked at me. I walked back and took his hand. "Come on."

Craig smiled. "I told her what you said in the changing room. About fucking her in Central Park." Ricky went ominously still, a hiss of air in his nostrils. He let his bag fall off his shoulder, his fists clenching. Craig grinned like a thief with a knife between his teeth. "Kee, he said he porked you a bunch of times."

Ricky threw himself at Craig, shooting his fists—but Craig kicked him in the stomach. "Ricky, no!"

He jerked, grunted, charged in, and Craig laughed as his lips drew back from his teeth. Ricky pumped his arms and Craig blocked, locked his elbows, they seethed together, snarled, grunted, toppled, "Stop!" and hit the tar with a frightening clunk of bones. "Ricky, no! No!"

Burly men from the fish markets and the sidewalks surrounded them, grabbed them, pulled them, pried at them. Ricky's grip broke off Craig's body, the cloth of his shirt ripping into raw edges down his chest. As they dragged Craig away he kicked at Ricky's face.

"Wimp!" His toe missed Ricky's nose by inches. "I'll kick the shit out of you! Wimp!"

"Liar!" Craig flung himself back and forth while three boys grappled and Ricky twisted and swore. "Lying son-of-a-...!"

They wouldn't stop and I couldn't stand it. I turned and ran up Bayard Street, pushed into the crowds on Mott, ran on the curb, dodged cars, bumped an old woman, reached Canal Street, darted into the street. A car halted with a screech of rubber, the driver shouted, and I realized what I was doing. I stopped and pulled myself together. In the crowds on the walk, the stink of fish and clam shells in the air, I stood until my lungs stopped heaving and the air stopped hissing in my nose.

A broken goldfish lay on a manhole cover. I crossed beneath the traffic light and stopped to let my thoughts go slower. Candy wrappers, cigarette butts. No distinct thoughts, only fear and different forms of one thought. He'll get hurt! Ricky!

Ling came running with her hair flying back. "We're late!"

I called, "Auntie! Auntie Yen!"

She appeared in the window frame, up the side of the building. "What's the matter?"

"I have to talk to you!"

A truck rumbled, echoes rumbled in the canyon of buildings, she had to shout. "Sunday!"

"Okay!"

We started home. The concrete walks seemed harsh, dark, shadowed, the gutters lined with dark filth. I was quiet so long that Ling asked, "What's the matter?"

I shook my head. Ricky will get hurt! We reached the subway stairs. She skipped down past me, past an old man with a wire basket on wobbly wheels. I gazed into the grainy light of the platform. Ricky Tibbs separated himself from the rivets and painted steel faces of a pillar. He came toward me before I was down the stairs.

"I didn't say that, Kee, I didn't, I swear it."

"What do you say, Mister Tibb?" Ling asked.

"I never said a word to him. Actually, he never stoops to speak to me."

His lips, I thought how Craig's kick had come so close to them." We stepped onto a train that arrived with a hardly noticeable roar. I couldn't look at Ricky's eyes. In the crowded car he spread his arms around me, gently held me close, a feeling so good to me that I leaned my head against his bony chest. I could not see the Pagoda Woman, but her smell of motor oil and overripe nectarines surrounded us.

Ricky whispered in my ear, "I love you. Don't think anything else. I love you."

How could he know what love felt like? I asked, "Did you love a girl? Before?"

"Yeah, once. But not like this. I loved you the first time I saw you. It's true. The first time I saw you do the Tiger and Crane Poomsey. I've loved you ever since then." He kissed my forehead. He kissed my lips, in front of everyone on the subway, and the Pagoda Woman with her head on top of six layers of fat watched us.

I was surprised. Ling didn't tease us. She did not tease me even after we got off the train and climbed the stairs to Astor Place and followed the soft grey tar of St. Mark's Place, still warm in the evening light. I was still changed from seeing Ricky. Kissing him left such a wonderful right feeling inside me that my upset was settled.

I looked at Ling. When we could hear the sighing of the trees in Thompkins Square Park I asked, "Why don't you tease me about Ricky Tibbs?"

She sidestepped a bum picking garbage from a can. "Because I know you're serious."

I lowered my bag from my shoulder. "I'm not serious about him. He's just my only friend. Why do you think so?"

She rolled her eyes. "When you kiss him you look goofy. Hello, Appa."

"Hello, plum." My glance went to the wound on Appa-nim's arm. He was staring at me when I looked up from the scar. "Well, that Mu knicked himself again. Trim lettuce."

"Yes, Appa-nim."

In the gloom of the storage room the slats of the crate sagged beneath Mu's big body. He raised his thickly-haired head and straightened out of his hunch.

"I cut myself. Again." He waved his bandaged finger, stood up and said, "The men in this store, we have trouble with knives. You're the only one who knows how to use them."

I accepted the knife from Mu.

"I study with Choi Su-nim so I...," I smiled at the thought. "...can trim these bad leaves." I flipped the glittering knife. The handle hit my palm with a spat. "'Lettuce Su-nim'. One who knows lettuce."

"You certainly do." He rubbed his belly and backed toward the doorway. "Oh well, goodbye."

Mu said goodbye to Ling as he lumbered into the dusk. I felt good as I watched him go. I turned and flipped the knife, and its edge glittered and flashed until I pulled its wooden handle out of the air and stopped its twirling. I glanced at the knife as I sat on the crate. The wooden handle was worn blonde by my hand, showed the pattern of my grip, a record of my days spent trimming lettuce.

Chapter 18

On Friday afternoon Ling and I rode the subway to Canal Street. I went with her all the way to the stoop of Auntie's building because I heard singing. A man's voice echoed off the buildings, farther up Elizabeth Street, a growl that rose into a reedy falsetto that ended in a squeak. It was the man who threw the persimmon back at me, the street singer singing the blues, swaying behind his keyboard on a busy corner.

People who walked by him walked faster, pulled their children by the hand, and wouldn't look at him, as if it was shameful for him to growl into a microphone and stumble his fingers drunkenly over the keys. A can before his shabby amplifier propped up a record album with mashed corners. No one stopped, no coins plunked into the coffee can, but this time I did not feel sorry for him. He was very drunk.

His jeans were filthy, with a hole at a knee, his shirt hung out messily in the front, and a brown bottle stuck its metal snout out of his back pocket. "Ling?" She had ducked in past someone coming out of Auntie's building. I turned away after a last glance at the street singer. He drinks because he's weak.

Women really are stronger than men.

I reached the corner of Mott Street, the pagoda bank, and newspaper kiosk, the smells of shrimp and newsprint in the air. I trotted down Bayard Street, past the fish markets, past a man hosing down the sidewalks, the cement so hot it smoked. I climbed the four steps before the dojang and went into silence. My routine went routinely until I knocked on the office door.

"Choi Su-nim?" A shuffle of feet. The door opened. His bleached lips were set together with...bitterness? "Sir? Is something wrong?"

His voice grated like wood against stone. "Go change," he said, and gestured me into his office.

I changed into my dobuck quickly and came out again. Choi Su-nim waited near the door to the street. He said nothing as I mopped and sat in meditation. The dojang was absolutely still until other students came in from the street. Though they talked and let the changing room door clap shut, and the street door rattled and fractured the peace, I was not much disrupted.

Choi Su-nim disrupted me. His shout echoed around the walls. "Not you. Out!"

My eyes fluttered open. I rose out of the cross-legged lotus. Choi Su-nim stood with his cane raised, Craig stopped on the threshold, bag in hand, his mouth open. Choi Su-nim shouted, "For you, no more komdo! You have no respect for this dojang, no respect for the sword. Go!" Craig blinked. Choi Su-nim pointed to the street and shouted, "Go!" Craig backed out past the first glass door and watched as his master locked the door, the tumbler clacking like a trigger being cocked.

Through the glass I saw Craig lift his hand as if to appeal, mouth open, and I felt sorry for him. He'd studied komdo so long. I did, I felt sorry for him; I knew what losing my Way would have done to me.

Choi Su-nim clapped his hands and everyone hurried onto the bare boards. Tension crackled in the air, but otherwise class was the same. Sinclair gasped and tried so hard to do poom-sey correctly that he could not. Choi Su-nim shouted Hangugo, spit out syllables like a beaked turtle spitting out pieces of fish. *"Kum-pung-o Poom-sey! Hundu-lida Poom-sey! Won-sung-i Poom-sey!"*

For the final moving poem I stood alone on the glowing floor. I performed Tiger and Crane Poom-sey, leaped, kicked, suffered the pains in my body, "Hah!" and my bamboo sword swished like a willow in a storm. When I finished I was pure energy, except in my chest. My whole body hummed, except inside me where the moving shapes were larger, my lungs ballooned and shrank and squeezed, the drumming of my heart like the tight sides of a funnel.

I was a funnel. I was a channel for the rhythmic surging of life.

A drop of sweat trickled behind my ear and tickled my throat. Choi Su-nim shuffled along the edge of the practice floor. He stopped under the American and Korean flags, his usual position for the end of class; but he snapped, "Ahn Kee-Yong, *ke-yo ap!*" To the front!

I circled respectfully behind Sinclair, put my feet together, clapped my hands to my sides and bowed to Choi Su-nim. He lifted his cane and let it drop with a thump of its rubber foot on the floor.

"We are privileged to have practicing with us," he said in English, "the first woman ever to study in Saebyoke style of komdo. It has been practiced for eight hundred years! Still, no other female has ever studied Way of the Dawning Sword. Ahn Kee-Yong is unique, and she is an example of the dedication needed to follow this Way."

Me? Really?

The flags shivered behind him. "Saebyoke Komdo is a path to the One Truth. Down through the centuries teachers of this Way have used a final, difficult trial to bring students to the One Truth. That trial was a walk across the Young Falling Water. Kee-Yong's teacher walked the Young Falling Water. I walked the Young Falling Water. Before she came to New York City, Ahn Kee-Yong also walked the Young Falling Water." Choi Su-nim spoke to me in Korean. "Please describe your experience and I will translate."

I bowed. "Yes, Choi Su-nim."

I spoke and then Choi Su-nim spoke in English.

"Not long before I left Nun-yo, my home village in Korea, Peng Su-nim ordered me to come to his garden early the next morning. We rode for a long time along the coast in his son's car. On the seat between them was a *jang san kum,* the long sword fashioned by Peng Su-nim's grandfather. During the occupation, when the Japanese were trying to destroy all Korean culture, the sword had been buried under a yew tree for twenty-four years. Seeing that blade, I knew something important was taking place.

"We skirted a village, passed a Buddhist temple, and came to the Young Waterfalls. In a time long ago the Old River changed its course. When the river changed its course it also lost its name, and came to be called the Young River. There at the coast the Young River was shallow but wide, twenty meters wide."

Choi Su-nim said, "Sixty feet wide."

I nodded. "But it ran very fast, white and broken, and the water flew far out from the lip of the cliff. That's where Peng Su-nim's son parked the car. Then I followed them to the edge of the cliff that overlooked the sea.

"Peng Su-nim just pointed. I couldn't believe it. He wanted me to do a poom-sey across the river, where it flowed fast and flew off the edge of the cliff. The lip was still flat, the river had not rounded it, but algae made it slick and the water from the mountains was very cold. The thought of doing a poom-sey there terrified me. If I slipped and fell I would be swept off the edge and killed on the rocks a hundred meters below.

"Peng Su-nim insisted. The water roared as it fell onto the rocks and a mist rose to support a rainbow. When I allowed a thought to enter my mind I lost control, I was terrified. Peng Su-nim insisted. I knew I would be disgraced if I disobeyed him. I pleaded with him not to make me walk the edge. He shook his head. He said, 'All of nature follows the Tao. All that moves in accord with the Tao will not be thrown down by conflict.' Then he handed me the sword, bowed, and stepped back.

"I was also terrified because the long blade was very heavy, at least twice the weight of any sword I had ever wielded before. A heavier sword means adjustments have to be made in steps and positions, and I did not see how I could make those changes and still maintain my footing on the edge of the cliff. I pleaded with Peng Su-nim and grew frantic. In reply he said, 'You do not wield the sword, the sword wields you.'"

"Finally I accepted that Peng Su-nim would not relent, I could not avoid a walk across the Young Falling Water. Staying mindful, silent, and centered—I sensed the truth—it was the only way to survive, to keep from being swept off the edge.

"I sat in the lotus. Peng Su-nim sat on the ground beside me. The sun rose in the sky and burned away the morning mist. The skin of my hands grew hot, the sun burned my face, but I still did not open my eyes. Peng Su-nim's son went to the car and ate lunch. He played his bamboo flute. The water roared. Finally I rose, stretched the stiffness out of my hips, took off my shoes, raised the sword, and stepped into the river.

"Water rushed up to my knees. The current had the opposite effect from what I expected. Instead of cutting my feet from under me the rushing water seemed to root the soles of my feet to the rock lip. Far below, the water hit the sea rocks and exploded. It did not matter. I was not afraid. I performed the poom-sey across the river, turned with *ilban* step and returned to Peng Su-nim and his son."

The sound of my voice trailed away like a shiver dying in the air. The dojang full of students stood quiet and poised, as if it too were waiting, ever waiting. Choi Su-nim broke the stillness.

"What did you learn," he asked, "from Walking the Young Falling Water?"

"To rely on Way of the Dawning Sword," I said. "Peng Su-nim later told me that the river, water, all things material, are drawn toward the still center of the Earth. That is gravity. It is also a universal law of Tao, of all lesser and greater beings. If I wholeheartedly practice Way of the Dawning Sword I too am following that universal law. My thoughts, words, and actions gravitate, without coming into conflict with my will and with each other, toward the stillness of my center. However, Peng Su-nim told me that my center and the center of the Earth are not physical places. They are the one pure state of Being."

I stopped speaking. Choi Su-nim stopped speaking, and in the silence we bowed to each other. He went to a big lacquered teak chest by the door of his office. He lifted out of it, from a purple silk-lined shelf, a sword so beautiful it stopped the breath in my chest. The blade curved long, mirror-like, its ivory handle yellowed with age. Choi Su-nim said, "Tito!" A boy he rescued from the street, Tito hurried forward. Choi Su-nim placed the sword into Tito's upraised hands and beckoned for me to follow.

Leaning on his cane, he led us out through the glass doors. As we descended the four steps to the walk the sky opened over us and the noise of the city rushed in. Children screeched and screamed on the merry-go-round, chanted and slapped a jump rope on the macadam of the park. Craig stood by the gate. Waiting for me, he uncrossed his arms and clenched his fists. Horns honked, a truck rumbled, trees rustled, and two men speaking Italian in the doorway of a restaurant stopped speaking and watched us.

Choi Su-nim raised the sword from Tito's brown hands and placed it in mine. The sword was heavy, almost as heavy as the sword buried under the yew tree for twenty-four years. Choi Su-nim said, "Choon-be!" Ready Stance! He pointed to the curb. I stepped to the curb and took readiness. He described the poom-sey I was to do, a simple phrase of steps, attacks, and stances.

"This exercise," he said, "is called Walking the Edge of the Street. Every day for the next year you will follow this curb, doing this poom-sey, always at this time of day. As you perform this moving poem remember: komdo is not for the dojang. The purpose of Way of the Dawning Sword is to still the tumult within you, wherever you are." Across the street Craig narrowed his eyes with hate. Choi Su-nim said, *"Say-sha!"* Begin!

I began the poom-sey along the curb, its curved steel edge cool to the soles of my feet. Choi Su-nim turned, led Tito up the steps, and they disappeared into the dojang.

As I knew he would, Craig rushed across the street. He drew back his fist and snarled, "You're *dead!*"

Chapter 19

I began the moving poem Choi Su-nim prescribed, began to move along the curb, feeling the pits of its steel edge with the soles of my feet. I brought down the beautiful sword. The sword flashed in the sun just before Craig's fist hit my arm. I felt a burst of pain and seemed to fall for a long time, the sidewalk jarred me, and for a moment I lay stunned on the concrete. Stunned, in that still moment I realized it.

I was going to suffer.

"Bitch!" As I got to my feet Craig spit into my face. I wiped my cheek and returned to the curb. He shouted, "You're too damn weak to hold it steady!"

It was true. The curved sword rose long and heavy, it made my wrists ache. It was so heavy that as I sank into back step, turned and stroked to the rear, to support the long sword even my stomach muscles had to tighten. I pivoted, shifted onto my forward leg. Stroke to the front.

Craig's fury heated him. "I should be doing this, not you!" He leaned back to avoid the blade and leaned close to shout, "You bitch!"

He punched my arm. The sword wobbled. I kept my gaze forward. I reached the corner, the brine stink of the fish markets in the air.

Craig's eyes held hate. "Why isn't Ricky here to protect you, the little buck-tooth twit. I'll kick his ass any time he wants!"

In the fish market two burly men dumped squid onto white beds of ice and a boy dragged a crate to the gutter with a loud grating. The sword shivered as I stroked to the front; I could not keep it still. Old Chinese women stopped to watch as I approached, doing the poomsey up the curb.

Craig found a slat broken from a crate. I rose into Crane Stance, poised high on one foot, and when he jabbed me in the ribs I teetered over the gutter. He chuckled. "I know you'll like this." *Crack!* He hit my buttocks with the broad side of the stick. Pain spasmed through me. *Crack! crack! crack!* on my thighs and buttocks, and he laughed and ducked to avoid my strokes with the long curving ceremonial sword.

Near the fish markets an old woman snapped at him in Mandarin and people stopped gabbling to watch. Craig said, "I'm supposed to do this. For Choi Su-nim!"

I pivoted in a tight space among housewives, workingmen, tourists craning their necks, and the blade hit a parking meter. *Clunk.* Craig laughed. He hit me hard with his stick, I saw a flash of pink pain, and an old woman came off her stoop, screeching at him. Shrimp jumbled in a box twitched their antennae. My leg brushed the box, I stumbled as the old woman thrashed at Craig with a newspaper. He was too smart to defy her and turn everyone against him, so he skipped out between the bumpers of cars and circled ahead to wait for me.

I left the fish market as Craig found a grape among the gutter filth. When he threw the grape it stung me like a bee. Cold splotch of juice on my cheek. I thought, why don't they stop him? Old men watched from the stoop of a dry cleaners. Feet shuffled on the walk, Chinese filled the air, English words, Spanish, carts rattled, baby carriages squeaked, but nobody stopped him.

Craig hissed into my face. "You think you're going to finish this? Over my dead body!"

He jabbed and beat me with the stick as I climbed the inclined curb of Bayard and followed its arc onto Mott Street. Craig had a taste for ice cream. He went into the ice cream store on the corner. Trucks rumbled. A taxi honked. School girls gossiped in Cantonese, a bicycle bell tingled, cameras went zip-zip-zip, and I planted my foot farther along the curb. The sword was so heavy my joints screeched in my shoulders. Craig came out of the ice cream store with two cones. I did not see him. He mashed a cone of cold ice cream on top of my head.

He laughed, "Dunce cap," and I made six steps before the ice cream fell off my head. The cold remained.

Mott Street ran past a vegetable stand, import shops where dragons roared behind glass, small groceries, dark doorways, a bakery smelling of nutmeg and almonds. Craig licked his ice cream and prodded me with the stick.

"Look! She can't even hold up the sword." I couldn't keep the blade from shivering. He cuffed the back of my head. "Wimp!"

We came to a school, a stone fence topped with black iron spikes, and beyond an iron gate, a flagstone courtyard. Girls with textbooks giggled in the sunlight of the court. I brought down the sword and my muscles felt like they were pulling away from my bones. Craig swung the stick—*crack!*—pain flaring across my kidney.

"Where's Ricky, your knight in shining armor? Afraid to come out and protect you?"

A man's hoarse voice came from above. "Leave her alone!"

Craig looked up and across. "Up yours, old man!"

I rose into Crane Stance, elevated on one foot. I sank smoothly forward into charging step, stroked, the sword flashed, and the old white-haired man in the window snapped, "Leave her alone. She's doing her art!"

"Up yours."

"You little jerk!"

"Up yours!" But Craig did toss his stick into the gutter. "Enough for now, I have to finish my ice cream." He grinned into my face. "I'll be back. And if you think I was mean today, bitch, wait until tomorrow."

That first day he was not vicious. I continued moving through the phrase of steps and sword work. Craig went, I was relieved, the curb lay open, and I was free to focus on the poom-sey. No-parking signs stood before the school and the old church joined to it like a siamese twin. After the closeness of Bayard Street I breathed deeply of the smells of green tea, rice, black bean sauce, and hot peppers that filled the open space. The smells distracted me from the buzzing, the shapes of pain left by Craig's stick.

Transfiguration School and Church were beautiful old buildings with smooth sandstone trim and windows pointed at the top. Moving through the poom-sey worked the tingles of pain out of my buttocks and thighs, but because of the weight and length of the sword it was agony. My face grew hot. I reached the corner of Mott and Mosco Streets, a tea shop across the way. Rankles of pain came from under my shoulder blades. Old men standing on the curb did not move. They pointed at me, cracked jokes in Vietnamese, laughed, and did not step aside until I was a foot from them.

Not everything was bad that first time walking the edge of the street. I followed the curb down Mosco Street, a steep alley shadowed by the church and a tall tenement building, lined by garbage cans, to where a Chinese funerary hung out its sign. A funeral march was about to begin, the men of the band waiting with their mallets and drums and brass horns. As I passed among the musicians, doing the moving poem, the trumpet player raised his horn to his lips, blew a trio of slow elegant notes, and I took heart because I sensed that he played them for me.

I reached the dojang, returned to Choon-be Stance and lowered the ceremonial sword. My shoulders slumped and I waited a long moment to let my lungs breath slower. Sweat soaked the back of my dobuck, my hands shook and my palms were printed by the scallops of the sword handle. I felt the sharp pains of too much torsion in my thumbs, shoulders, all the joints between them and down my spine. I held the sword against my chest and climbed to the dojang.

When I let the doors close on the shrieks of children and entered the silent cool of his dojang, Choi Su-nim stood waiting. He nodded. We went to the teak chest. He showed me how to clean the sword with a soft cloth, the ceremony I would use to replace it in the chest, kowtowing to the five directions, North, South, East, West, and Center, and when all was done I sighed.

He chuckled. "A master craftsman in Cholla Province fashioned that sword. Do you think it's as heavy as the one made by Peng Su-nim's grandfather, that was buried under the yew tree for twenty-four years?"

My body ached. "About the same, sir. The curb is so long!"

"The Young Waterfalls is a short path to enlightenment, the curb, a long path." He motioned, and I followed him into his office. He gave me a brass key on a cord. "The dojang is closed on Saturday and Sunday, you will need this."

"Thank you, sir." My bag on the floor reminded me of the store and Appa-nim. Every day? What about Appa-nim? I bowed to Choi Su-nim as he backed out of the office. I undressed slowly, my body sapped of energy—I could not dress quickly—and I winced as I fastened my pants. I was bruised; but when I stepped out of the office I made a quick decision and did not mention Craig's cruelty.

I bowed. "Thank you, Choi Su-nim. This is a great honor. Thank you, sir."

He bowed slowly. "Ahn Kee-Yong, thank you."

I hurried down the steps and around the corner of Bayard Street, winnowed through a celebration on Mott, crowds packed tighter on the walk than schooling needlefish, dodged telephone poles, trotted across Canal Street, and found Ling at the corner of Elizabeth.

"Where have you been? Appa's going to scream now!" We ran to the subway. After leaving the dojang I worried about being late. I also wondered how I was going to ask Appa-nim to let me come to Chinatown every single day.

I knew he would never agree to that. Not a chance!

We skipped downstairs to the subway, the waistband of my pants sawing against a bruise left by Craig's stick. A train came and we sat on a bench. I settled gingerly, the backs of my thighs and my buttocks striped with pain.

"Where's Ricky?" Ling asked. "He didn't wait for us?"

"He only comes every other day, like me, but sometimes on Thursday instead of Wednesday."

But now class every single day? How do I ask Appa-nim for that? I pondered that question all the way home. On St. Mark's Place I pulled Ling away from displays of bows and hair decorations, and I realized a plan. I squeezed the strap of my bag, jogged with Ling, and when we crossed First Avenue I saw at the far end of the block the thick body and big-haired figure of Mu, wrenching apart wooden crates.

Crack, crackle. When we were close enough to hear the splintering of wooden slats I called to him. "Mu!" He glanced up. I motioned for him to come along. "Come, please. Please, come in!"

He dropped a broken crate. "I have to go."

"No," I said, beckoning, "come, come. Come in."

He filled the doorway behind us. Appa-nim shouted, "Where have you been! You know Mu has to leave at—"

"Something special happened." I said it breathlessly. "I'm sorry, Appa-nim, but I'm supposed to work in the dojang tomorrow night too; so I was hoping..." I looked at Mu and switched to speaking English. "I give Mu ten dollar, so he can work? Tomorrow night?"

"Kee-yong, we agreed. You go down there three times a week and that's it!" Appa-nim rang up a customer's purchases. "Thank you, come again. I'm serious." I pulled the ten dollar bill that Appa-nim gave me on Monday out of my pocket; but Appa-nim's face hardened. "No! We agreed! Mu, out. Kee, you get to work!"

Customers had stopped to listen, and they watched as he threw up his arms and stormed into the storage room. Mu looked at me with his fleshy lips pursed as Appa-nim cursed in Hangugo and rasped his feet up the kitchen stairs. The door at the top slammed.

Silence. A fly buzzed.

Mu's big hands hung at his sides. "Can I go now?"

I nodded, my spirits sinking painfully into my stomach as he turned away, blocked the light coming in from the street, and then he was gone. Appa-nim was also gone. I rang up mangos and soy sauce. I asked Ling, "Is the storage room clean? Did Mu trim lettuce?"

She peeked through the doorway. "It's clean, no empty boxes. But it doesn't look like he trimmed anything."

"Was anything delivered?"

She shook her head. What did Mu do? Did Appa-nim let him stand around? Didn't he tell him what to do? I worked with quick nervous energy. The longer Appa-nim remained upstairs the more uneasy I became. Of her own accord, Ling settled onto the crate and slowly trimmed lettuce. An hour passed and then I said to her, "Come in and take over the register. I have to go see what's keeping him."

"Okey-dokey." She flounced out to me, at the register, and said to a man with a cowboy hat, "That be all, Joe?"

I climbed the stairs and silently pushed the door a few inches into the kitchen. Babbling. Appa-nim's voice. I pushed my head into the light of the kitchen. Beyond the stove and table the bathroom door stood closed. I listened to his babble, a mix of Hangugo and English, and I thought, who is he talking to? I opened the door, and I was going to sneak closer and listen, but the hinges creaked. He heard and stopped babbling.

Silence.

The demons, I thought. They're still here.

Carefully I closed the door. I carried an eerie feeling with me back down the stairs, the same feeling I felt after he rushed out of the kut. Dread. I sensed it again, faintly, that some terrible story was catching up with us.

Chapter 20

The next morning the air in the store was different. Appa-nim smiled, joked with customers, said to a bleary-eyed man, "You drinkin' big beer last night, hey?" As usual, I sat trimming lettuce, perched on the edge of the crate to spare the bruises on my thighs and bottom; but the deep bruise over my right kidney hurt each time I reached for a head of lettuce. It nagged me along with a swarm of questions and numbers. Hours before lunch, after lunch, hours after I get back from Chinatown, hours I didn't go, Saturdays, Sunday mornings, I added them all up.

Eighty-five hours a week, that's how much I worked.

How many hours do I owe him? But how do I get out? And what if Craig is there? What then? And who was the man in the window, who shouted at him? Sunlight streamed through the doorway. Children shouted in the sunshine, clapped their sneakers on the sidewalk, and artists with broad tablets of newsprint, talking and drawing in the air, passed the doorway. The bruises hurt me, I wondered how to get away, and hoped Craig would not be there.

What if he is?

The sun climbed the sky, a white rectangle of light brightened on the floor by the doorway, and at noon Umma appeared at the top of the stairs. She smiled down at me when I looked up from my crate half full of trimmed leaves of lettuce. "Ki-Teh," she shouted, "your boloney sandwich!"

"Good stuff, boloney," he said, coming into the storage room. "Take the register."

"Good? Better than odong in garlic sauce?" Umma made a face as they passed on the stairs, and together she and I stepped into the store. "What's the matter with Korean food?"

"No more Korean!" His feet disappeared up the stairs. "In America we eat American!"

Umma rolled her eyes. I said to a boy with an orange, "Seventy-five cent total," and to Umma, "Now he won't eat Korean?" She shook her head. She wiped the coffee counter and kept her face away from me. I persisted, even while I made change for a pale businessman with a nose like a piece of cauliflower. "Thank you, please come again. He hates everything Korean."

She threw the rag down on the counter, stepped to the doorway, said "Time for work," and ducked out onto the street, the thick soles of new shoes that did not hurt her feet squeaking. Squeaking sixty hours a week, I thought, how can she like going to work? Then I felt bad because suddenly I understood: it kept her away from home. From him. I felt bad because it also kept her away from me.

She gets away every day. I need that too. But how?

In mid-afternoon I came out of the storage room. Appa-nim stood behind the cash register, his shirt baggy around his waist, his too long pant legs bunched on top of his shoes. I dumped a dozen green heads of trimmed lettuce into their place, and even as I turned toward the street door he snapped, "Where are you going?"

"To check the sidewalk bins. They were low last night, they might be empty now."

"Let me worry about that! Who do you think you are? Boss?" Through the doorway I saw no bouquets on the flower rack, hoops empty, and the front lip of the onion bin showed its slivers and dents. Does he think I'll slip away? But then he said, "Take over here" and strode into the storage room.

He climbed the stairs and slammed the door at the top. I was glad for the break from trimming lettuce, but it was an hour before his feet made slow cautious steps on the stairs. What does he do up there? Oddly, though, when I passed him to go to my gloomy crate he kept his glance on the floor and would not look at me, embarrassed. I glanced over my shoulder and watched the bones of his back, a column of knobs his sweaty shirt clung to. He hurried out to check the bins still empty along the sidewalk, and that's when it was my turn to sneak upstairs.

In the living room I found a number on a scrap of paper in our box of telephone numbers, and while I glanced out the window at a policeman frisking a teenager on the corner I heard the phone ring on the other end.

Hello?

"Mu? It's Kee. Can you work? Today?"

Sure, Kee. I said I would last night; but your father...

"Uh-huh, I know. So we will see you then, huh?"

Yeah, he said slowly, *I guess so.*

"Thank you," I said, and even as I hung up I hurried toward the door. I crept down the stairs, as nervous as a cat, and when I settled onto my crate I winced when it creaked. He knows. I bit my fingernail and tried not to think. He knows what I'm going to do.

In the store it was my turn to be afraid to pass him. Beyond the door horns honked, cabbies shouted at a drunk staggering in the street, and customers shuffled in a line before the register. Appa-nim said to an old man with a melon, "See spot? That got rot," but when I glanced over he was looking at me. "Another. Get a good one for him," he said, looking at me, and I shriveled inside because he knew I was planning something. As I hurried to get the old man a good melon I thought, did he see my bag under the stairs?

Didn't matter. An hour later, behind me in the store, I heard Mu say loudly, "Hello, Mr. Ahn."

I grabbed that bag as Appa-nim shouted, "Kee!"

I rushed out of the storage room, but Appa-nim was too fast. He cut me off in front of the counter. "Kee, enough! Enough of this nonsense!"

I dodged around the island. He cut me off at the door, bumping Mu aside. "I'll pay him. Appa-nim, I'll pay him."

"No!" He backed me up against the leafy greens. "We made an

agreement!"

"But I need to go to the dojang. Please, I..."

"Three times a week isn't enough? We settled it, with your aunt, and you said yes!"

"But I..." His chest expanded, his fists clenched, and I was forced back against the bumps of fresh fruit. "Please, I have to do what Choi Su-nim says."

"No!" Rage narrowed his eyes, flared his nostrils, and frightened, I split out from between him and the fruit bin. He shouted, "No! You do what *I* say!"

"Appa, please..."

"Does he feed you? Does he put clothes on your body?"

"It's a special exercise. I..."

"No! You need us! You need to work! Here! Now!" He pointed toward the storage room. "Back to work!"

I don't know where the courage to speak came from, but my voice was shaky. "I need to practice too. Every day."

"That does it! The deal is off! No more komdo! None! I'm done with this! Done!"

I watched him stab the air, ordering me, and suddenly my desperation turned. After all the years he had pounded the table, or shouted, all the times he was drunk and foolish, all my anger at being ripped away from Nun-yo boiled inside me. My teeth clenched so hard my jaw hurt and I heard one sharp hiss of air in my nostrils as I leaned toward him.

"I work here eighty-five hours a week and I *hate* it! I hate being around *you!*" I wanted my words to slice open his face. "You just want to keep me here! Keep me trapped! *Keep me!*"

His whole face clenched with rage, but some pain or some very old guilt made his shoulder jerk, and that's when I darted past him, past Mu, out into the sunshine, bolted up St. Mark's Place, ran clutching my bag, dodged couples, and burst through a crowd.

About that moment Appa-nim burst into the storage room and

hurt himself. Mu told me later what had happened. He said Appa-nim had rushed into the storage room. He grabbed a watermelon, raised it over his head, and threw it down, broke it into jagged chunks. He grabbed the broom, snapped the handle over his knee, threw the pieces up the stairs, then kicked a stack of crates. He kicked it so hard that the top crate flipped, the others tumbled over, other stacks fell, wood crackled, and heads of his precious lettuce rolled into the darkness under the stairs.

Mu told me, "I saw him through the doorway. He turned around, like he was looking for something more to break. Then he found it. He leaned against the wall, his hands on it, and I could only see his shadow, but I heard him do it three times. It was awful. Thunk thunk thunk, like he was hitting a melon against the wall." He rubbed his cheek nervously. "It was his head. I yelled at him, Don't! But by then he already did. Then he fell down and I went in to help him."

I was free to walk the curb, but, I did not know its terrible price. I ran across the soft tar of First Avenue, down the sidewalk in the city so unlike me, gay and carefree when I felt so hated.

Why! Why does he hate me!

It was August and the city was light with the air of a festival, tourists everywhere, everyone out to have a good time. He wants to keep me in his pocket like a piece of change! A piece of change he hates! Five or six different languages peppered the air of Astor Place, and the poor people selling books and dirty magazines on blankets sniggered contentedly and showed their grey teeth.

Tourists clogged the sidewalks in Chinatown; I had to budge between people through to Mulberry Street, until I gazed up the long sidewalk that rose along the park across the street from Choi Su-nim's dojang. I was relieved. No Craig. I hurried upward, looking forward to the peace, the sanctuary from my problems and from myself.

Why does my father hate me? I thought. Why does he...

"Hey!" I stumbled, my bag flopped off my shoulder and hit the ground. Craig shoved his face close to mine. "Did you think I wouldn't show? Thought I'd forget?" His eyes were rimmed with red. I grabbed my bag off the ground and ran for the dojang. "I'll be out here when you walk the curb. Then we'll dance the dance, bitch!"

I bolted up the five steps and burst in past the two glass doors, into the silence of the dojang, breathing hard. I stopped. What? I couldn't think. What do I do? Choi Su-nim's office door was closed and the silence in the dojang lay as thick as sea water. I gazed around the space, the wide expanse of dull floorboards, the strip of threadbare carpet. For a moment the fear swirled behind my eyes, confusing what I could see. The ritual asserted itself and I thought, do what you're supposed to do. Take off your shoes. I took off my shoes. I bowed to the flags and strode toward the closet where the mop and bucket waited. Mop. Calm down. Meditate. Do class. Get some peace.

No chance. Not that night and not for a long time after.

Chapter 21

As I put away the mop and closed the closet door a student came, a tall thin boy with platinum blonde hair. He smiled to me, kicked off his high-tech sneakers, and hurried into the changing room. I needed to change my clothes too, and talk. I knocked on Choi Su-nim's door. When his muffled voice came through I stepped into his spare office. Desk, chair, him, the picture on the wall.

I bowed and closed the door. "Sir?"

He nodded, gazed at me over the tops of his too big eye glasses. I said, "Sir...um...my father won't let me come every day. He hates komdo." I looked down at my toes because Choi Su-nim pushed up his glasses, looked through them, and saw me clearly for the first time. "One reason he brought us here, to America, was to end my study. And now..."

"But he can't end your study." My toes curled as if to hold onto my place in the dojang, but I was ashamed and couldn't look at him. He spoke quietly but firmly. "Is komdo only for the dojang? No. It's for everywhere. That's why I'm having you practice along the edge of the street. You trim endless heads of lettuce in the store. You wield a blade there, and that's your way too. But toilet plungers and mops are the same as a sword. Life itself is the way, Kee. You can do most anything, most anywhere, and be practicing with the sword."

The shame was startled out of me. I looked up at him and said, "How can I be doing komdo in the store, or in the subway, or walking down the street? When I don't have a sword, sir?"

"How? Simple. Wield the sword that is always with you. What is the sword of the mind?" He gazed at me and waited, but I couldn't answer. He said, "Mindfulness. Your undivided attention on what you are doing makes it your art and your way. Mindfulness is the sword that cuts through the clouds of ego and personality. Cut through the clouds of ego and you will become enlightened."

There was a shift, a swirling inside me, as if he was stirring me with a fingertip. Feeling the shift and the swirling, I mumbled, "Yes sir."

He let me settle for a moment before he said, "Change now, it's time for class. We can talk more after you walk the curb."

"Yes sir." I stepped aside and bowed as he came around the desk. "About walking the curb, sir, I...while I did the poom-sey on the curb yesterday Craig was hitting me with a stick."

He stopped with the door open. "He was beating you? With a stick?"

I nodded. "He said he'd be out there today, waiting for me."

"If he is, I won't let you walk the curb. Hurry up and change."

When I stepped out of the office, barefoot and wearing my dobuck, relief spilled through me. Ricky was not there. Choi Su-nim clapped his hands. We students hurried onto the floor, feet rumbling, dobucks rustling, and I stepped into my place at the front. Class began. I remember nothing of it except the moment when Ricky came, a few minutes after we started. I could feel his upset, his rush, and all through the class I felt him watching me struggle with my bruised body. I tried not to let the bruises affect me, but my cheeks crimped hard.

Ricky watched me struggle. Some fear gathered at the top of my chest, tied lines of tension to my adam's apple and tugged it, tugged at my breastbone so that I felt hunched. My neck ached by the time class ended.

Choi Su-nim shuffled out the door. After a long minute he returned, hadn't seen Craig, and nodded to me. I went and lifted the ceremonial sword from its purple silk shelf. I bowed in four directions. The blade rising before my nose, I stood in silence to kowtow to the fifth direction, the center.

I descended the four steps to the sidewalk. I stepped to the curb, and as I looked up the long shining blade, into the blue sky, I glimpsed movement in the park. Craig. He slipped through an opening in the fence and crossed Mulberry Street, a flat stick in his hand. He looked so handsome with his clean skin, perfect white smile, and lean muscular body. He also looked cruel as he said, "Baseball, the all-American game," and swung his stick.

Crack! An explosion of pink pain filled my eyes. The sword swayed in my hands, Craig chuckled, and I began the moving poem. Stroke to the north. Craig drew back his stick. I stiffened, *crack!* and lightning burst through me. "Is your boyfriend coming out to play?" *Crack!* "I'll whack him out of the park." *Crack!*

I have wondered why I kept moving along the curb, why I even started the poem. I didn't want to disobey Choi Su-nim and stop. Craig was only the latest block in my way, and I didn't want to stop. But I think too that some voice within me, silent yet loud, told me I deserved Craig. Some damaged place inside me already knew I deserved to suffer.

I rose into Crane Stance as he danced an odd jig all the way back to Choi Su-nim's steps. I sank forward and brought down the sword, it flashed, and Craig circled back to me, humming a patriotic tune. My breath stopped as I tensed for the blow.

"Swinging for the fences!" *Crack!* "Or are we dancing?" *Crack!* "I forget." *Crack!*

We reached the corner of Bayard Street where he bent low and jabbed me in the calf. The blade shook before my eyes. I rose into Crane Stance, descended, the blade flashed, *crack!* and as we passed up the rising curb of Bayard Street an eerie silence filled the markets. The people of Chinatown stopped on the sidewalk, in doorways, and on stoops to watch us.

Craig shouted, "What are you looking at!"

A woman came thrashing at him with a page of a newspaper. He raised the stick. She backed away, scolding, and the burly men in the fish market stopped dumping buckets of ice. The air turned faintly cooler around the displays of iced fish. A man pointed at Craig and said, "You stop. Don't do that."

Craig shouted, "I'll kick the shit out of *all of you!*"

The sidewalk was a mass of people, shopping carts, bicycles, so Craig circled ahead, past four parked cars, to wait for me. I rose into Crane Stance, sank forward, and the blade shook as I controlled it. The aching of my body and the noise of the world flooded in on me. I was like a sinkhole. When a wave reaches those sinkholes the water explodes out of them.

I reached where Craig hopped from foot to foot, waiting for me. An old man rebuked him from the doorway of a dry cleaning store. "Oh yeah?" He swung the stick, but it made no swishing sound because he turned it flat. The edge hit me with agony. The street, the sky, the sooty buildings shuddered as I jerked and gasped. "Piss me off and see what happens? See!"

No, I could not see. Only the buildings, passing cars, Craig's clenched white teeth and scowl, everything shattered into prisms, blurry glistening lights and shadows. We travelled the curb on Mott Street, Craig swatting me as I stepped, pivoted, wheeled the sword overhead, and for a dozen yards I don't know how I continued. We passed an import store, a grocery, the bakery, and people stopped to watch. When he hit me I saw bursts of red, tears filled my eyes, my hands shook, the sword shook, and the world seemed like a huge crushing weight.

We reached the first black pikes of the fence before Transfiguration School and Church. "You son-of-a-bitch!" It was the old man at the second floor window, a silver air hose clamped to his face. "I'm calling the police!"

Craig shouted, "Yeah? Watch!" He turned the stick, it made no swish, and a crease of pain split through me as the edge split the skin of my buttocks. A cry broke out of my throat, which seemed to be someone else's throat, and I dropped out of Crane Stance, tears leaking down my cheeks, and I saw the blue sky through a pane of shattering glass. It was too much pain. The buildings smeared into a uniform black. I thought I was falling, I was about to collapse.

Craig's shout kept me from falling. "Ricky! I've been waiting, *Ricky!"*

I went still inside. Bare feet pounded the sidewalk. Ricky screeched through his teeth as he ran toward us, still dressed in his white dobuck and yellow sash. The thumping of his feet grew loud, louder, and his screech made something powerful surge inside me. Fear.

"Come and get it," Craig shouted. "Come on, *Ricky!"*

With the sword raised, I sleeved the tears out of my eyes, but everything was cracked and blurry except for Craig and Ricky beyond him, rushing in. I shouted something, but it was too late, Craig was set up for a kick. I heard two words. *Kill him.* Ricky charged, legs and arms pumping. I lifted the sword. Fine silver hair and two little bumps of vertabrae marked the nape of Craig's neck where the sword would hit him. *Kill him now.*

Craig waited until the perfect moment, rose off the ground in a leaping kick, spinning for maximum power, and his foot shot out like an ax. Ricky folded around it and dropped with a gagging cry.

"No!" I heard the plunk and raw scrape of his skin and bony knees hitting cobblestones. *"No!"*

He gagged, curled up, and rage exploded from the sinkhole inside me. I raised the sword. Craig's back was turned to me as he screamed down at Ricky, "You stupid little *toad!"* Two steps. *Kill him!* Craig stood two steps away. I raised the sword high. I was going to hack off his shouting head.

Like a piece breaking away from the building, a man rose from where he was sitting in a doorway across the street. It was the street singer, the organ player. He had a bottle wrapped in a bag, he was drunk.

Craig turned, saw my raised sword, my still feet—I had stopped, he had won—and his head went back as he laughed at me. "Go ahead," he shouted, "cut me down!" The street singer came up behind him. "Come on, Kee, cut me down! Cut me down!"

He startled me, and I felt the shock rather than thought the words. He wants me to kill him. My elbows dropped. "Do it! Do it, Kee, I dare you, come on!"

I let the sword sink, finally seeing who Craig was—a man who hated himself and wanted to die. Stunned, I let the sword settle against my shoulder.

Behind him, the street singer gripped his quart bottle by the neck as he stripped off a brown paper bag, the bottle half full of sloshing red wine.

"Kill me, Kee!" Craig shouted. "Come on, do it!"

He didn't see the street singer, who grabbed him, jerked him around, and swung the bottle. Glass exploded, wine splashed, glittering shards tingled on the cobbles, and a bitter smell filled the air.

Craig dropped. The street singer bent over him and shouted, "Lay off her!"

Craig moaned. Blood welled out of gashes in his face, out from around glistening shards of glass stuck in his brows and cheeks, and wine and blood ran down his throat. It dripped to the cobblestones and creeped toward the gutter in thin red tongues.

The street singer made an odd flip of his hand as he saw what he'd done. His mouth opened and closed. He let the bottleneck drop and shatter. "Don't mess with an artist. At least my daddy taught me that."

The old man in the window said, "Jesus." The street singer was his son. "Jesus, Junior. Jesus."

People surrounded those three, the street singer, Craig, and Ricky on the ground, and I was forgotten in the tumult. I again felt the cool steel edge of the curb under my feet. What I was doing came back to me. I raised the ceremonial sword. I resumed the moving poem, no poetry in that motion. I was shattered.

Persimmon

The tracks of tears were cold on my cheeks. The places where Craig hit me with the edge of the stick were like burns, but I resumed that exercise. Stroke, stance, pivot. I passed the funerary at the bottom of Mosco Street. Children screeched joyfully on the swings, the sweet aroma of tomatoes escaped an Italian restaurant, a breeze whispered among the leaves of the trees, and as I neared Choi Su-nim's dojang the wail of sirens came over the park.

Chapter 22

When I opened the chest and took out the cloth to clean the blade, I saw that a drop of wine and a drop of blood had dirtied it. I wiped the shining edge and returned the long curving sword to the purple silk shelf in the chest.

I bowed to Choi Su-nim.

"Sir, Craig and Ricky are hurt."

He nodded, his mouth tight. "Ricky said he had a feeling. I tried to stop him, I knew he'd make matters worse, but I couldn't."

He waved his cane at the other students and ordered them to leave. Young boys and businessmen hurried into their shoes. As they opened the door and hurried out, the wailing of sirens came in. The doors closed, shut them out, and Choi Su-nim looked at me.

"What happened?"

"Craig kicked Ricky. He might be...hurt badly."

"And Craig? He was beating you again?"

"Until a man hit him in the face with a bottle."

Red lights flashed across the door as a police car appeared at the curb. I drew close to Choi Su-nim. Three uniformed policemen lifted their big black shoes up the steps and pushed their way into the dojang, thick in the middle with holsters, bullets, pistols, night sticks of brown lacquered wood. One man whose name tag said he was Sergeant Brown cleared his throat, ill at ease. He glanced around the dojang and nodded to Choi Su-nim.

"Yes," he said, "I understand this sword stuff is a cultural thing, protected and all that, but we have to take her in for paper work." A pink scar ran along Sergeant Brown's jaw, which he hid by shaving his sideburns into long triangles. "She has to give a statement."

Choi Su-nim spoke perfect English. "I will accompany her."

"Sure, why not." He looked at me. "You want to change into street clothes?"

I thought of how painful it would be and shook my head. Sergeant Brown pushed open the door for us. As we descended the four steps to the walk I grew weak, I felt sick. It felt as if something inside me snapped and was moving around, doing damage to my steadiness. I faltered, so Choi Su-nim held my elbow. A policeman opened the car door before me. I looked into a tunnel-like back seat, hard, stained grey, and I shook my head.

"I cannot sit." Sergeant Brown looked closely at me. I felt faint. "I...lie down?"

"Go right ahead." I crawled onto the seat and collapsed with a moan. They closed the door at my feet. Choi Su-nim got in through the other door, let my head rest on his thigh, and the squad car moved with a drone of its engine. Sergeant Brown, a man with a callous glance, said, "We're just going around the park, to the Tombs." The car hit a bump. Bolts of pain shot through me, I gasped. He said, "Take it easy, Brooks."

The driver snapped, "Tell it to the D.P.W."

Choi Su-nim's thigh was soft and warm under my cheek. I lifted my head, pains shooting down my spine. I asked the police, "That boy, Ricky Tibbs. He's hurt?"

"They took him to the hospital. I don't know what's the matter with him. Is he your boyfriend?" The driver watched me in the rear view mirror. "Just be glad it isn't the other one. The other one isn't too pretty."

The car stopped at the base of a skyscraper. We did not go up. They herded us to dirty concrete steps and I slowly, carefully went down them, into the basement. It was called the Tombs and the name fit. We shuffled into a cage made of thick iron bars. One set of bars closed on us before the next set hummed open, three men watching from behind a window; then the second set of bars closed behind us too.

Everywhere there were police in pale blue shirts and dark blue pants, pistols on their hips, and I shivered because I knew each of those pistols could kill me. Then again, the policemen were leading men with empty eyes, drugged or drunk, men with hard glittering defiance in their eyes, handcuffed criminals with filthy beards and greasy hair, and I was glad I was not alone.

Sergeant Brown led us past a line of cells that stank of urine and vomit. Men, dozens of men stood around the pens or lay on the floor, waiting to go before the judge. Choi Su-nim stayed at my elbow. We passed a huge room with a hundred desks and came to another room with a dozen desks. Keyboards clacked, cigarette smoke burned my nose, and the smoke competed with the stink of burnt coffee.

Sergeant Brown motioned to a chair by a desk. Groaning, I sat.

"We need you to make a statement," he said. "Tell us exactly what happened. Understand?"

I nodded. I briefly described what happened before the church and school on Mott Street, and Choi Su-nim translated into clear English. Sergeant Brown wrote fast with a ballpoint pen that made a faint zipping sound. I sagged forward onto my arms, supported by my knees, and swallowed as my stomach clenched with illness. My eyes wanted to close but the pain kept me awake.

Finally Sergeant Brown said, "Want to lie down? Kee-Yong?"

I nodded. "Can you..." I glanced at Choi Su-nim. "Would you call Appa-nim, sir? Tell him I'll be late?"

"Her father," he said to them, "must be notified that she will be getting home late."

"She's not gonna make it home. Not tonight, you better tell him." Choi Su-nim picked up the receiver of an old black telephone on the desk. He dialed as Sergeant Brown led me to a sofa with crushed foam cushions.

"Kee," he said, "you're going to the hospital. You're not looking too bouncy. Madelyn?" A woman looked up from a desk. "Before you can lie down, Kee-Yong, we have to get some pictures. Madelyn, would you?"

Sergeant Madelyn wore a pistol on her hip, stripes on her sleeve, and a widow's peak of sand-yellow hair over her forehead. She said, "Right this way. What's your name?"

I looked at her bleerily. "Kee."

"Well, Kee, let's go where the men can't." She opened a door, turned on lights. Spotlights stood on stands. "This is the evidence room. What should we take pictures of? You tell me. This is your chance to be in the spotlight."

"Back. Back of me."

"Stand between the lights. Yeah, that's good."

I undid the strings of my dobuck, let the bottoms drop to the floor, gritted my teeth as pains criss-crossed my back. I raised the cloth top. Sergeant Madelyn went silent. Typewriters clacked in the other room. She said, "I would've chopped his head off."

The camera clicked and hummed and she tossed snapshots onto a table. "Pull them up, that's all we need. That sword stuff, good exercise, huh?" Everything was hazy. She led me back into the other room, to the hard couch. "Let me get you a blanket."

"Damn!" Sergeant Brown hung up the telephone and turned on his squeaky chair. He said to Choi Su-nim, "Craig Donafrio, your student, why didn't you tell me?"

Choi Su-nim pushed up his glasses. "Tell you what?"

"That he's the son of the Assistant District Attorney of Manhattan." Other policemen raised their heads to look. Choi Su-nim did not reply. Sergeant Brown said to Madelyn, "Screw me. My promotion, you watch, Madelyn, it's gonna get sticky now. You watch."

She chuckled. "Poor Jerry."

The door opened and two policemen came in, one holding the elbow of a man in a shabby dinner jacket and jeans torn at the knee, his wrists handcuffed behind his back. It was the street singer.

"Time to lay down, Kee," Sergeant Madelyn said. "Time to take it easy." She spread a blanket to soften the bench and draped a second coarse green blanket over me. Choi Su-nim sat beside me. "Relax," Sergeant Madelyn said. "The ambulance will be here in a minute."

"Ambulance?"

"You're going to the hospital," Choi Su-nim said. He nodded toward the street singer. "Is that the man who hit Craig with the bottle?"

I struggled to keep my eyes open, to fix on the street singer's voice.

"You're charging *me?*" he cried. "For what? That surfer boy was whackin' 'er—I'm not kidding you—I mean *whackin'* 'er!"

"Sit down, pal." They sat him down in a chair by a desk. He swayed back and forth, the chair creaking under him as a policeman got out a form. The policeman said, "Tell it to me slowly, pal. What happened?"

The street singer was very drunk. "She's comin' 'long the curb, doing her sword stuff—looks beautiful, it does—but Surfer Boy's whacking her with a stick and nobody's doin' a damn thing, nada, and he keeps on whackin' her. My old man starts yelling. He's always yelling, tell the truth, but he got cancer and can't do it, not from the second floor."

"Do what?" Sergeant Brown asked.

"Stop Surfer Boy from whackin' 'er; and then this skinny black kid, god bless his little stick arms and legs—got skinny stick arms and legs—he comes chargin' down the street like a kamikaze. Bang! Down he goes. Takes a shot like I never saw, except for the shot I gave a Jersey chump in a bar on...wait a minute. You're the police, why am I tellin' you about *that?*"

"Slow down, pal. How much wine did you have? Half a quart?"

"Well, no. It was quart number two that I used in such a useful fashion. Wasn't a waste, no way. Man, I feel *good!* Felt good to smash that asshole. Busted it right over his face." He burped, and the policemen grimaced at the smell. "Yeah, cheap, I know. On a budget."

"Anyway, I couldn' believe what Surfer Boy's doing, I hear my father swearing, Surfer Boy swears back and whacks her, and she lets out a yelp. It woke me up. Takes at least a quart to go see dear old Dad. He always been disagreeable, but he got cancer, so now he's awful. True pain in the butt."

The policeman sighed. "Leave out the family stuff, will you. What happened next?"

"I took the bag off the bottle, 'cause I'm neat, an' I walk over and clock the guy. That's that. Now you want my autograph? I used to give autographs alla time. I signed a woman's nipple once. You believe that?"

"Sure, pal. Now let's do the hard part. Fill in the blanks. What's your full name?"

"Francis Joseph Bonn…Bonnarotti Junior."

"Wait a minute." The tone of Sergeant Madelyn's voice opened my eyes. "You're Francis Bonn?"

"That's me," the street singer said. "Lead singer for Dayz. Remember us? Back 'n the day?"

"Twice over," Sergeant Brown said. "Screw me twice over."

Sergeant Madelyn patted Sergeant Brown's shoulder sympathetically and chuckled. She said to the street singer, "I liked you in my maladjusted youth. What happened to you guys?"

The street singer nodded his head. "The Dayz are numbered. I am the only…one…left…alive."

The policeman with a pen in his hand snapped, "Address?"

"No address, thank you. Dad's there on Mott Street."

The policeman rose from the desk. "Okay, rock star, the tank is this way."

"I get to call him, don't I? He's famous, famous painter, got millions in the bank, he'll throw my bail."

"Not this minute he won't."

"My ex-wife? She got alla it." As they led him out the door he laughed. "I feel good. Damsel in distres' and all that. Made dear ol' dad proud, I bet. Finally."

His voice trailed away down the hall outside the door. I had nothing left to fix on, went in and out of a haze, and I cannot say how much time passed before Choi Su-nim touched my arm.

"Wake up, your father is here."

I struggled up and the blanket fell off me. Appa-nim, Umma, and Ling were at the door. I whispered, "Appa?"

I needed him. I couldn't see clearly, they were surrounded by fog, like a cameo picture. I stood up, hurting everywhere, my chest crumpling inside when I saw the bruise on his forehead, black and swollen thick. Some control finally broke inside me and I started to cry.

He rushed over and put his arms around me, which made me cry harder. Choi Su-nim said, "Don't touch her back."

"Why not?" His shirt smelled of sweat, and I cried against his chest as he held me softly. His body hummed against my cheek as he asked, "What happened?"

No one spoke. Sergeant Madelyn came with the pictures, the snapshots that were going to make a lot of money for someone. I shook and sobbed. Appa-nim looked at the pictures. I felt his chest expand, then he shouted at Choi Su-nim, "You old *fool!* What did you do?" I stumbled as he let go of me and grabbed Choi Su-nim. "What! What did you do?! *What!*"

"Appa," I cried, "it wasn't him!"

The sergeant grabbed my father by the throat. He held onto Choi Su-nim, shook him, and shouted, "What! What!"

The detectives got him in a choke hold. Appa-nim gagged. He couldn't breathe, he flushed dark red, but they couldn't rip his hands loose from Choi Su-nim's dobuck.

My master, a little old man, freed himself with a simple twist and backward step.

Chapter 23

The EMTs carefully laid me out on a wheeled bed. They wore baggy white clothes, but the male EMT had a twitch that twittered the brow over his left eye. He handed straps over me to the female EMT, a skinny woman, and she snugged the straps down on me. They rolled me on the gurney down the long hall past the cells holding angry drunken men, into a freight elevator that groaned as it lifted the nine of us—two EMTs, Sergeants Madelyn and Brown, who stayed between Appa-nim and Choi Su-nim, me, Umma, and Ling.

Machinary rumbled. We stopped, then the elevator shook as one side opened onto the night that had settled down around the Tombs. Red lights splashed us. Ling and Umma clung to my gurney, wide-eyed, but Appa-nim's teeth were still clenched. He watched suspiciously as they rolled me to an ambulance, past a man asking, "Was it his son? Donafrio's son?"

Sergeant Madelyn and Sergeant Brown shouted, "Out of the way! No comment!"

Among all the gleaming hospital equipment in the back of the ambulance there was little more than room for me on the gurney. Appa-nim still climbed in and sat hunched beside me on a box marked with a red cross. The twitchy EMT slammed the doors behind us. The ambulance started, moved in fits and starts, and red lights flashed in the windows. I was looking out through a thick fog in my head. Voices, shouts sounded like dream violence.

"Who was he?" I asked. "That man?"

"A reporter, I think," Appa-nim said. "Is there somebody important in there? There's more coming."

The engine droned. Equipment gleamed and rattled in the darks and lights. For a long minute we were jostled and swayed by the ambulance moving through traffic. No howling sirens or splashing lights, in the relief and calm something rigid in my father finally snapped. As we trundled under a street lamp, it lit us and I saw Appa-nim reaching out to touch me. He pulled his hand back, rubbed his face, his hand shaking as he dug it through his hair. His voice came out strangled. "When they told me you were hurt I…got so…"

"I'm all right. They just want to be safe."

"I know, but…but I can't lose you." He choked, hunching over me. "I'm afraid of losing you. I'm sorry. I'm so sorry!"

I reached up toward the ugly bruise swollen on his forehead. He flinched though I didn't reach him. I said, "I'm sorry you hurt yourself again."

He looked into the dark, stared back through the years, and didn't say anything.

"Remember when I first took you to Chen-puin? For tutoring? When you were five? When she led you away, into the garden, it felt like I was sending you away…a piece of myself. Ever since…"

I followed his glance and saw that he was seeing himself reflected in a window. The stringy cords of his neck played as he swallowed.

He shook his head. "No, I…I'm always afraid. I've always been afraid. But…of what? Of what?" He started to rock back and forth on a box with a red cross on it. It creaked as if it would give out beneath him. His cheeks knotted beneath his eyes, the bruise on his forehead speckled with scabs of dried blood. He whispered, "Something's wrong. Something's wrong with me."

A sob shook him, ripped the dark. An EMT asked from the front, "Everything all right back there?"

Appa-nim's head sank between his shoulders as he cried and shook. I touched his knee. "Just because I need komdo it doesn't mean I'm leaving you," I said. "I won't. Until you say it's all right. Like you did in Peng Su-nim's garden. Okay?" He choked on himself. "Appa? Okay?"

He stared at the window and nodded his head. When we passed beneath a street lamp a stripe on his cheek glowed in the light, and for the first time I saw the path no one could save him from, a path of suffering and tears that began a long time ago.

But it was too much for me. The pain killer fogged my thoughts until I was lost in the fog of sleep.

Chapter 24

By the window, Mr. Hurtog leaned over to cough and his face turned reddish purple. Even the skin that showed through the hair combed over the top of his bald head turned red. Her husband's hacking did not disturb Mrs. Hurtog, a fat woman in the bed next to mine. She and Umma and I were watching News at Noon, on TV. Mr. Hurtog stopped coughing and his mustache, growing out of his nose, twitched as he spoke.

"I need a cigarette."

Mrs. Hurtog's jelly arm shook as she pointed at the TV. "Shut up, Harvey. It's her, she's on the news."

The TV bolted to the ceiling bore a plastic card below the screen. Bellevue Hospital Visual Services x6990. On the screen people stood at the back of an ambulance as they loaded someone in, then one little figure climbed in. Me? And Appa-nim?

Umma grunted. "You got out just in time. They're like barracudas."

On TV I saw a familiar skyline—the buildings standing around the park in Chinatown. Mulberry Street stood crowded with people. What, I thought, are they doing? Heads and shoulders, cameras, microphones in outstretched hands. The crowd churned as the door of Choi Su-nim's dojang opened at the top of four steps. The camera shook and the scene wobbled crazily on the TV as reporters rushed at him.

"What are they saying?"

"You know English better than I do," Umma said. I lay on a special watery sand mattress that squished, burbled, and shifted under me. "There's the fallen rock star. What's his name?"

"Bonnarotti." The mattress burbled. I winced, the TV showed the street singer coming out of the Tombs, and I knew some of the announcer's words. Donafrio. Tibbs. Sword. I asked, "Siren with a sword? What's a siren?"

The world seemed unreal to me after a long sleep. Umma shrugged. I glanced at the fat woman. She seemed to know what we said, though we were speaking Hangugo.

"Little girl," she asked, "are they really all your boyfriends?"

"What?"

Her husband snuffled, twitched his mustache, and pointed to the door.

"I had a heckuva time getting in. Fifteen, twenty of them out in the hall. They got a guard too. They're not nice, the cop or the newspeople. Honey," he said to his wife, "I saw Cynthia Valenzuala, from Channel Six. She is good looking."

"Harvey, shut up."

The door opened. A woman in a white coat entered, the disk and coil of a stethoscope in her pocket. Beyond the swirl of her long colorful skirt printed with tropical birds I heard mechanical things chattering and snapping like the teeth of feeding barracuda. What was that? She nodded to Umma; they'd met while I was asleep. She smiled to me and spoke in perfect Hangugo.

"There's my TV star." I was so surprised I turned my head. Pains shot down my back, my face clenched, I groaned. She said, "It's going to hurt for awhile. Kee-Yong, I'm Doctor Rosenberg. How are you feeling?"

I glanced at Umma. "Okay."

Doctor Rosenberg unhooked a clipboard from the end of my bed. She glanced at it and spoke, a bit amused with the effect of her Seoul accent.

"Surprised that I speak Hangugo?" I blinked. "I served my residency in Seoul. My husband is a Kim. Your mother tells me your home is near Kwangju. I liked the spring in the south, but the summer was too hot. Are you ready for the x-rays?"

"I need x-rays?"

"Maybe."

"But it was only a thin slat of wood, that's all he hit me with. It just hurt a lot."

Her nose was big and rounded, like one of the toucans on her skirt, but she had sea-green eyes and flowing black hair. "Let me take a look. Here."

She held out her hand. I sat up, clenching my teeth. My back felt like a turtle shell broken into pieces that sliced me as I moved. I winced as they helped me off the bed, then Doctor Rosenberg pulled the curtain closed around us.

Umma untied my robe. When she saw my back she inhaled sharply. "How many times did he beat you?"

"Twice."

Doctor Rosenberg spoke into a hand-held tape recorder.

"Large multiple contusions. Laceration, left buttock." I stiffened beneath the wind of her fingertips. "That was quite a beating; but no, I don't think there's any fractures." I let out squeaks of pain as she turned my sorry body. "You didn't fall? It was a light piece of wood?"

"A slat from a packing crate."

As Umma tied the strings of the robe at the back of my neck, the curtain billowed. It was the door being opened. Flashing lights, chattering camera teeth, quick steps beyond the curtain, and Ling's quicker skipping. Appa-nim's face appeared between the curtains.

"You see them? Sharks in a feeding frenzy."

Ling's face appeared. "Isn't it great?!"

"Aigo! It's a madhouse at the store." Appa-nim watched Doctor Rosenberg lift the telephone. "Who's that?"

"Kee's doctor."

She spoke into the phone. "This is Doctor Rosenberg. I'm with the patient... Yes, an escort, and send a cab to the loading docks. Thank you." She put down the receiver and spoke in Hangugo. "Mr. Ahn, I'm Doctor Rosenberg. I don't think x-rays are necessary, so I'm releasing Kee-Yong to you." She waved at the door. "You have to sign a release, and you'll have to wait for Security before you can leave, and I have to write a prescription for pain killers. She's going to have pain for awhile."

"Wait a minute." He spread his hands and looked from me to Doctor Rosenberg. "What's going on? Kee, what happened down there? Doctor Rosaburr, what are they saying? I can't understand, they speak so fast and ask so many questions that I can't answer a single one."

Doctor Rosenberg settled her glance on me. "They're saying that Craig Donafrio, the son of the Assistant District Attorney of Manhattan—a very powerful man, Mr. Ahn—was competing for Kee's affections with Ricky Tibbs, the African American boy. They're also saying Francis Bonnarotti, the rock star, was fighting for you too, and it grew violent." Her eyes held a flicker of amusement. "Kee, you're a new version of the femme fatale."

Appa-nim asked, "The what?"

"A woman who drives men crazy. I'll be back with the release and prescriptions."

When she went out we heard chattering teeth, the mumble of feet, voices, spiking shouts. Appa-nim stepped outside the curtains so I could dress. Umma and Ling helped me, then when the doctor returned there were loud voices issuing orders.

"They'll move the paparazzi," Doctor Rosenberg said. "Here's the prescriptions. Fill them at any pharmacy. Mr. Ahn, please sign here." She indicated a place on a form, he signed his name, Hangugo characters looking out of place among the tiny printed English. She glanced at me. "Ready?"

I nodded. "Thank you."

I walked slowly, my clothes rasping on my bruises. Patients who stood in doorways, in blue smocks, gazed at me curiously. I felt like a freak. I clenched my teeth. The pain in my back made me hang my head and look at the floor. We went in an elevator to the second floor, detoured to another elevator, rode to the ground floor and stepped out. Doctor Rosenberg led us to a loading dock where a taxi waited by a dumpster that stank of rotting food.

"If you have any questions," she said, "please call me."

"Thank you," Umma said.

"Ah!" I gasped and had to clench my teeth as I settled into the taxi. "Umma, it hurts."

The cabbie had a gold ring in his ear. His dark brown eyes found me in the rearview mirror.

"Hey you," Appa-nim snapped. "Avenue A and St. Mark. Go slow!" The taxi moved onto First Avenue where a line of white vans sat by the curb and people milled around the mouth of a walkway. Appa-nim pointed. "See those people, Kee? They're waiting for you."

"Me? Why?"

"Because of what you did! We haven't sold a single piece of fruit today. The sharks were outside at six this morning and nobody could get in to buy even a cup of coffee."

Ling laughed. "But we have a plan. Don't we, Appa?"

The cab hit a pothole, the broken turtle shell sliced my back, but I hung my head to stomach my moan. "Ki-Teh," Umma said, "it's not her fault."

Ling prattled, "The Rhee twins said you're a three-timer."

"A what?"

Appa-nim's eyes skewered me. "Is it true? Were they all your boyfriends?"

Umma said, "Ki-Teh—"

"Quiet! Were they? Were you fooling around with them? That's what they're all saying. How embarassing! What am I going to do in church? Keep my head down?"

I was glad the cabbie could not understand Hangugo. I whispered, "They're making it up. That fallen rock star, I don't know him."

The sidewalk in front of our store was gorged with people that overflowed onto the street, men in suits spilling out between vans with lettered sides and satellite dishes mounted on their tops. Men hefted cameras, perched camcorders on their shoulders, while a man sat on a seat behind a machine with a long metal snout that rolled on three legs.

"What's that big thing?"

"A movie camera," Ling said. "They're all reporters and news people. Isn't this great?"

"Great," Appa-nim said. The taxi stopped across from our store. The newspeople turned, saw us, and it was like blood dumped into the sea. The sharks began to swirl and mill around as Appa-nim stuffed a bill into the cabbie's pay slot. His mouth hardened as he said, "Stay right behind me."

Ling laughed. "Here we go again!"

I slowly climbed from the cab, groaning. A cry went up. That's her! The thrummelling of hundreds of feet. They surrounded us before I took one step. "Any broken bones? Were you sleeping with them?" Camera teeth chattered and snapped, camcorders hummed, lights flashed; faces shouted; lips moved; hands, knuckles, microphones jumped at me. "How long have you been seeing them?"

"When did they find out about each other?"

"Was it a feud?"

"Any broken bones?"

"Pressing charges? Are you?!"

"Appa-nim?" Shoulders, battery packs, microphones, clothes on bodies crushed in on us. "Appa!"

"Get back!" Umma appeared by my elbow. "You back off!" They pushed in, those in front staggered by those behind. Umma shouted, "Get back!" She flushed a bright and dangerous copper color, swung her arm and knocked aside the microphones. "You! Get! Back! *Off!*"

The newspeople thrust their microphones at us, cameras fired, lights blinked, recorders hummed. Is komdo a cult? Did you have sex? Was it a plot to kill Donafrio?

"Appa-nim!" All I could see was the top of our building against the clouds. How long? Who most? What? Why? "Ling! Appa-nim!"

A camera bumped me, I gasped. Appa-nim shouted, "Over here!"

A hand appeared, a skinny little forearm. Ling giggled and pulled my hand. Umma and I broke between microphones, skipped between chrome bumpers, stumbled over the curb. The doorway of our store rose over me and thankfully I scuttled inside. Appa-nim slammed the door, sealed out the daylight, and we stood in our cool gloomy store letting our breath out slowly.

He glanced at me and nodded, letting me catch my breath. What's he thinking? Ling stepped up onto the stool behind the cash register. Appa-nim said, "Ready, Ling?"

Umma said, "What are you doing?"

"Ready, Appa. Get ready, Kee."

"For what?"

He opened the door wide and the reporters rushed up to the jambs. His arm blocked the doorway.

"One question," he shouted, "one piece of fruit!" The newspeople went still and looked at him. "No no no." He spoke in Hangugo. "Ling, I changed my mind. Five pieces of fruit."

"Okay, Appa, I'm ready."

He shouted, "One question, you buy fiiiiive piece of fruit!" Out of the crowd on the sidewalk I heard snorts of disgust and ridicule. "You see customer? No customer, so *you* are customer." Appa-nim's brows wrinkled over his eyes and he pointed at us. "Ask question, buy five piece of fruit. Good deal, who first?"

"Hey." Elbows jerked, men scowled. A chubby woman with bulldog cheeks budged out of the crowd. "How many questions for a spaghetti squash?"

A man elbowed her and snapped, "I'll take some flowers!"

"Out of the way!" The woman built like a fire hydrant forced her way over the threshold. Her head was covered with corkscrew vines of red hair, a camera and tape recorder hung around her neck. "How many questions for a turnip?"

"Baggo potato," Appa-nim said, "one question. Squash and...and four turnip, one question."

"Two turnips."

"Three."

She said, "Deal," and Appa-nim slammed the door. The woman pushed buttons on the tape recorder, wheels turned in a little window, and she said, "I'll take five green peppers, ten white onions, a bag of potatoes, flowers for Cheryl..." She ducked her head to the tape recorder. "...you hear that Cheryl? A spaghetti squash, five oranges, and ten kiwi fruit. Questions, how many is that?"

Ling figured and said, "Seven."

She pulled a wallet from her hip pocket. "What's the damage?"

"Li, get what she ordered." Umma looked furious but turned with tight lips to the island. She let turnips, kiwi, peppers, oranges, and a squash thump on the counter as Ling's fingers skittered on the keys. Appa-nim said, "Bouquet too. How much?"

Ling sang out, "Twenty-six dollar and sixty-one cent, please come again!"

The woman paid green dollar bills and slapped exact change onto the counter. "Okay, the first question is..."

Knuckles rapped at the door. Appa-nim shouted, "You next!"

Hangugo, a woman's sharp voice, and Appa-nim pushed open the door. It was Auntie, her mouth painted like a red butterfly; but she took one look at us and out came stinging bees.

"What's going on here? Are you all right?" She touched my arm and looked into my eyes. "I heard that you..."

"Who are you?" the reporter asked.

Auntie Yen turned on her. "Who are you?"

The woman produced a business card. "Joella Marks, Publisher, *Feminist Weekly News.*"

"That rag you find in laudromats?"

Ling said, "Three question left."

Joella Marks shook her mass of corkscrews. "No, I paid to ask Kee questions, not this princess."

Auntie snapped at her, "Get out."

"No," Appa-nim said, "she bought fruit."

"Yeah, I paid and so..."

"Get out!" Auntie flung open the door, it banged against the counter, and cameras chattered and hummed. "Ki-Teh, I can't believe you! And you too, Li?"

"Me? What did I know?"

I stood there, the pieces of my broken turtle shell cutting and slicing me, and Auntie Yen glared at Appa-nim. He straightened himself as the newspeople shot pictures. Auntie snapped, "Kee's not for sale. That's what you're doing, selling your daughter."

He slammed the door. "I'm trying to stay in business! You see any customers? What's the sales for today, Ling? Twenty-six dollars?"

"And sixty-one cent."

"I don't care!" Auntie pointed toward the storage room. "Li, get two crates." Even as she pushed open the door, shutters snapped and questions burst. She shouted, "Press conference. Press conference!"

Out on the sidewalk, in front of our bin for navel oranges, Auntie and Umma stacked one crate on top of another and draped the plastic cloth from the kitchen table over the slats. The newspeople covered the top with foam-covered bulbs, microphones each with the call letters of a TV or radio station on the stem. Reporters bumped and shoved for position until Auntie Yen smiled and nodded to a man she obviously knew.

"My turn!" Joella Marks, a bouquet of flowers in one hand, shook her red corkscrew vines and shouted, "I paid, I go first!"

Appa-nim nodded. "She's first."

Auntie looked strong for being furious; I felt protected by Appa-nim at my elbow, Ling and Umma on the other side with Auntie. The sun heated my cheeks, I squinted, back pains stuck me, but I stood still as video cameras whirred like hummingbirds, bees, mosquitoes, and camera shutters chattered.

"How does it feel to be sacrificed by one man to another?" asked Joella Marks. "How does it feel to be the latest victim of our male-dominated, patriarchal society?"

What? I looked at Auntie Yen. She said, "Do you feel like a victim of a society run by men? Do you feel Choi Su-nim sacrificed you to Craig Donafrio?"

"Oh." I squinted and spoke Hangugo. "Um...Choi Su-nim didn't know Craig was outside." Auntie translated me into English. Did I feel like a victim of men? I really didn't want to discuss myself so I said, "In Korea we say the big society is run by men and the little society is run by women."

Joella's red corkscrews quivered. "What little society?"

"The family."

Auntie spoke English. The reporters scribbled, I squinted, and a policeman waved the traffic on Avenue A away from St. Mark's Place. The importance of speaking the right words made me nervous. Auntie said, "Next?"

Joella Marks asked, "Master Joy said..."

"Master Choi?"

"Right. He said you're the first female ever allowed to study that particular martial art. How did you manage to crack a male dominated social group? How does it feel to be a symbol of female success in a male political system?"

Auntie translated, and I realized the woman was planting her ideas like rice, all in a row.

"No mastery." I shook my head. "'Su-nim' doesn't mean mastery. Su-nim means 'one who has special knowledge'. I'm not a su-nim. What I do know," I said, "is that I don't feel like a success. I feel like a turtle with a broken shell."

When Auntie translated me the newspeople scribbled. I felt tired. Auntie pointed to a man in a suit and a striped tie. He asked, "Why were you walking the curb? What's the purpose?"

"To reach enlightenment."

"What's enlightenment?"

"Well...I'm not, so I can't say. It made my teachers wise, and they keep things peaceful. That's what enlightenment did for them, and the people around them."

Auntie pointed to other newspeople. About the rock star: Was he your lover? Were you sleeping with Ricky Tibbs? With Craig? How long have you been in the U.S.? How much do you work? How much do you make? Are you pressing charges?

My neck stiffly bent as I cranked my head up to glance at Auntie Yen. "What does she mean, pressing charges?"

"If you press charges against Craig Donafrio," Auntie said, "he'll be tried in court for beating you, and then he'll be punished."

I looked down the microphones, down the crate to a crack in the sidewalk. Moss was budding up from between two blocks of cement and slowly heaving them apart. I said, "Yes, I will press charges. But..." I felt wilted. "...but Auntie I..."

She saw. "That's all for now. Kee, inside."

They herded me into the store, into cool smells of fruit sugars and onion shells. Appa-nim slammed the heavy metal door and threw the bolt, clack-rattle. I needed to lean against Umma, who held me tenderly.

The store seemed dark after the bright afternoon sunshine. I sighed, Appa-nim fidgeted, and we stood looking at each other.

Ling said, "That was fun, but now I feel like a prisoner."

"Get used to it." Auntie stepped close, and with her fingertips swept strands of hair off my forehead. "The craziness," she said, "has just started."

Chapter 25

Mindful agony. As I climbed the stairs to our kitchen pain stabbed between my shoulder blades, edges sliced my back, my pants chafed my bottom and thighs, and the bruises on my calf muscles felt like fingers digging in. But the pain I suffered as I followed Umma up the kitchen stairs kept me mindful. Each moment I raised my foot to another stair, pain kept me focused on that moment.

Appa-nim was the opposite. His forehead was layered with worry lines, his cheeks stitched in around his eyes, and his shoulders looked frozen. As we reached the kitchen Auntie asked, "What exactly did he do to you, Kee?"

I beckoned with a finger and we filed into our bedroom, leaving Appa-nim alone in the living room. The four of us filled the floor between the window and the futon. How odd. The room had shrunk, the rubber plant drooped, the bed looked different. It was different because I was different.

I unbuttoned my shirt and slipped it off my shoulders. They did not speak. I said, "It's worse down below, where he broke the skin. Umma, I'm hungry."

The air shaft let in the sounds of life in our building and the next, life that went on no matter what happened to me. The longshoreman's wife in the next building was humming a tune. Her husband shouted, "Shirley, where's the ketchup?"

Auntie mumbled, "How many times did he beat you?"

"Twice."

Ling cried, "I wish I could beat him!"

"Ow!"

"Sorry," Umma said. She eased the shirt over the bruises at the nape of my neck. "You slept like a dead person until noon, of course you're hungry."

"Why didn't you wake me up?"

She shrugged. "If a spoonful isn't enough..."

When she opened the bedroom door we found Appa-nim looking out the window. Before he could cover himself I saw his tense scowl, the nervous flutter of his hand.

"All those press people," he mumbled.

I peeked out. Vans with satellite dishes crowded the curb, the walk clogged with reporters, photographers, cameramen, passersby, a drunk begging with a paper cup. One lens spotted us, glinted as it turned up, and we stepped back as the camera teeth began to chatter and feed on us.

Umma rattled the kettle under the water faucet. "I'll boil some shrimp; and Ling, I'll show you how to mix up garlic sauce, quick, and there's some rice left in the pot. How is it at the U.N., Yen? Are they talking about her?"

Auntie tossed her head and mocked jealousy. "All they can talk about is Kee and her men." Umma made a lid clang and Auntie turned to me. "How do you like the circus?"

I shook my head. "Walking the curb won't be fun."

"No," Umma said, "you're not going down there, not today."

"For God's sake, you need to heal." Auntie rolled her eyes. "Ki-Teh, talk some sense into your daughter's head."

He shrugged. "As long as nobody beats her, why not?" Surprised silence. Ling's laugh tingled among us. "It's not for us to decide. Is it?"

Auntie said to me, "And how are you going to get out? They'll be all over you. And walk the curb? Forget it."

I'd thought about it. "I have my way."

We ate dinner, and when the time came I led them into my bedroom. It was simple to climb down a step ladder, with my bag, to the roof of our storage room. They crowded the window as I stepped away. The roof creaked. Ling gasped, "Uh oh!" but I crept across the black tarpaper, the rotten roof sank under my feet, creaking, the air shaft filled with tension. Then I felt the rough brick wall of Super Redsy's building and started to breathe again.

I knocked on the window of the long-suffering wife who lived with her longshoreman husband. From their arguments, when he was drunk and shouted and cursed her, I knew her name. I said, "Hello? Shirley?"

She appeared at her window, a heavy woman with huge breasts and pouched cheeks. She saw Umma, Auntie, Appa-nim, and Ling crowded at my bedroom window and looked down at me with her brows curdled. She said, "What are you selling?"

I nodded. "I'm Kee. I sleep there." I pointed, and Ling waved and giggled. "I have to keep out of the news people."

"Oh. Yes, you're that girl on the news!" She dried her hands with a rag wadded in the pocket of her apron. "Sure, here, let me give you a lift."

Shirley hauled me into her window like she was boating a fish. When I stood inside her bedroom I smiled for my family, though I was dizzy and sweating from the pain. I hid my suffering and waved goodbye.

Shirley smiled, her huge breasts quaking inside her dress as she led me away from the window.

"Front door's this way. Say hello to your boyfriends for me. But not that Craig." At her door she unstrung a chain, threw a bolt, twisted a knob with the brass worn off. "If you see that Craig, punch his lights out. Okay? And give Ricky a kiss."

"I will." I will kiss Ricky, I thought. If he's there. "Thank you, Shirley. Bye bye."

As she closed the door she said, "Good luck, sweetie."

I skipped down the cracked granite steps of Super Redsy's stoop as the door of our store opened with a bang. Auntie appeared. The news people converged like scraps to a drain, feet drummed, shouts, equipment rattled. I hurried up St. Mark's Place. More trucks with satellite dishes were parked along the curb, three big cameras rolled on tripods, and two police cars sat on Avenue A. But I was free of it. Free to think.

Ricky Tibbs. I sighed, gazed down at the sidewalk, and my steps turned bouncy. I love Ricky Tibbs. The thought was a wonderful new thing inside me.

I love Ricky Tibbs!

"Kee!"

Huh? I stumbled. I was fifty feet from First Avenue. Auntie sat framed by an open cab door, her long legs shining in her stockings. I got in beside her, carefully, clenching my teeth.

"You get into a cab like a grandmother," she said, "and you're going to walk the curb, swinging a sword?"

Whenever the cab hit a bump I suffered. Auntie noticed. Her lips pressed together, which warned me that I was going to get a lecture. We reached Houston Street, divided in the middle, and divisions were on her mind.

"You have to stop thinking about yourself. I know komdo is important to you; but look what it's done to you! Your back is a mess, and now the store is shut down while those vultures hang around. What if this keeps up for two or three weeks? Think of how much income the store will lose." Huge murals blazed on the sides of buildings, cartoon figures painted in bright colors. "What if the store goes bankrupt? Your life won't be so pleasant. This sword stuff will go right out the window."

"Out the window?"

"Figure of speech. Kiss it goodbye. The end."

She looked out the window and put the nail of her pointer finger between her teeth. The day was sunny bright and the city went about its business, people on the walks hawking stuffed animals, handbags, socks, batteries, sunglasses, scarfs, cheap radios, kitchen gadgets, and people strolled by the tables with their friends, their dogs, their lovers, sisters and brothers.

"I didn't mean for this to happen, Auntie."

She snorted. "Oh? I don't know what to think. Harold broke up with me. Now this. What fun."

"Harold broke up with you? Why?"

"Because he's a jerk." I did not know that word. She bit her fingernail so hard that blood-colored paint stayed on the edge of her front tooth. She sighed and knocked on the dirty plastic divider.

"Stop here!" The corner of Elizabeth Street and Canal. "I'm very upset with you, Kee...and with life in general, I suppose. It's just that you're being so selfish."

"Sorry." Getting out, I put my feet into a puddle of water swirling with gasoline colors. "Bye." She pulled the door shut. The cab droned away, leaving me standing in the open at the edge of traffic. Exposed.

I crossed the street and walked down Gregg Street to where Mott bent around it, past the church and school. I stopped and looked down at the place where Craig had fallen. Blood still stained the cobblestones. A memory of his face, streaming blood, appeared in my mind, shards of glass stuck in his forehead.

I almost got sick.

I hurried toward Mosco Street. A Vietnamese man at the corner tea shop called to me, but I turned downhill to Mulberry, the street half-crowded with newspeople. I approached the dojang from the south instead of the north, but it did not matter. Just before I reached Choi Su-nim's steps a man thrust a microphone at me.

"Miss Ahn, were you in love with Craig Donafrio?"

"No."

Other microphones shot at my face. How do you feel? Any broken bones? Were you sleeping with all three?

"No. No! *No!*"

The newspeople shouted at me as I rushed up the stairs. The first door only muffled the shouts, but past the second glass I found relief, stillness. In front of me, Choi Su-nim's office door stood open, funny papers on his desk. He chuckled as I bowed to the American and

Korean flags.

"Sir?"

"Kee?" He rose from his desk. His cane thumped against a chair leg as he shuffled out of his office. "I heard you were released from the hospital, but I didn't think you'd come."

I bowed to him and smiled. "I saw you on the news."

"Yes, but it's strange. I don't remember getting so old." He looked down at his hands, spotted with age, and chuckled wryly. "How is your back?"

"Painful. It hurts so much I don't notice it...much."

He went back into his office after taking a last glance at me and nodding. "Mop. Best thing for you."

Steaming water splashed, pain spit out from under my shoulder blade, and the bucket clanked against the door frame. I settled into the quiet stillness of mopping. My back complained as I pushed and dragged the mop, the backs of my thighs ached, my pants were sandpaper to my bruises, but I mopped the practice floor until it glowed. After I put away the mop and changed into my dobuck I looked down at the place where I sat in meditation. Gonna hurt. I didn't want to sit, but for twenty minutes I was right, it was painful.

Class began. Ricky Tibbs wasn't there. I could feel eyes looking at me, dozens of eyes. Choi Su-nim barked the names of poom-sey, my body rankled, loosened, unkinked, but I was thankful he didn't call for Tiger and Crane Poom-sey.

He nodded. I went to the teak chest and unwound the cloth from around the ceremonial sword. It was sweet agony to raise the shimmering blade. I thought how I had given so much for that, to raise that sword. I kowtowed to the five directions. While I stood silently to acknowledge the fifth direction, the center, he said to the other students, "Sit. Assume the lotus position and begin to meditate."

Meditation had returned to Choi Su-nim's dojang.

When I stepped outside with the ceremonial sword the barracudas were waiting. They schooled in on me, pushing, shoving, jamming in with chattering teeth, questions, and shouts. They staggered me off the curb, the railing of the steps jammed into my back, and I cried out.

"Stop!"

Choi Su-nim's voice froze the crowd. He descended the stairs with his old man's dignity. Cameras chattered, recorders whirred, the reporters waited for him to be dramatic.

He waved his cane. "Please do not disrupt her," he said, "while she performs the poom-sey on the curb. Please."

I stepped to the curb and raised the long shimmering sword. Looking up the blade, I saw two helicopters chopping the air over the park. I lowered my eyes to the crowd.

"To be safe," I said, "do not come close to this blade. Thank you."

Some of the newspeople converged on Choi Su-nim, some followed me as I moved along the cool steel crown of the gutter. They respected my warning, but others peppered Choi Su-nim with questions that faded from my hearing. What's a poom-sey? Why is she doing this? What's the purpose? How long? Why?

Inside and outside me were alike. Pain. Pain slashed across my shoulders, down my spine, shot through my hamstrings and buttocks like electric shocks, fire brands, hot pokers. Lights flashed, cameras clicked, chattered, whirred, horns honked, people shouted, pointed, voices spiked the air, helicopters chopped overhead. Shop workers on Bayard Street stopped to watch. The walks were always crowded, cars parked wheels to the curb, but the newspeople flooded the street, traffic came to a standstill, horns bleated. Windows opened, heads of black hair popped out and housewives talked back and forth.

I passed the ice cream store and travelled by the bakery, the terrific din echoing in the narrow slot of Mott Street. A policeman's motorcycle spuddered, mopeds beeped, trucks honked, engines rumbled, and a trucker cursed as the big cameras on tripods rolled along the street in front of his bumper. I advanced slowly along the curb, a tide of churning newspeople, traffic, and noise roiling along with me.

I reached the fence before the school and church, black iron pikes, where the clattering cameras were noisier than a flock of pigeons bursting up from the pavement.

A cameraman said, "Against the fence, she's beautiful. Beautiful!"

How many pictures do they need? The cameras snapped and filled Mosco Street with chatter. They were like a single beast chugging and lurching along beside me, down Mosco, along Mulberry, until I finished the poom-sey. Reporters shoved microphones at me: Is komdo a cult?

I ignored them. I climbed the four steps, my body not so painful, and when I stood before the chest I performed the ceremony to return the sword to the purple silk. As I straightened from that final task I realized, even with the pain—maybe because of the pain—my whole body tingled. I felt like a billion shivering granules molded into the shape of a human body.

Choi Su-nim sat in his office, his hands folded on his desk. I bowed in the doorway. "May I come in, sir?"

Students talked quietly in the changing room. I closed the door. He asked, "Did they bother you?"

"A little. Well...when they stopped traffic all the drivers got mad. That distracted me." The corners of his mouth lifted in amusement. My big toes were getting calloused, white on the side. I said, "I wanted to talk about what happened on the curb yesterday. I'm...confused."

"Violence is often confusing."

"But Choi Su-nim, I was almost the one who was violent." I gazed down at the holes worn in the carpet before his desk. "When Craig kicked Ricky I stopped doing the poom-sey. I was going to cut his head off. I was going to kill Craig."

The humor was gone from his mouth. He gazed at me, but I

couldn't read his eyes. He took a deep breath and exhaled slowly.

"I tried to keep Ricky from leaving the dojang, but he disobeyed me. For that reason, he is barred from here." I looked up from the foot-shaped holes in the carpet. Choi Su-nim sat unruffled. He said, "I called and told him that he was not to come here again."

From the changing room came the tink tink of a belt buckle, the jingle of pocket change. Ricky barred too? I remembered how it shocked Craig to be barred, and while Ricky was only a yellow belt I knew he loved komdo.

"Please" I said, "don't kick him out. I was the cause of it. It was a strange situation, it won't happen again."

Choi Su-nim shook his head. "Doesn't matter. And you should feel lucky Ricky will not be coming here."

"Lucky? Why? I feel awful!"

He gave me a few moments to settle.

"You are committed to a path," he said. "You must have unbending intent. You cannot strike with both edges of a blade at the same time."

"He won't disobey you." I didn't understand what he meant, but I was focused on Ricky's loss, and my own, that Ricky would not be there with me. "And I won't be disobeying Appa-nim anymore, when I come down here." I shrugged at the curiosity of it. "All of a sudden he changed his mind."

"How is he handling all this?"

"All right, I think." A spasm of pain darted down the back of my leg. "Why did he change so suddenly?"

Choi Su-nim rose from behind his desk. Leaning on its edge, he came around to me.

"Fear drives us to resist, but the Tao is a relentless teacher. It rains, the streets are scoured, the gutter is washed clean."

The door creaked as he opened it. He gave me a glance full of encouragement and the glistening lights of humor, and closed the door. In the still quiet of his office I thought, when did it start to rain?

Then I untied my black sash, already old and faded though I was only seventeen.

After I changed into my jeans, sneakers, and two shirts—I carried a bra with me, but it was too painful to wear—I opened the door. I bowed to Choi Su-nim and he bowed to me.

"By the way," he said, "a hint. Cameras don't work if you're too close to them."

Why tell me that? "Thank you, sir. Good night."

When I opened the door I realized why he told me that. The newspeople were massed and waiting for me. So...what about being too close? Men flicked cigarettes into the gutter, rushed forward, raised their cameras, lights flashed, they jammed around the steps. I looked down at them, camcorders on shoulders, rolling cameras, women with pads of paper, pens, microphones, cameras. I skipped down the steps, shutters chattered, shouts, large faces, big lips, eyes wide to engulf me.

They were a heaving mass, one slow-moving many-headed beast. I leaned close to the snapping, biting shutters, and when I got too close the people behind the lenses had to pull back. A man shouted, "Back up!" as I stooped and burrowed between two pairs of pants. Another man shouted, "Where'd she go?" He threw himself backward, "Back up!" and someone swore and shouted, "Son-of-a!"

The beast split apart, heaved against itself, scrambled to expose me. Curses, grunts. "My foot!" Hips, legs, knees, I scuttled. Shuffling feet, shouts. A rift opened among the shoes. Bare cement. I ran. Clattering machines, a herd of footsteps, shouts, rustling cloth. An old man laughed from his doorway. I ran. Up Bayard Street? No, can't. Trucks with satellite dishes sat along the curb, cars double-parked at the corner. Beyond the gap between car bumpers an orange taxi blocked me, I slowed, and the herd caught me.

The door of the taxi swung open. "Kee!"

Ricky? I ran between bumpers and jumped into the cab.

He shouted, "Go!"

Tires squeeled and the door slammed as the cab jumped up Bayard Street. We were thrown back against the seat. Ricky grunted, I gasped in pain, but he laughed, and I laughed and cried out as we jostled against each other. I quickly rolled to lift my back off the seat. Or was it to face him? My arm fell across his, on the seat, and our fingers laced together. He squeezed my hand gently.

"Where you wanna go?" The cabbie was a chocolate man with thick dreadlocks flopping over his shoulders. "Where you wanna go now?"

We reached the top of Bayard Street. Ricky said, "Anywhere."

He looked at me with joy. We leaned together and kissed. Our mouths met with wet fire. I kissed him with a hunger for his breathing, the heat of him, all of him, I wanted all of him. He kissed me urgently, our mouths rubbed and clutched together like halves of a fruit trying to be whole again. He groaned. I kissed him and mumbled, "Tang shinl...sarang...heyo."

"Ow!" he said. "Watch it, my ribs."

"Sorry. Ow!"

"Your back?" Holding each other gingerly, close together, he looked deeply into me as I saw the goldfish swimming way down in his eyes. He asked, "Tang what?"

The taxi lurched, we swayed, and the cabbie called, "Yoo hoo, lovebirds. This meter be running and I don't wanna be fightin with you about the fare. Where you wanna go now?"

I kissed Ricky. "I love you. Ricky Tibb, I love you."

"I love you too." We kissed with mouths of sweet heat. "Kee, I love you so much."

"Yoo hoo!" The cabbie rapped on the plastic divider. "Come up for air. Love doves, now tell me where to go. Where to, huh?"

"Seventh Street and Avenue A." Ricky stuffed a bill into the slot. "Take your time."

"No problem. Baby needs new running shoes. Okay birds, twenty dollars, twenty minutes on the meter now."

The cabbie stuffed the bill into his shirt, the taxi lurched, we settled back on the seat, and I don't remember riding uptown. The taxi hummed around us. Ricky's arms went around me. "Ow!"

"Sorry." His breath whispered steamy silk across my ears, his hands warm to my throat, his chin smooth, and the moisture of my mouth glowed around his lips. Three hundred kisses, a liquid bond, glinting gold, and the pains from his hands on my back were delicious.

Our humming love cab went still. I gazed past Ricky and noticed the trees. Thompkins Square Park. The taxi sat at the curb fifty feet from the corner of St. Mark's Place.

The cabbie rapped on the divider. "Hey!" He wasn't shouting at us. "Hey!"

By our window there was one big eye. Lightning flashed. A woman lowered her camera. "Gotcha!"

"Ricky, I love you!"

I scrambled out and ran, ran and thought, he loves me! Joy burst out of me, I laughed, and as the news people stormed me I didn't care because Ricky shouted, "Tang shinl! Sarang heyo! I love you too!"

Chapter 26

Columbus Park covered a city block with basketball courts, cracked tar paths, trees, scraggly bushes, benches, and a band stand that for a long time had been too old and rickety to hold a band. A mulberry tree had grown clumped against its side, paint peeling off the wall, dirt and a bum's ratty blanket at the bottom. There I waited, hidden by the scraggly bushes.

I leaned to peek out. On Mulberry Street the schooling news barracudas swam about, waiting for me, smoking cigarettes, checking their equipment. "Kee?"

I turned and there he was. "Ricky!" I threw myself into his arms, he gasped, I groaned, and our pain was our pleasure. We kissed and he whispered, "Tang shinl...sarang heyo!"

"I love you too!" We rubbed and struggled and hurt and kissed and clung and clutched as if we were starving for each other. "I love you too, Ricky, I do. I do!"

I held him tenderly, his ribs sensitive. His hands hurt my back, but it felt like the pain of healing. We kissed, our wet lips became the greedy center of the world, and the smell of cologne he stole from his father's cabinet and the spices of his skin made my thoughts swirl and I was unable to think.

Anxiety woke all over me. I didn't want to, but I broke our lips apart and looked at him. "Ricky I, I must tell you something. Two thing."

"What?" His hands slid down to my hips to pull me firmly against himself. I loved his face, his brows like caterpillars inching over the humor glistening in his eyes, his cute nose sloping down to his sweet lips. I loved even his big white teeth. "What? I love you, what?"

"I ask Choi Su-nim to take you back."

He hummed in his throat. I pushed against him gently. He looked me in the eyes. We kissed and he wanted to kiss more, but the anxious feeling gathered below my stomach. I broke the kiss and so he whispered in my ear, "What's the second thing? You had two things to tell me."

My breath caught on the desire in my throat. I said, "I go to see the Distric' Attorney tomorrow."

Ricky's lips pursed, his jaw hardened. "Don't let him talk you out of it."

I blinked. "Out of what?"

"Pressing charges. Craig's daddy is the Assistant D.A., they're gonna beg you to drop the charges. He beat the crap out of you, so don't you dare!"

His anger was so loud and sharp I leaned back out of his arms, a version of Ricky I never saw before.

"I am gonna nail him," he snapped. "He'll get his face fixed, he won't suffer because of that, so he'll get off scot free." A spell was broken, different anxiety woke in me, and I glanced out of the bushes. Footsteps. Ricky was too caught in his anger to notice. "Now I can't practice komdo because of him. It's because of Craig I got kicked out, so the hell with him!"

Shoes. It was a man with a camera whose shutter teeth started chattering. "Get the hell out of here!" Ricky jumped out of the bushes and pushed the photographer. I bolted out past him and ran. Ricky shouted, "Leave us alone! Kee!"

Grey path, curves, old man feeding pigeons, and a flock of grey exploded up around me, wings slapping my legs. The newspeople were a mass of grey beyond the fence, stirring with metal glints, equipment angles. They weren't ready to see me, I think, because I charged through a gate in the fence, dodged, hit one, rolled off his hip, barged through a few more, flew over the walk, leaped up the four steps. Breathing hard, I stopped between the inner and outer doors.

Muffled steps, trapped air, and I let the camera lovers chatter their teeth and take pictures of me.

Why don't they just go!

Breathing slower, calmer but worried, I stepped into the cool stillness of Choi Su-nim's dojang. I kicked off my shoes and bowed to the flags. I was too long in the park with Ricky and hurried to fill the bucket. I dunked the mop, slung it over the floorboards, the pain that hid under my shoulder blade slipped its tooth into me, but the rust of dead blood was much broken up and washed out of my back. The shell of my turtle self was almost whole again.

I couldn't focus on mopping. Anxiety lingered in my throat and body, the buzz of lust in my fingertips, and I thought of what Choi Su-nim said: two edges of one sword. Strike with one edge or the other. I realized what he meant: romance or komdo. I finished mopping and rolled the bucket of grey water across the shining floor.

Does that mean Way of the Dawning Sword is like love? Love for whom?

After knocking, I opened the office door to find Choi Su-nim looking disturbed. I bowed. "Sir? Is something wrong?"

He tilted his head to the left, then to the right, as if looking at something from different angles. "I got a call from the Chinatown Association. Close the door."

Other students were already coming in. "The Chinatown Association? What's that?"

"A political group for Chinatown, an umbrella organization, really, for the tongs. The tongs are like big gangs, and they can be violent. But the Association said that they want you to press charges against Craig. They want him to go to jail."

"He beat me with a stick, twice. He should go to jail. Shouldn't he?"

"Maybe. For the right reasons." The wrinkles on his forehead deepened. "It's not simple. The Association wants Craig to go to jail because he's the son of the Assistant D.A. The D.A., Kenneth

Graham, is in the middle of a re-election campaign. The Association has proposed legislation to the City Council, but Mr. Graham has always been against it. So the Association wants to discredit him. They want you to press charges against Craig to make the D.A. look bad, hoping that he'll lose the election."

"Oh. That must be why his secretary called me." The woman sounded like the pay phone voice asking me to deposit more money. "I go see him tomorrow morning, the D.A. But I don't understand. Auntie Yen told me that people don't press charges, that the Distric' Attorney's office decides who gets them pressed." The door from the changing room clapped shut as students came out; it was time for class. I opened my hands. "Why are they asking me? It's not my decision."

"Yes, it is." He rose from behind his desk. "It happened in Chinatown, it's legally separate." He opened the door. "We'll talk more later."

From that class I recall Choi Su-nim's clapping hands. White lines, feet and hands slap slap, strike and shout, *ha!* Hissing bamboos, tan blurs, my heaving lungs, shouts, echoes, then my solo Tiger and so lonely Crane, and that was class. I lifted the ceremonial sword off the purple silk shelf in the chest. I bowed to the four directions, clothing rustled, and little boys let their bones thump on the floor, sitting to meditate as I kowtowed to the silent center.

When I opened the door over Mulberry Street the sky opened over the park, blue, cloudless. I was surprised. The newspeople converged, but unlike before they let me step into Choon-be Stance on the curb. I raised the sword. Cameras started to snap, click-clatter zipzipzip, I pivoted, wheeled the sword overhead, and camcorders hummed as I rose to the peak of Crane Stance.

I floated along the steel edge, the center of a churning mass of people, machines, noise that roiled along the curb, swallowed cars, filled the walk, spilled around the corner mailbox and the lamp post like a stream around a rock and a stick. It was different, as if the newspeople had become a cooperating part. I neared the markets where the fishmongers and housewives dickered. My joints ached. I wheeled the flashing steel spoke. My shoulders rankled, the heavy steel blade flashed over my head, and I realized all the cars along Bayard Street were parked a foot away from the curb. All around the block the curb was swept clean.

The people of Chinatown were taking care of me.

The pains in my body, the pull of my muscles, the weight of the sword that tightened the cords of my arms, shoulders, and back, were already routine endurable pains. Chinatown flowed around me. The air eddied against my elbows and knees. I noticed small details I could not before. A gum wrapper fluttered, caught in a crack. Marigolds rustled in a window box. The breeze drove a tuft of pigeon down along the pavement. Shoes clomped, the tuft rolled, no one stepped on it. On Mosco Street a banana peel draped over the edge of a garbage can shivered. I reached Mulberry Street. The invisible energy of the breeze swished the trees in the park, and somewhere someone was cooking persimmons. The sweet aroma gusted around me as I lowered the sword.

Pandemonium broke. Ms. Ahn, Kee, over here! What drugs? who? how long? what charges? But I scampered up the four steps and let the doors silence their shouts.

Choi Su-nim was in his office, the door open. Uptown boys, dressed in expensive polo shirts, bowed to the flags, to me, and pulled on their sneakers. Choi Su-nim came out of his office. I wiped the sword and lay it on the purple silk. He watched me close the teak chest, then we stepped into his office.

He nodded. "How is your back?"

I was relaxed and calm, my hands loose at my sides. "Much better, sir."

He leaned over his cane. I felt his *nun-chi* probe me. "And the newspeople?"

I dipped my chin. "Not a bother, sir. Not really."

"Uh-hmm." He gazed at me, his eyes distorted by his bifocal lenses, and I looked at the floor peacefully. I waited for him to speak about the charges against Craig, immediate concerns, but instead he spoke with a vibrance in his voice that stirred in my chest.

"Did Peng Su-nim discuss the Tao with you?"

"Only that one time, sir, after I walked the waterfall." He raised his grey brows to encourage me. "That's when he told me to trust in the Tao, and that whatever is in accord with the Tao will not be thrown down by conflict."

He said, "Uh-hmm." A su-nim is someone who has special knowledge. Choi Su-nim had special knowledge of the Tao. He asked, "What is it? What is the Tao?"

"The Tao?" I looked at the worn carpet in front of his desk. I said, "All things?"

He shook his head.

"It's easier to say what the Tao isn't, than what it is." He was standing so close to me I smelled the bleach of his dobuck. "The Tao is not matter, the physical world, what they have called the ten thousand things. The Tao is not the genetic code in living things. Do you know about D.N.A.?" I nodded. He said, "The genetic code did not start itself, it was started by something else—but the Tao is also not that initial urge to organize."

"The Tao is not our bodies, and it isn't the animating force in the body, *chi* energy. The Tao is not big Mind or little mind. The Tao is not thought or emotion. The Tao is not the ego or the unconscious, the spirit or the soul; it's not religion, culture or government, the family, the clan, any of that social ordering. The Tao is not good or bad, right or wrong, yin or yang. The Tao is not God, Yahweh, Shiva, or Visnu, Brahmin, or any other deity. The Tao is not those because it is all of those, and more. In fact, the Tao is not even the Tao."

All the other students had left so that when he stopped speaking the silence flowed in to immerse us. I stirred that liquid by saying, "If the Tao is not the Tao, what is it?"

He leveled his glance on me. I felt the power of his presence, and I would've been unnerved except there was his kindness and sense of humor. He said, "'Tao' is a word for what cannot be contained by the human mind. Tao is unknowable."

I glanced up at him. "If the Tao is unknowable, sir, how do we know it's there?"

He smiled, and I felt him release me. He said, "The Tao cannot be comprehended, but it can be experienced. You chose a practice through which you experience the Tao. Way of the Dawning Sword. And you felt it today. Didn't you."

I didn't realize until then, but instinctively I knew. "Yes, on the curb. The newspeople, and people who live here, and me, and even how the breeze made a banana peel shiver, I knew everything was working together. That's why...that's why the newspeople didn't bother me."

He nodded. "The Tao cannot be known, but it can be experienced." He leaned on his cane, he was tired, and I saw the toll our difficulties had taken on him. "That's why I told you that Tao means 'to express.' You experience Tao when it is being expressed through you, and through others, unimpeded. There is no waste for the Tao, no accidents. There is a reason behind every change."

"Then there was a reason Ricky disobeyed you. When Craig kicked Ricky it got the street singer to hit Craig with the bottle. So could you forgive Ricky and let him study here again? He won't disobey you, I know he won't."

Choi Su-nim shook his head. "The Tao brings everything into balance. It did not need Ricky's interruption. Craig was drunk on rage and the street singer was drunk on wine. They do what they do out of fear and anger, which come from their sickness. Craig and the street singer—his name is Francis Junior. He's the son of a famous artist—their fears brought them into conflict with the Tao. The result? Each cancelled out the other." He nodded, regret weighing on the corners of his mouth. "Painful return to balance."

He glanced at my bag, my clothes stuffed inside. I said, "Why shouldn't Craig go to jail? He beat me with a stick, twice. Shouldn't he be punished for beating me?"

"Wasn't he? He's in the hospital." He exhaled slowly. "By the way, have you seen the *Village Voice?*"

"The what?"

He slipped a newspaper out of his desk and turned it to face me. On the front page was a picture of a woman in panties and a bra, taken from behind, her white clothing lifted to her neck and dropped to her knees. I leaned close, squinting. The picture was black and white, grainy, but what made the woman look odd were the dark blotches and stripes that crossed her ribs, that marred her buttocks.

My mouth opened. Me? Naked on the front page?

"I hope Appa-nim doesn't see that!" I straightened and stepped back, then leaned forward to look. "What does it say?"

"The truth." He showed me the long article. "It says everything is sensitive because the D.A. is running for re-election." There were columns of tiny print and pictures of me, Ricky, Craig, and Francis Bonnarotti Junior, who they called the Fallen Rock Star.

Everyone is seeing me with my clothes off!

Reading me, Choi Su-nim closed the newspaper. "How is your father?"

The sudden change of subject caught me unprepared. "He can't stand having the store closed so we're opening tomorrow, no matter what."

Choi Su-nim nodded and turned to shuffle out. "You have to get home and trim lettuce."

As he closed the door I said, "Yes sir," and started to untie my sash. As I pulled on my pants the cord-like welts embedded in my buttocks, the most painful reminders, pulled and went slack. I turned over the newspaper to hide the picture, shouldered my bag, opened the door, and said, "Good night, sir."

"Good night, Kee."

Outside the door, the questions peppered me. Kee-Yong! Which drugs? Over here! Which guy? Who did you screw? Kee! Kee! I put my head down and leaned to push my way through their filthy thoughts of me. Bayard Street was crowded, I lost the mob in the traffic, and on Elizabeth Street Ling met me at the corner of Canal Street.

"Did you see?" she shouted. "The *Village Voice* is talking about you!"

I touched her arm. "Not so loud."

"Why not?" We scurried past shop windows too bright for my comfort and down the dank subway stairwell blotched by green and white lichens. I gave Ling a brass token and used one of my own. She asked, "Why not tell everyone? They'll want your autograph, and pay you for it."

"My autograph? Don't be dumb."

On the subway people never spoke to each other, so I didn't worry about that; but as I glanced down the car, empty but for a man in army surplus green, black leather punk rockers, tired old men and women, I had to wonder. Did she see me naked? Did he?

At least I wasn't wearing my black bra that night. Ling was irritated that I called her dumb. We stepped off the train and she hurried up the stairs ahead of me. The night air lay warm in the streets, heavy and resistant, and Ling hummed to herself as we passed the black cube balanced in Astor Place.

I'll wear the black one for Ricky. Yes, I love Ricky Tibbs!

Ling and I skipped across the wide light of First Avenue, then slowed in the shadows and weak lamp light on St. Mark's Place. Our street ended with the trees of Thompkins Square Park, and before our store were the crowding newsmen. Ling asked, "Through Shirley's?"

I nodded, and when we could we stayed beneath the hard luck trees, in and out of their jigsaw puzzles of shadow. I dropped my chin and kept my glance on the sidewalk. We veered toward Super Redsy's stoop. They weren't seeing us. We skipped up the stone steps.

A man at the top. Two steps to go. The man stepped in front of us. "Where you going?" Wild grey hair, crazy eyes, crisscross teeth, a stubbly chin. Not a newsman, but he shouted, "You can't fool us. I know who you are!"

Ling hissed, "Let us go in."

"You're *not* gettin' in my building." A knife appeared in his hand. He waved it near my nose and shouted, "This is mine! My country! America for Americans!"

Chapter 27

The knife glimmered, sliced the air near my nose, and I leaned back from the crazy man on Super Redsy's stoop. He shouted, "I fought you! In Korea!"

Down the sidewalk, a newsman saw us. "Don't!"

The crazy man waved the knife like he was conducting music. "I'm an American. We're everywhere! And I...uh..."

He swallowed as all the newspeople rushed on the walk, flooded up the steps, lights flashed, motors hummed, a hundred shutters clattered a thousand times, and for once the shouting helped me. You're on TV! Hey! Put it down! Hey pal! He swallowed, the stubble on his throat jerked, and he looked confused. Put! down! the knife! Snapclatterbite, lightning, whir and hum, he was dumbfounded by the nightly news.

Super Redsy opened the door. His overalls were unsnapped and the bib flapped below his waist.

"Clarence," he shouted, "what in god's name are you doing!" He snatched the knife out of Clarence's hand, shoved him against the wall, "Girls, get inside," and shouted at the newspeople, "Beat it! What do you think this is, a circus?"

We ran down the hall toward Shirley, standing in her doorway, who called, "Clarence, you half-wit!" as she ushered us in. "Hey, Ringa-Ling-Ling."

"Hi, Shirley!"

We ran down the hall of her railroad flat, into her bedroom, to the open window. After a moment we were across the roof and climbing the step ladder we'd left below my window.

"Thanks, Shirley!"

"Any time, girls."

After I waved to her from inside our bedroom I dropped my bag and let myself breathe. Ling giggled as she skipped into the kitchen. She yanked open a drawer by the sink. "I'm gonna make some cherry stuff!"

I crept down the stairs into the dim storage room. I stopped and glanced around. One milky light bulb. Cobwebs rippling among the ceiling pipes. Hm. Scabby concrete walls, dry sink, dull tubers in a box, bright fruits, cases of soda. Something was new and quiet. The floor lay bare, clean and dry around two crates, my makeshift seat and an empty catcher for the trimmings. Clean, still, waiting. I tapped my foot in the puddle below the sink, plish plish.

"Appa?" What new silence had found the storage room? "Appa-nim?"

I walked out into the lighted store. He was cleaning the bins empty along the wall, rag in hand. "You're back. Any trouble?"

"Some. Should I wash potatoes?"

"Tag soda, get it by the cooler." We had salvaged thirty wrapped heads of lettuce by stuffing them into the soda cooler. "You'll have time to re-trim that lettuce, it needs it again, before you go downtown. Are you nervous about seeing the D.A.?"

I nodded. "Behind every tiger is the tiger's mother. Or its father. That's what Mansin With a Bump said."

"Bumpkin with a bump. I'm opening up after you leave." As if I'll cause trouble? I tagged and stacked cases of soda. He said, "I got rid of the old grapefruit today." He shook his head. "But even bag ladies don't want wilted flowers."

"Kee! Appa!" We hurried into the storage room. Ling shouted from the top of the stairs, "We're on TV already!"

We ran up. In the living room a TV commercial showed a sleek car taking curves. A news lady appeared. *The story for Newsbreak at Nine: Generosity and craziness.*

"Appa, it's you!"

Ling pointed and laughed as the TV showed him walking through the gates of the park, a box in his arms. *Unable to open his store since trouble began for his family, Ki-Teh Ahn showed us what generosity is all about.* On screen Appa-nim handed grapefruit to men huddled in boxes. His face appeared, the wrinkles of suffering plain. *Cannot open to sell fruit—too nuts here, huh?—so it gotta go.* He lifted his eyebrows. *Right?*

The insanity worsened tonight. While coming home from their nightly visit to Chinatown, Ahn's daughters were accosted at knife point. On screen, Clarence the Korean War veteran waved his knife, Ling and I frozen on the steps.

Appa-nim's mouth fell open. "Kee, you didn't tell me! Again!"

"But… Appa-nim?"

He threw up his hands, his face red, but he was too upset to speak and slammed the bathroom door, the air buzzing as the lady said, *Trouble began for the family when...*

I turned off the TV. Silence. Ling and I looked over at the closed bathroom door. She blew out a ragged whistle, shrugged, and said, "Want some cherry stuff?"

I didn't see him again that night.

The next morning I skipped down the stairs to help unload a truck and he was back to his normal self. "Empty the cooler!" A box smacked the walk. "Re-trim the lettuce!"

Gladly. I settled on my crate and took up my old friend, the knife. Slats squeaked under me as I raised a head of lettuce, cold from the cooler. I love Ricky. I twisted, the blade glimmered, and clutched around the heart, leaves edged with dark rot fell into a crate with humble sounds of loss. The head was pale green, cool, perfect, but not much left to it. What happens if I trim away all the leaves?

I unwrapped all the heads and started anew. Grab, twist, wrap-and-toss. My rhythm quickened. Grab, twist'n'slash'n'wrap'n'toss. Slice away all the leaves? Twisslice, slashsheet, wrap'n'toss. I'd be left twisting and slicing the air. Doing komdo. I glanced at the crates of sweet fresh lettuce stacked around me. Witnesses. They'd watch me make a dojang out of a storage room.

"Kee?" Umma called down from the kitchen. "Come up and get dressed." I lay down the knife and went up. "Hurry, we don't want to be late. I have to be at work by twelve. Why he has to open the store I don't know."

The telephone rang.

"Hello?" I listened to her voice as I pulled a dress over my head. "Yes, it is." I slipped into the black shoes that squeezed my toes. "Oh, okay. When?" I stepped out as Umma nodded and hung up the phone. She wore a knowing look. "He really wants you as a friend. The Distric' Attorney is sending his personal limousine."

And two police cruisers. Four uniformed policemen made a rift through the newspeople, and we ran and leaped into the long black car. It stank of new leather, the two seats in the back facing each other.

Umma snorted. "Police escort? He really wants you."

The blue and white cruisers rode before and behind us. People rushing on the walks, or crossing the street, stopped and watched us go by. They couldn't see in the tinted windows, see it was just us, so the whole show felt like something false.

Umma nodded knowingly. "He wants you to see things from his point of view."

There were telephones between the seats, and in the center of the carpeted floor stood a small bar with glasses, red wine, bottles of liquor, a radio and CD player on top. "I wish Auntie was here."

"The Ambassador is in town." She opened the refrigerator, took out a can of Coke and opened it. "Are you nervous?"

"Aren't you?"

My bird-like mother fluttered her hand. "We got the tiger by the tail. Is this it?"

The limousine nosed through a stone archway and stopped inside a parking garage. The chauffeur, wearing a brown business suit and tie, opened the door and we got out as three policemen appeared from the cruisers. The six of us shuffled into an elevator, mute, and I smelled a cigar. The butt of a policeman's pistol stuck out of his holster. The wood was carved with a cross-hatched pattern and the trigger shone blue. The gun made me nervous, or maybe the elevator made my stomach flutter. Numbers over the door lit up right to the highest, 34.

As the doors opened Umma said to a policeman, "Hold this," gave him the empty soda can and stepped out.

My shoes sank into a blood-red carpet. Office doors stood closed, faces of cherry wood polished and glossy, with bright brass knobs. The woman who strode toward us looked two feet taller than Umma, her hair coiled high, and she wore two golden roses on the lapel of her jacket. She nodded and smiled.

"Mister Graham is expecting you." She led us down the carpet, her neck long like a swan on parade. "Can I get you something to drink? Coffee? Tea?"

Gazing at the molded trim along the ceiling, Umma whispered, "No thank you."

I gawked too, feeling small and trivial among all that wealth and power. Then the secretary with the golden roses knocked on a door, opened it, and let us into an office.

"Mister Graham?" He looked up from papers on a wide green blotter on a broad oak desk. The woman said, "Mrs. Ahn, Kee-Yong, this is Mister Graham, the District Attorney."

"Thank you, Sarah." Mister Graham, the District Attorney of Manhattan, stood up and said, "Come in, come in." He was tall and handsome, with salt and pepper hair, thick brows, and his cheeks had not sagged as he aged. His jacket opened to show a tawny shirt, a striped tie, and a tie clasp with a gem like a tiger's yellow eye. "Can I get you some coffee?" he asked. I noticed that behind the tiger's eye his chest was sunken, as if he had no heart to fill it. "Tea?"

Umma said, "No thank you," and settled into a chair he suggested, with carved wooden arms and thick cushions that made her look as small as a child. I sat too, and glanced back as the door closed. A small studious woman and a chubby man came to the side of the desk and sat down. I cannot remember that man except for his lips like a grouper fish. But the woman had a high rounded forehead that looked hard like a pestle for Mister Graham's mortar, as if together they ground their enemies to dust.

Was I their enemy? Didn't look like it. Mister Graham, the most powerful policeman in New York City, opened his manicured hand toward the other two.

"This is Mr. Paulson, our translator, and my associate in this matter, Ms. North." He spoke, then Mr. Paulson's grouper lips opened and droned out his textbook Hangugo.

"The charges against Craig Donafrio are serious," he said, "and the prosecution—that's what we do—is complicated by several factors. The first factor is, obviously, that Craig is the son of the Assistant District Attorney. That makes the circumstances difficult for everyone here." He leaned on his desk and gazed at me. "However, Kee, I promise you that we are not going to spare Craig Donafrio because his father works in this office. Craig deserves equal treatment under the law, and the charges are serious." His hands were large, clean, and squid-belly white. He saw me looking at them and straightened. "The second complication—"

"What are the charges against Craig?" Umma asked.

Mister Graham settled his wide hips into his chair. Somehow, he still looked large.

"The charges? Two counts of aggravated assault, stemming from his beatings of Kee-Yong," he said, "and one count of assault and battery with a deadly weapon, due to his use of martial arts against Richard Tibbs." He nodded. "They're misdemeanors, but the one Mr. Tibbs will be filing is Class A, the most serious. Craig has significant legal difficulties. But as I was saying, the second complication adheres because the alleged offenses took place in Chinatown."

I said, "Alleged offenses? What's that?"

Mister Graham's hair rippled as he glanced over at the grouper-lips interpreter.

"We call an offense 'alleged' until someone is found guilty, at which time it becomes a conviction and a fact under the law." Umma nodded, I nodded, and Mister Graham continued. "But the complication here is that Chinatown is an ethnic enclave, and as such it's been granted a special status. It's called a LLEZ, a Limited Local Enforcement Zone. In other words, because of the..." He shifted in his chair. "...the predominance of Asian ethnicities there, the area is somewhat self-governing. This office cannot press certain kinds of charges there, those involving cultural activities such as walking the curb. That's why you're here, Kee-Yong. You have to press charges against Craig Donafrio."

Ms. North offered him a manila folder with papers in it. He opened the folder; but before he could speak I spoke.

"Choi Su-nim told me," I said, "about the Chinese Association. He said they want you to throw Craig in jail. For a long time."

Mister Graham shot a glance at Ms. North, as if I had dropped a piece of the Chinese Association into their pestle and mortar. Then he lied to me.

"Yes," he said, "the Association and I are old friends, we often work together. That's true in this case too. Now, Kee, if you'll sign here, we'll begin legal proceedings against Craig." He compressed his lips as he set the folder before me, then he looked away. "These are serious charges against him."

The paper was there in front of me. Ms. North poked a pen into my hand as I looked at the paper. Silence. They sat there and looked at me, Umma, the interpreter with his closed grouper lips, cold Ms. North, and Mister Graham, the most powerful policeman in the city.

My stomach felt wrong. The room was silent. They looked at me. Umma pointed to an X. "Go ahead," she said, "sign it," and so I did.

The wrong feeling grew stronger as Ms. North gathered the papers. The folder vanished. I noted her satisfaction.

"Will Craig go to jail?" I asked.

For the first time Ms. North spoke.

"Oh yes." Her eyes widened, as if she welcomed the idea. "These are certain convictions. Yes," she said, "Craig will be going away for quite some time." She sent a sharp glance to Mister Graham. "Especially in light of the current political climate. But I must be going. Thank you for coming, Kee." She rose, stuck out her hand, grabbed my hand and shook it. "We'll notify you about court dates and your testimony. Thank you."

She and the grouper lips interpreter were gone out the door by the time Umma and I struggled out of the big chairs and stood up. Mister Graham led us to the doorway. I stopped there and asked, "Did Ricky Tibb...um...press charges?"

He looked eight feet tall, a tiger's eye in the middle of his empty chest.

"I'm certain he will," he said. "The family attorney hasn't been available, however, so they won't be coming in until next week. By the way..." His voice dropped to a private tone. "...it took a hundred and sixty-two stitches to close the cuts on Craig's face, and he also lost his right eye."

I whispered it. "He lose his eye?"

Umma spoke in Hangugo. She looked up at the most powerful policeman in New York City and said, "When a house burns down you also get rid of the roaches." Mister Graham didn't know Hangugo, but he understood her tone of voice.

He blinked.

"Kee," Umma said, "let's go."

Chapter 28

Umma flagged down a taxi. As it approached I said, "What did you mean about the roaches?"

She carefully checked the seat for dirt and stains—she was wearing her red dress for work—then she got in and scooted across to make room for me. The cab smelled of moldy plastic. I pulled the door shut. The cab lurched ahead.

She said to the cabbie, "Avenue A and Six Street."

"Umma? What did you mean?"

"About what?"

"How you get rid of the cockroaches when you burn down the house."

She opened her pocket book. "You press charges and you get rid of him. What do you think I meant?" She raised a silver plastic tube and twisted it until a tip of rose red lipstick appeared. I stared at her. "Your father knows I wear it, I told him. Mr. Bobby asked me to."

She colored her lips, then popped open a tiny case with a mirror. I said, "What about the house I'm burning down? What house?"

"It's just an old saying, you know that." There was a tiny foam brush in the case, rows of colors. She dabbed a red tablet and feathered her cheek bones. "Eat the salt, drink the water, that's what I should've said. Beat people, go to jail." Her mind snapped shut as she closed the compact, snap, and dropped it into her pocketbook. "Why?" I gazed out the window. The cab rattled onto the Bowery, which was lined with rough buildings and struggling shops. "He beat you black and blue. He deserves to go to jail for that, doesn't he? Didn't it hurt?"

"But he lost his eye."

"That's what he deserved."

The cab turned onto Sixth Street, into Little India. A man wearing a purple turban strolled past McSorley's, an old pub squeezed between windows painted with Hindu mosques. Ceramic elephants stood on ledges, and then we neared the restaurant for the deaf, Bobby's Place.

"Mr. Bobby's joke," she said. A wrist watch was painted on the window. "We got Thai-Mex food, named after an American watch, ha ha." She rapped on the plastic divider. "Stop here!"

"Here?" The little cabbie had a spotted bald head, his ears prickly with white hairs. "Didn't you say Avenue A?"

"I say here, wise guy, so you stop." She stuffed a ten dollar bill into the slot. "Now to Avenue A and Nine Street. You hear?" She switched to Hangugo. "They always act like I'm stupid." She climbed out, let in smells of rice and curry, and fluttered her hand goodbye. "Be careful at the store!"

She slammed the door, then I watched my changed mother drive herself with strides across the walk. In Nun-yo she never wore lipstick, and she never screeched. The cab rattled me away.

Maybe I was feeling badly, but the image of Craig on the cobblestones of Mott Street, blood streaming from around the shards of glass stuck in his face, came back to upset me. He lost that eye…forever. Sadness touched me like a fingertip. And he will go to jail. On my say so.

I felt such sadness at the pains my body suffered, Ricky's pain, and Craig's too, that I began to cry.

Didn't last long. The cabbie scratched his hairy ear and said, "I aint drivin' into that mess."

Police cars, splashing red lights, a clog of people around our corner. "Uh-oh." What now? Traffic guards waved cars away, east along the park, so the cabbie stopped us by Eighth Street. I sighed and got out. When is this going to end? Dreadfully I walked toward the crowd. People craned their necks to see what was going on. No one looked at me, a nobody Asian girl in a dress and clacky tacky shoes.

A policeman stood with his hand on his night stick. I asked, "What going on?"

He was young, silvery thistle sideburns by his ears. He looked down from under the brim of his hat. "Can't go in there."

A photographer jostled me. "Why not?"

He relaxed a little. "The vet who threatened that girl with a knife, he got arrested, so a buncha old guys came from the V.F.W., then all these Koreans, and the press, and so you can't go in there."

"But that's me. Clarence threaten me an' Ling." He pushed up his hat brim. He had beautiful blue eyes. "I come from see…from seeing Mister Graham. The D.A."

That name scared him, so he pushed away between two gawkers and went over to another uniform man with three stripes on his arm. More gawkers gathered, hid them, hid me, I went unnoticed. The bins along the sidewalk were empty. Didn't he get to put out the fruit? The air felt savage. Near me a man smelled of raw shoe leather from the bottom and beer from the top. Shouts came over the heads, and he shouted back, "What about Americans? What about jobs for us!"

Jobs? What jobs? People stretched their necks to see. Not me. I stood unknown, resigned, sinking into carelessness. The world seemed awful and broken, I couldn't care, something was gone, and the people around me looked ugly. Who cares for anyone else? It's a game. Isn't that what New York City is, a game for getting what you want? I thought again of Ms. North's glee after I signed the papers that would send Craig to jail.

What did she want? What was her game?

I felt so careless I stopped being careful. I leaned against the wall near the end of our sidewalk bins. An old policeman came, his eyes watery, folds around his mouth, his jowls sloping out and down to a huge beer belly held up by his gun belt.

"Are you her? From in there?" I nodded. "And you wanna get back in there?" I nodded. He rubbed his mouth, gazed over the heads, jerked his thumb toward the park. He said to the young policeman,

"Go get Green, Jigarjian, and Springer. Discreetly, know what I mean?"

The silvery young policeman slipped into the crowd. The old cop's name badge said he was Sgt. Scanlon. He rested a big soft hand on my shoulder and looked over the crowd. "Bowl of mixed nuts, huh." He grinned as he looked down at me. "Don't look so sad, it'll all blow over. None too soon for you, huh."

"None too soon," I repeated, and he chuckled.

The chuckle faded. The young cop appeared, towing three uniformed officers. Sergeant Scanlon said, "You call that discreet? A dress parade?"

"Kee?" A man with a camera. "Kee-Yong?"

Clattersnap, shutters bit, and Sergeant Scanlon shouted, "Get around her!"

"It's her! Over here!"

The crowd heaved. Reporters barged through the gawkers. A woman fell screeching and vanished from sight. I backed up, my back hit the wall, blue uniforms closed tight around me and the beast in the crowd roared in my face. Lenses like glassy eyes, flat snouts with clattering teeth leaped at me—Kee! Over here! Kee!—faces shouting between the policemen as the metal shutters knashed, shearing at me.

Sergeant Scanlon's teeth clenched, his hat knocked low on his eyes. Behind him I saw an elbow plunk a machine. The camcorder slammed a man's head, crunched his spectacles, and blood ran from his nose. Shouts, blue uniforms, my back against bricks, cries, grunts, shirt buttons up close, and the young cop's silvery sideburns rippled as he clenched his teeth.

Sergeant Scanlon's stomach was so big there was room below it. I slid down the brick wall. I glanced over. Two pairs of legs, but a few feet away, a dark space. The sidewalk bins! I wiggled between a woman's legs, she screeched, I bumped against the bins and slithered under. Rotten apple, cigarette butts, gum wrappers, wooden uprights, the bottom of the bin low over my head.

Darkness. Room to breathe.

No time! The crowd heaved, bodies hit the bins, they creaked, and the old crosspieces scissored as I clambered over the joints. The noise was terrific. Shouts, groaning; dirt sprinkled me, the bins shuddered and creaked, shoes rasped on the concrete inches away, all of it punctured by the steady pointless clattering shutters. No one could see me, the cameras kept going, a woman cried out, crushed against the bins, and her shoe fell off her foot as she got lifted off the ground.

Over there! Hangugo cursing. Is she? Can't tell! I turned the corner, wiggled over crosspieces. Nails popped, wood groaned, and I bumped my head. "Ow." Shouts, feet shuffling, legs, gasping, curses, wood crackled, shouts, I squirmed and reached the bin beside our door. The screen door stood closed, the metal door open, shoes tightly planted before the threshold. We're open? I looked up the pant legs. All men. Men all with black hair. Koreans.

Ling appeared. Excited, grinning, she put her hands up to the screen. I reached past a pair of business shoes and knocked. She glanced down at me and giggled. "What are you doing under the fruit bins?"

Appa-nim appeared. "Open the door!"

A man in business shoes looked down. "There you are." He helped me stand up as they cracked open the door. I scurried in, the businessman stepped in, and they smacked the door shut. A proper American, Ling threw her arms around me. "You're okay!" She let go quickly. "Yick. Your dress is dirty."

I saw Appa-nim. Uh-oh, not good. He looked frantic, pale, his hand spasmed against his leg. Ling said, "I tried to tell you, Appa, everything—

"Everything was going so well!" He turned, spun away from me. Back and forth he walked, scowling, his hand jumpy. "Look at the cooler, it's almost empty! We sold as much soda this morning as any two days before. The newspeople came in—coffee too, I had to make more, they gulp it by the quart—people were coming in, nobody stopped them. I did four hundred dollars in two hours.

"Then those damn vets showed up, came in, started shouting at me, angry stuff, garbage I can't repeat, and that's when I called the Association." He glanced at the man in business shoes, a handsome man in an open collar shirt. Then he shocked me. "Kee, I should've waited until you got back—you could've handled it better—but they were angry, arguing, customers were leaving and I, I just got—"

"Mr. Ahn, calm down." The businessman glanced at me. "I'm Larry Chua, president of the Korean Association, glad to meet you. But Ki-Teh," he said, "you're in business now, you have protections. The city doesn't want another Howard Beach, and the D.A. won't let it happen here anyway. He's not that kind of guy." He glanced at me to confirm it. "But we've been wondering why you didn't call us sooner. We Koreans have to stick together, protect each other. Capeche? That's Italian. Understand?"

"More slogans?" Appa-nim kneaded his brow and leaned against the island. "That's why we have my sister, to interpret all the slogans. Aloha, that's hello and goodbye in Hawaiian. I'm so confused. Tired and confused."

I said, "Auntie's here?"

"Upstairs. She came when she heard a fight was brewing."

My shoes rasped the treads as I hurried up. Auntie's voice grew loud.

"The hell with you, you jerk!" Whack! She slapped the phone into the cradle and glanced over at me. "The V.F.W., the Veterans of Foreign Wars, I tried to tell them we only have a problem with vets who threaten us with knives. Did they listen? No." She rolled her eyes and stood up. "Did you file charges? Are they going to crucify Craig?"

I told her about the meeting, about Ms. North's eagerness and Mister Graham's legalese. I said, "Why was she so eager? Why did she say Craig had to go to jail 'in the current political climate'"?

"That's simple. Graham's running for re-election. If Craig doesn't get sent up everyone will think he leaned on you to drop the charges." She tugged at a notebook in her purse, "Dammit," jerked it out and said, "Where the hell," as she scrounged for a pencil. "We have to write—here we go—you have to make a statement to the press, quick. You're becoming a symbol and that's not good."

"But why was Ms. North so gleeful? She works with his father and she looked happy to send Craig to jail."

"She probably wants Donafrio's job." She tapped a pencil on the kitchen table and motioned for me to sit. "First we have to say you don't have any grudge against vets. What a pain." She nodded and scribbled. "Then we'll give them what they want. Craig's head on a platter. Everyone hates him now, you know that." She wrote, crossed out words, rewrote, bit the pencil eraser, recopied the English, then gave me the paper. "Aloud now, read it."

Regret crinkled one side of my mouth. "I, Kee-Yong Ahn—" I stopped. "Shouldn't it be the other way around? It sounds strange, the family name at the end."

"All right, gimme it." Does she have to be mean? She shaped the message for me, I got past my name, and read aloud the first point—how I had no dispute with war veterans. She said, "It has to be in fourth grade English so these clowns can understand it."

"Easier for me too," I said; then I read, "Number two: after meeting with the Distric' Attorney, Mister Graham, I decide that I am pressing charges against Craig Donafrio. I had no relation of any kind with Craig, and his attacks were unprovoked." I glanced up at Auntie Yen. "Unprovoked? What does that mean?"

"You didn't give him any reason to beat you. The rest is just for emphasis."

I read, "I repeat: I had no dealings with Craig Donafrio, and I am pressing charges against him."

"How's it sound? Better yet, how does it feel?" she asked. It felt sad and not right, but I couldn't say that to her. "You read it well enough in English, but I could write it in Hangugo and translate." She was pleased with her handiwork. I twitched one shoulder, a resigned shrug. She saw my dismal heart but jumped up and went to the stairs. "Larry? We're ready."

Handsome Larry Chua appeared in the doorway with a small box and a microphone. He said, "A personal size P.A. system," and smiled with his white teeth.

I did not smile back. He led us into the living room. As he set the amplifier down by the front window Ling clattered in behind us, drawing attention to herself, and as she watched every move the President made I knew she had a crush on him. He opened the window. The mumble of the crowd broke in, rumbled like high tide on rocks, voices spiking from an undertow of belligerence.

The President set the amplifier on the sill and plugged in the microphone. He glanced back at me. "Ready?" I glanced at Auntie Yen. She motioned with her chin, so I stood, and with the paper in hand I crossed the living room. I glanced back. Appa-nim had come upstairs and was behind me too. It didn't matter when I saw outside the window. I stumbled. A sea of faces stared up at me, thousands, a surf of voices, a churning undertone of anger and frustration.

I froze, a clinch in my breath.

"Kee?" Larry Chua touched my arm. He didn't smile as he handed me the microphone. His eyes lost their friendly lights and became darker than steel. I sensed it. His *nunchi* was well developed, he knew how dismal and wrong I felt. He said, "Seeds go through the bird and get planted. So remember: the bird is eating the seeds in your hand now."

What he said hit me like a stick. A steady ringing sound. The crowd went quiet. The thoughts that always filled my head like non-stop radio suddenly stopped. Silence. Larry Chua flicked a switch, turned on the amplifier, then stepped back. I looked at the microphone. I was alone. This was me, I had to speak, small and nervous, but still and silent inside myself.

I stepped to the window. The voice of the mob settled so that between the pepper clatter of shutters I heard the hum and mosquito whine of camcorders.

"Um...ne." My loud voice startled me. I looked at the microphone, at the amplifier, and I stammered, "Ne—Hangugo—it means yes."

From behind me Auntie said, "Stick to the script."

I nodded. "Yes, thank you for coming." She was right, I had to read. I glanced down at the paper shivering in my hand. I read my name and then I said, "I have two point to make: One. Clarence Miller, next door, threaten me with a knife. I have no problem with the veteran. Service to country is to be honored. We should honor all those who serve."

I glanced up from the paper, over the sea of heads settled like a clog in St. Mark's Place, rippling out to the gates of Thompkins Square Park. I said, "Number Two. This morning I meet with the Distric' Attorney, Mister Graham. We decide that I am..."

I couldn't read more. I knew for certain. I had to change my mind. I wasn't angry, but the microphone blared my words. I said, "I am not press charges against Craig Donafrio. I'm not. No charges!"

Auntie grabbed me, jerked me around. "What are you doing?!"

"I can't. I don't want him to go to jail. I don't!"

Outside the window it started, a voice booing. The mob picked it up, dozens, then a hundred people shouting, boo! boo! boo! The wrath hit the building like spit, spattered in the window, the wrath swelled and Auntie's scorn showed in her eyes. I glanced around. Ling and Appa-nim looked shocked. My eyes met Larry Chua's. His eyes were troubled too.

I flung the paper at Auntie, threw the microphone onto the sofa, ran into my bedroom and slammed the door. The shouts, the booing hit my door like rotten fruit. I dropped to my knees by the window overlooking the air shaft. My choice! I covered my ears. My life! Why? Why can't they understand? Hasn't Craig suffered enough?

The fallen doll lay abandoned on the bottom of the air shaft, its hair stringy and bleached orange by the weather. I needed to do something. I clambered down the ladder propped below my window. I walked across the floor of the air shaft, unafraid, and cradled that abandoned doll in my arms. I thought she was broken, that her left eye didn't work, but when I swept the hair off her forehead with my fingertips both her eyes blinked together.

I carried her inside, settled onto my futon, and carefully brushed her hair. The booing had stopped. Didn't matter. I already felt okay. Disturbed, not good, but okay.

My life. This is my life, I thought, and I rocked with my rescued child and enjoyed the silence.

Chapter 29

Three days passed. The eighth day I walked the curb I wheeled the sword in a space as private as a poet's desk. I returned to Choon-be and stood silent before the steps of Choi Su-nim's dojang. My lips tasted salty, my shoulders ached, my wrists ached, and the blade rose shivering out of my shaky grip. As I let it settle against my shoulder my gaze went beyond the steel blade and through the fence across the street, into the park.

My small dark love waited for me. He waved to me and smiled.

I climbed the steps and slipped into the dojang. It was a beautiful summer day, many students had not come and the rest were already gone. Silence. I kowtowed to the five directions, wiped the blade with the soft cloth, and relieved, lay it onto the purple silk shelf in the teak chest.

"Sir? May I come in?"

Choi Su-nim sat in his office. He nodded, pleasure in his eyes, and I was pleased as I stepped into my familiar place before his desk, and relieved and curious too. Yes, mostly curious.

"They're all gone," I said. "The newspeople are gone, except for one, and he doesn't bother me. They're gone from around the store too. We were open all day today. But...why?"

"Congratulations," he said. "You've become stock footage."

"Sir?"

"They have enough pictures, they don't need you any more. And you don't look the same to them now."

I glanced out through the glass doors to the curb, cars parked a foot away from it, the empty street beyond. "Why don't I look the same?"

He shrugged. "Mercy is not popular in America. When you

dropped the charges against Craig you surprised them. You showed him mercy. They wanted revenge. But the hoopla would've only gotten worse."

"I'm glad Mister Graham let me change my mind. He was glad I wanted to." I wiggled my toes pleasurably. "It would've been cruel if Craig was in jail. He suffered enough."

He glanced toward the door as if he knew Ricky waited for me. "Everyone wanted him to suffer. And Ricky? How is he?"

I clenched my toes and looked up. "Please give him another chance. It was a strange situation, it won't happen again, and I know he respects you. Please, Sir?"

He rose and shuffled around his desk, his cane in one hand. I waited until he reached the doorway.

"If he drops his charge against Craig," I asked, "then would you let him come back to the dojang?"

He paused, about to close the door. "He must apologize to me. How he deals with his anger is another matter."

"Thank you, Sir. Thank you!"

He shut the door, its tongue clucked softly, and I changed into my street clothes. The bruises in my back were little more than blood memories, their painful shapes worked out of me as I did moving poems, mopped, worked the cash register, trimmed lettuce. Who knew that mopping the floor was a healing art?

I opened the door and stepped out of the office, my bag over my shoulder. Choi Su-nim stood gazing up at the Korean flag.

"Good night, Sir."

"Good night, Kee."

In my shoes I bowed to him, to the flags, then skipped out and down the steps, across the street and through the gate. Ricky came to meet me. I threw myself into his arms, desperate to hold him as love rushed through me and swooshed out to him.

"Tang shinl," he said, "sarang heyo."

We kissed and hugged, hugged and kissed, then I looked until I found the swimming goldfish that glinted deep in his eyes. "I love you too," I said.

We let each other loose and began along the path that wound through the park toward the band shell. I glanced at him and felt an egg in my chest, full to bursting, break open and let out its glow. It was a relief to love him, as if I had never loved the world before, loved anything that way, and it was safe because he loved me too.

He was so pleased to be with me that he chuckled and kept showing off his white teeth. We walked arm in arm, my head against his shoulder, and he grew quiet and thoughtful.

"Maybe I should drop the charge against Craig too," he said. He rubbed his cheek against the top of my hair. "Yeah, you're making me think. He lost an eye, and he won't ever look the same again. But I don't want to go to court either. What a hassle."

"Hmm, good." I squeezed his arm. "Choi Su-nim said if you say sorry, he maybe let you back in."

"Into the dojang? Really? You asked him?" He stopped us and looked at me. "You really are amazing. I love you so much."

He kissed my lips. The wind of love swooshed out of me again. Children screeched on the slide, basketballs beat the tar in the courts, and somewhere a radio crackled with the daily news.

We kissed.

In the streets the traffic lurched, rumbled, honked, and groaned. Subway trains roared in their tunnels and shook the sidewalks. All over the city, people hurried to work, to home, and to play. Still we kissed. Love swooshed out of me, swooshed out of Ricky, swirled around us like a protective whirl of wind, and I knew that until we wanted it, nothing in the world could part us, nothing could end our kiss.

Or so I thought.

END

Preview of *Persimmon Tree*, the second book in the Sword of the World trilogy:

Persimmon Tree

History is full of big horrors. Those big horrors often begot little ones.

I did not know it, but my family fled Korea to escape its own little horrors. Didn't matter. They were with us in New York City, as much as the air we breathed.

Air? We were breathing ghosts.

I was in Chinatown the day the ghosts rushed in to fill my father's head. I did not know it was the day they'd take him, because I was with the boy I loved. I was kissing Ricky Tibbs.

My lips felt the edges of Ricky's big teeth. I tasted his sweet mouth. My hands felt his hips, knobby like coral. That's how skinny Ricky was. Then my hands rose to hover over the bandages that bound his ribs, cracked ribs, an injury he had suffered for me.

No, Ricky was not the handsome boy you see on beer commercials, but it did not matter. He tried to save me, so I loved him, and the heat of his kisses dissolved me.

What did matter was that Appa-nim, my father, knew the little horrors, knew those ghosts that pursued us. I didn't know them. All I knew was that I loved Ricky, loved the smell of him, how tenderly his lips touched mine, his hands that held my waist. I knew the rightness of being in his arms.

I whispered it. "I love you."

He replied in Hangugo Korean, words of love I'd taught him. *"Tang shinl sarang heyo."* I love you too.

Ricky and I were in Columbus Park, in Chinatown. Traffic droned all around us, beyond the trees whispering secrets into the breeze, hints of the way of the world. Ricky and I were innocent of those secrets. We were too new to explore the urgings of lust, so our lips met like two halves of a pure fruit, desperate to be whole.

Squeak…squeak…squeak. We were still kissing when two mothers pushed baby carriages toward us, one carriage with a squeaky wheel. As luck would have it, they were Korean girls new to mothering.

One mother had fingernails painted bright blue. She spoke Hangugo, not realizing that I understood her.

"Ha, look at these two. A black one with a horse's face and a Chinese bumpkin girl."

"Fresh off the rice paddy," said Squeaky Wheel. She wore a tank top that displayed the red straps of her bra. "Plain too, look at her."

"Made for each other." They laughed hard. "Bad luck. So sad!"

"So homely! And so dumb!"

We broke our kiss, Ricky and I, and moved aside to let them pass. We were in the newpapers for the last week, so I leaned against Ricky and hoped they wouldn't recognize us.

Squeak…squeak…silence. "Isn't she the curb walker?"

Blue fingers pointed at Ricky.

"Hey, you be Ricky Tibbs." A smile broke on her face, and she forgot that they had heaped insults on us. "Hoo-wee! *Is* you, Ricky Tibbs, right here. Hi, Ricky Tibbs!"

"Uh…hi," he said. "I guess."

Squeaky Wheel threw up her hands, incredulous. "Kee-Yong," she said to me, "how do you let that Craig off the hook? He should be beat too!"

Craig Donafrio, a vicious boy, had beaten me with a stick as I walked the curb in Chinatown, doing a *poom-sey*, a moving poem, while wielding a sword. Ricky tried to save me, that's how he got hurt.

Blue Fingers fluttered them. "You right, they should beat Craig too."

"Big shot daddy, so what?"

"And Ricky! Ricky, you so bad, goin' to save her."

"Well," he said, "I just…"

"No, you great! That Craig, he a black belt!"

"But that Fallen Rock Star," said the Squeaky Wheel, "he jus' a drunk. I see him—" She pantomimed slumping over, passing out drunk. "—just like that."

"Me too, fallin' down." Blue Fingers had the flat nose of a mountain Han. "Yeah, I see him fallin' down inna street."

"And his podder," Squeaky Wheel said, meaning "father," "he paint picture. Big man, he rich, but he sooo mean. Nobody like him!"

"Nobody *see* him." Squeak…squeak, they pushed on with a gossipy laugh. "Good to see you, Kee. Bye Ricky!"

It was a relief to be free of the news sharks, they disrupted everything; but those mothers were different. Choi Su-nim, my Chinatown master, was right. We were a news story that didn't need us anymore.

"Hey, Kee!" Blue Fingers called back in Hangugo. "If you two have a baby, make sure you're married first!"

The mothers giggled like school girls and squeaked their wheels away.

Three pigeons chortled as an old Chinese *abuji* grandpa threw them crumbs. Ricky took my hand. "That was weird."

"Uh-huh."

We ambled toward Bayard Street, northward past the old bandstand. We had met there once, when things were strange, and were discovered by a man with a camera.

"Remember how I was so mad about Craig?" Ricky asked.

I squeezed his hand. Craig Donafrio was the son of a powerful man, the Assistant District Attorney of Manhattan. Craig had kicked Ricky, when he came to save me, and cracked three of his ribs.

Ricky's chest still ached. We reached a gate open to the street.

"I don't hate him anymore," he said. "Not so much, anyway. I keep seeing his face all bloody, the shards of glass sticking out of his eye."

"Good. We must go to get Ling at Auntie Yen's."

The Fallen Rock Star had smashed a bottle over Craig's face. That was how he stopped the beating, how he saved me, when Ricky could not. But the Fallen Rock Star had been famous, his father was a famous artist, Craig's father was high in the government, so the story exploded onto the TV news and front pages.

It was warm, evening sunlight slanting golden over the Chinese lanterns that dangled over Mulberry Street. The air smelled of duck fat and brown rice. People clustered around the fruit bins of the Han May Meat Co., on the corner, and it felt calm like a neighborhood.

No calm on Canal Street! Tourists, truckers, shouting hawkers, fishmongers dumping ice, bums, children, shop windows, food bins, cafes, smokers exhaling clouds, Catholic school girls in skirts and shirts. Ricky led me through the crowds, bumped shoulders, and I crunched a crab's claw under my foot.

Ahead on Canal Street the Manhattan Bridge curved up to jump the East River. We stepped off the curb at Mott Street, in the shadow of a pagoda bank, and scampered across Canal. The crowds thinned before the store windows that displayed gold chains and diamond jewelry.

I came from a small fishing village. Few lights at night. New York City was so bright that, even before nightfall, the lights were coloring the clouds with the pinkness of mother of pearl. Jets streaked the sky, helicopters chopped it, cars rushed over the avenues, crowds ran on the crosswalks, people darted into and spilled out of stores, cafes, places to eat and shop.

Even the air in New York City was frantic.

We veered onto Elizabeth Street, a slot between high buildings. Parked cars further narrowed the street. The sweet crusty smell of cannoli met us. I heard the hammering of the cobbler who repaired shoes across from Auntie Yen's door, a little Italian man in a cubbyhole.

We reached the first banner of Little Italy. High up a building, a head appeared in a window, red lips and almond eyes, whispy black hair.

My beautiful Auntie Yen. "Hey, Ricky boy!" She gazed down to her stoop and said, "She's waiting."

My little sister, Ling, jumped up. Her pigtails bounced as she ran to meet us. Ricky smiled. He liked Ling as much as everyone, though she called him the name of a Disney character.

"Hey, Monkey Tibb!"

"Hey, little noodle brain." She slapped his arm and he tried to grab her. She ducked away with a laugh. We turned back for the subway. He asked, "How go the English lessons with Auntie Yen?"

"How go the monkey bars, Mister Tibb?"

I glanced back toward Auntie Yen, who hadn't spoken to me. She was still mad at me for letting Craig off the hook.

Ricky poked Ling. "You're the only person on the planet who could get away with that."

"Oh, Mister Tibb." Ling heaved a sigh. "Auntie Yen say we are *crazy* 'bout you."

We threaded our way back down Canal Street. Green ball over old cracked stairs, we skipped down to the underground turnstiles. Subway station, gum spots and cigarette butts, we pushed through to the platform.

Asians stood about, shouldering backpacks and computer bags. Ricky bumped against me. Ling bought a super grape lollipop at a magazine stand.

"Look," she said, pointing. "You nobody now."

No pictures of us on the papers. Fine by me.

A train roared out of the blackness, shaking our feet, hot air whipped and flailed, then we walked into a car. I sat between Ricky and Ling, who swung her shoes as she sucked her lollipop.

"Ricky." Ling leaned over me. "It the Pagoda Lady."

Across from us sat a huge fat woman. Her six layers of fat, topped by her head, made her look like the Royal Pagoda in Seoul, which had seven levels. We had seen her many times on the subway, so often that I could not understand how we happened to.

Maybe she lived on the subway?

Ricky leaned over for the conspiracy. He whispered, "What about her?"

"She hide the big blade in her fat." Ling nodded. "You got dime or cig'rette, she *kill* you."

He sat back chuckling. "Big blade, huh? Bigger than Choi Su-nim's sword? That Kee walks the curb with?"

Ling nodded, her tongue purple from the lollipop. "Uh-*huh*. That how it go, Joe!"

I wielded Choi Su-nim's ceremonial sword, a long curving blade, heavy for me, each evening when I walked the curb. Then we talked in his little office, below the picture of his wife, long dead.

Ricky's comment reminded me. "Choi Su-nim, he say something."

"Tonight?" he asked. "What?"

I nodded and looked at my sneakers. "That sword? You canno' strike with two sides...uh...in one time."

"You can't strike with both sides of a sword at the same time?" Ricky arched one of his inchworm eyebrows. "What's he mean by that?"

I shrugged. "Don't know."

I did know, but I could not say in English, or would not.

"Su-nim" is someone with special knowledge. Choi Su-nim had special knowledge of the Tao. He knew I loved Ricky intensely, as only first loves can be intense. He also knew I could not fully commit to *Saebyoke Komdo*, Way of the Dawning Sword, if I was committed to loving Ricky Tibbs.

"Has some...something," I stammered, "to do with...um...how do you say? A wake up?"

"Awakening?"

I nodded. "Something to do with…that."

"What is 'that'? Awakening?" Ricky squeezed my hand. "I mean, I get it, it's really important—it's the whole point of komdo, right?—but exactly what is it?"

He stayed looking at me. The train roared and shook, our box of light hurtling through the dark tunnel.

"So?" he asked. "What is it? Awakening?"

"I am not, so I do not know." I searched my limited English for the right words. "It is about Tao, being in Tao, with Tao."

 "Our stop." Ling jumped up. "Bye Ricky!"

"Bye Ling." The subway train slowed, ruckled on its rails. I squeezed his hand and we kissed quickly. "Bye Kee."

We climbed the stairs to Astor Place. Five streets met there, where a big black cube stood on one point. We hurried across the intersection, to the art school, two blue-haired artists exhaling cigarette smoke outside a doorway.

I followed as Ling skipped across the street to a pizza stand, a metal sign for St. Mark's Place. Our street, we lived at the other end.

Ling halted, the smell of pepperoni in the air, to confide her secret information. "Auntie Yen," she said, "has a new boyfriend."

"She just broke up with Harold!"

"That red-faced tomato?" Ling made a face. "Too old for her."

We walked past basement shops full of slogan tee-shirts and junky hair things. "He broke it off," I said, "not her. Auntie told me."

"He was too *old!*"

Ling was defending Auntie, so I changed the subject.

"Umma wears make up," I said. We circled a couple walking slowly, arm in arm. "After we met with the D.A., before she went to work, in the cab uptown, she put on lipstick and red stuff on her cheeks."

"Blush. I know," Ling said. "I saw her put it on before."

We neared First Avenue, wide lanes brightly lit. "When?"

"What's that?"

A scream. Down St. Mark's Place, red flashing lights. Somebody running, others chasing him. Men in uniforms ran toward us, chasing the skinny guy. The skinny guy broke into First Avenue, out into traffic.

"Appa-nim!"

The skinny guy was my father.

A car swerved to miss him. Ling cried, *"Appa!"* The car slammed into a parked car, *crunch*, its windshield shattering onto the street.

We ran toward him, shouting his name. A car swerved, tires screeching as it slid sideways. Appa-nim leaped the hood, rolled across, jumped down. He landed on his feet, wild-eyed, and saw us.

"Appa-nim! It's me! Kee!"

He didn't know us.

Terrified, he scrambled the other way. He collided with an ambulance man. Together they fell to the street with a frightening *clunk* of bone on tar.

"He's our father!" We ran toward them. "Don't hurt him! Please!"

Other medical men ran up. They pinned Appa-nim to the ground. He struggled and threw himself back and forth, wailing.

He cried out in Hangugo. "They all die! Burn! Oh god, *please!"*

"Appa-nim, stop!

"Stop fighting, Appa!"

A man with a syringe bent over him. He jabbed Appa-nim's arm. My father let out a scream, the cords standing out in his neck.

"That hero!" he cried. "No hero! *No hero!"*

Huffing, out of breath and sweating, Mu stumbled up. He was a thirty-year-old boy, tall and chubby, who worked in our store when I was in Chinatown.

"He just…" Mu shrugged. "…he started babbling. I was in the storage room. He was at the register, there was a baby crying, and suddenly he…just…he lost it."

The drug took effect. Appa-nim struggled weakly until, suddenly, his head settled to the tar. The ambulance men raised themselves off his arms and legs.

Ling watched, stunned to silence, her face a blank. The ambulance men lifted Appa-nim onto a stretcher. I glanced about. People stood along the curb, watching. Cars were stopped around us, a traffic jam, and police cars flashed, splashing us with red.

I felt it. Among those New Yorkers standing along the street, ghosts were watching us. They were watching those little horrors, which followed us from Korea, take over my father's life.

About the Author

Lawrence "Doc" Pruyne PhD has enjoyed careers as a contractor, a journalist and a poker player. As a college professor he taught writing and literature in the Albany, NY area, and in Boston. He is a trained film-maker and has been a consultant on literary and cinema projects for almost twenty years. He is the scriptwriter and cinematographer on films produced in partnership with his wife, Cheri Robartes. Together, they also raise rare ducks on a farm in western Massachusetts.